BISON
BOOKS

W9-BMH-635

OLD HOME TOWN

BY

ROSE WILDER LANE

University of Nebraska Press
Lincoln and London

Copyright 1935, 1963 by Roger L. MacBride
All rights reserved
Manufactured in the United States of America

First Bison Book printing: 1985

Library of Congress Cataloging in Publication Data
Lane, Rose Wilder, 1886–1968.
Old home town.
I. Title.
PS3523.A55304   1985   813'.52   85-8645
ISBN 0-8032-7917-5 (pbk.)

Originally published by Longmans, Green and Company
Reprinted by arrangement with Roger L. MacBride

⊛

CONTENTS

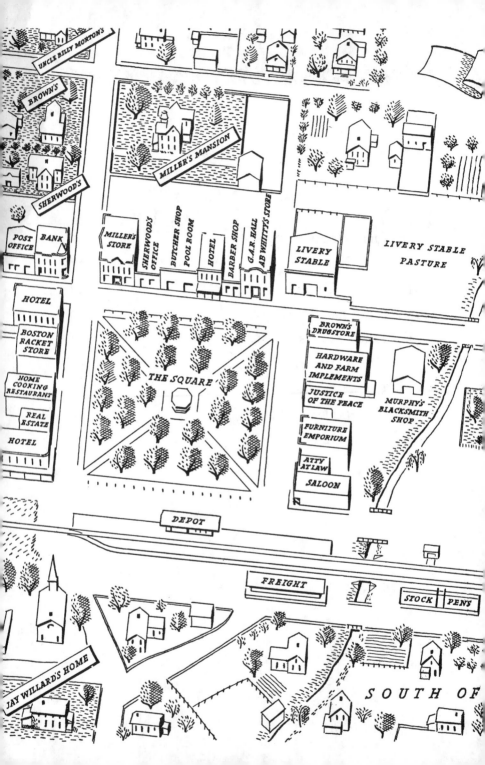

THE OLD HOME TOWN

LOIS ESTES LIVED HERE WITH HER MOTHER

MR. SHERMAN

MRS. SIMS LITTLE HOUSE

MINIVERS

MRS. BARBROOK AND LEILA LIVED HERE

SCHOOL

MRS. ROGERS

MRS. CLEAVERS MISS SARAH BOARDED HERE.

MINTY BATES

ERNESTINE'S HOME

BOLES · WHO KEPT A HIRED GIRL

MILL POND

GRAIN ELEVATOR

LUMBER YARD

THE TRACKS

SQUARE DEAL MILL

MILL POND

F. B.

OLD HOME TOWN

THERE was no sign to indicate the point at which country ended and town began. The jogging buggies and wagons moved along roads between meadows, cornfields and orchards; the town was in sight when its white church-spires could be seen. Bushes grew close to the wheel-tracks, so close that the road wavered between them, and often trees overhung it, making a leafy tunnel. As we traveled along those roads we read bits of the autobiographies of squirrels, rabbits, birds, lizards, snakes, written with claw and scale on the dusty wheel-tracks.

No visible indication marked the limits of town and country. But the frontier between them was definite in those days and now that highway signs mark it, it no longer exists. There is a city myth that country life was isolated and lonely; the truth is that farmers and their families then had a richer social life than they have now. They enjoyed a society organic, satisfying and whole, not mixed and thinned with the life of town, city and nation as it now is.

Country folks wore their best clothes when they came to town. The journey of two or eight miles was not to be undertaken on the spur of a moment.

During the week the horses were working in the fields or the men were too busy to hitch up. A farm woman could harness the old mare and sometimes did, but dealing with horses was felt to be a man's work. Usually farmers' wives put on sunbonnets or shawls, took their sewing, and walked across the fields to visit neighbors. They had quilting-bees, husking-bees, country parties and dances; on Friday evenings they went to spelling-matches, box-suppers, lectures and political speeches in their neighborhood schoolhouses; Sundays were given to services in their own churches and to all-day visits, picnics, basket-dinners.

On Saturdays they came to town, dressed for the occasion and bringing the week's surplus of butter, eggs, vegetables and fruits. They came to the stores, to trade.

The word lingers, though its meaning has been forgotten. Americans who never bartered eggs for calico will say, "I trade at So-and-So's," or, "He gets my trade." In those days, the small towns had never heard of going shopping.

From east and west the main-traveled roads came into town. At some unnoticed point the church spires were lost sight of, and schoolhouse or graveyard came into view. These were at the ends of town and in a subtle sense they were not part of it. The sidewalk dwindled to a path along the road before it reached the graveyard and if it extended as far as the schoolhouse, it ended there. And not only physically were graveyard and schoolhouse set apart from the everyday life of the town. They were places dedicated ; one to learning, the other to death.

The graveyard might have been any country graveyard except that taller slabs of marble were more populous in the shade of evergreens. The old, thin stones were yellowed by weather and slanted above a rich growth of wild grasses. Blue flags straggled through the fence and clung with bared roots to the dry bank along the road. Rosebushes grew unpruned and the gate sagged on a rusted hinge. The good churchladies were always saying it was a downright shame and a disgrace ; something must be done to fix up the graveyard.

But the schoolhouse at once struck you by its superiority to the little country schoolhouses. Two storied, with unshaded windows regularly spaced on all sides, it rose gaunt above an irregular space of trodden earth on which not a spear of grass survived. Its height was increased and seemed unbalanced by the cupola (pronounced, cupalo) rising from the eaves above the door. A large bell hung there, and when The Principal pulled the rope in the entry below, that bell clanged an iron imperative over the town. It was the voice of a place austerely devoted to toil, permitting no frivolity and righteously crushing any impulse toward merriment or play.

In school hours, whispering, fidgeting or a moment's idleness were crimes. Release from book and desk was granted only to urgent need properly expressed. "Please, may I get a drink ?" "Please, may I look at the dictionary ?" "Please, may I be excused ?"

The water pail and dipper were on a bench by the
door. The dictionary lay in state on its stand in a
corner. In the bright and lawless outdoors, the pri-
vies stood behind the schoolhouse, girls' and boys'
separated by a short length of tight board fence and
the whole overlooked by the schoolroom windows.

Supervised play was unthought of, but play was
strictly supervised. An indecorous outburst of
energy in the schoolyard at recess was promptly
stopped by a teacher's rapping on a window, or The
Principal himself descended on the culprits. No
pupil talked back to The Principal, nor indeed to
any lesser teacher. Teachers were always right;
there was no argument. A whipping at school meant
that any proper father would administer a second
sound thrashing at home.

With unconscious symbolism, the town stretched
from schoolhouse to graveyard. And there is another mystery; the direction of its main streets and
of its growth was from east to west. If some natural
obstacle diverted this course, it tended toward the
northwest. Chance does not explain this universal
tendency of American towns. True, the town was
built along the railroad. But why was it built north
of the railroad? Why did railroads follow the sun?
Why do all highways of man's historic migrations go
westward, northwestward? ·

The Indians said that the road of fleshly desire, of
material things, ran from east to west; that the path
of the spirit was south to north; where these ways

crossed grew the Tree of Life. But no one listened
to the Indians, and the Indians were gone.

There was only the fact which everyone knew and
no one questioned, that the direction of growth was
toward the west. And there was more than this
mystery in those Western Additions that cut the pasture northwest of town into building lots. Two deep
human desires were at war here; the longing for
stability, for form, for permanence, which in its essence is the desire for death, and the opposing hunger
for movement, change, instability and risk, which are
life. Men came from the east and built these American towns because they wished to go no farther, and
the towns they built were shaped by the urge to go
onward.

Main Street paralleled the railroad, on the north;
north and northwest were the pleasant street straggling into minor country roads. The railroad's raw
embankment limited the region where nice people
lived. South of it was "south of the tracks."

It is an American phrase. We all know what it
means. No logic explains its meaning. South of the
tracks the streets were no muddier or dustier than
our own. Houses were no more ramshackle or sour
with poverty than many houses scattered among the
neat ones north of the tracks. Often the country
was prettier, the summers more breezy, south of the
tracks, and often an effort had been made to build
the town there. Some of the old houses might be
south of the tracks, and perhaps the oldest church.

But "south of the tracks" was inevitably a limbo of shiftless ne'er-do-wells, section-hands, men who drank and their wives who took in washing, their children who mustn't be played with.   Nice people lived north of the tracks.

We lived in little houses of clapboards painted white or yellow, with contrasting color outlining their edges and framing windows and doors.   These houses had no more architecture than boxes.   Usually a gable faced the street, displaying in its window white machine-lace curtains looped back on either side of the many small panes.   Between these curtains the glass shone dark as deep water.   Dusk filled that room; it was the parlor, if the family could set aside one room solely for receiving callers.   If not, it was the front room and there would be a bed or two in it, adorned with the best pillow-shams and counterpane.

In either case, there would be a center-table decked with a crocheted doily, a parlor lamp, and such ornaments as the family possessed.   If it owned a book, the book lay here in state.   The table's legs supported, a few inches above the carpet, a shelf as large as its top, and on this shelf there might be a large seashell, or a stereopticon with its box of twin pictures, Niagara Falls, The Capitol at Washington, Views of the Chicago World's Fair, to be looked at through the hooded lenses.   But stereopticons were no longer fashionable.   What-nots, too, had gone out of style. There would be a rocking chair or two, with tidies ornamenting and protecting their tall backs; a few parlors could boast a parlor organ, its high top adorned with scroll-saw work, inset mirrors, and small shelves displaying family photographs. The walls were papered as richly as possible and every woman wanted an ingrain carpet for the parlor. But often she must make the best of tacking the rag carpet down again over the layer of newspapers and straw. She would be thankful if some of the glass-covered pictures had heavy gilt frames and a hand-painted silk scarf or two draped tastefully on their upper corners.

The parlors of the two or three mansions of the town were awe-inspiring with pale Axminster carpets real mahogany chairs, silken over-drapes at the windows, and pianos. The legs of their center-tables ended in carved claws clutching large glass balls, and in one corner a gilded easel held an enlarged crayon photograph of the baby.

Across the front of the house there was invariably a porch. At least one hickory rocker stayed on it in all weathers; on summer afternoons other chairs would be brought from the house and children sat on the steep porch steps. House plants in painted cans and tin pails too leaky to be mended, stood along the edge of the porch floor, and ferns in wire hanging baskets might depend from its ceiling, always painted sky-blue. The parlor door opened from this porch and usually another door led to bedroom or dining-room. And a path went around the house to the back stoop and the kitchen.

Behind the house there was the vegetable garden, the woodshed, the chopping block and the well. A path, or perhaps even a narrow board walk, led to

the privy near the henhouses and the barn. Every
family kept a cow and everyone wanted fine horses
and a buggy.

These little houses, all created to serve the need of
shelter as cheaply as possible, resembled each other
as sisters do. (Standardization did not arrive with
machines.) There was charm in their simplicity,
though no one saw it. They were candid and innocent, and poverty kept them free of affectations.
The utmost that individual taste could do was to
vary the pattern of scroll-saw work along their eaves
and to paint them a whiter white or a brighter yellow
than their neighbors.

The fenced lawns were mowed with scythes or
with mowing-machines. Rosebushes grew in the
tangled grass and lilacs fluttered their heart-shaped
leaves near the rain-water barrels. In the back yards
apples, cherries, plums and peaches blossomed and
ripened their fruits. Vines were trained on strings to
shade sunny windows and ends of porches and every
spring the fern-like tansy and ragged clumps of
white, yellow and purple asters—we called them
chrysanthemums—came up along the front fence.

Those white and yellow flowers were symbols. In
those years of hard times that followed The Panic—
when Coxey's Army, 60,000 strong, captured whole
railroad divisions in the west and marched footsore
from the Mississippi to Washington; when banks
failed everywhere and everywhere farm mortgages
were foreclosed; when Federal troops guarded government buildings against the mobs and on all the

mid-western roads long caravans of covered wagons were crawling east, west, north, south, filled with hungry families, driven by men desperately seeking food, desperately eager to work twelve hours a day for scraps of food — after that Panic, in the years of poverty that seemed unending, those white and yellow flowers became symbols of fanaticism. To me, a yellow aster still stands for the hated gold standard; the white aster means William Jennings Bryan, whose free coinage of silver would have taken us back to prosperity. But Bryan was defeated by the soulless corporations and our country was forever ruined.

Beyond these untended clumps of asters and tansy, on the other side of the fence of pickets or of horizontal boards nailed to posts, lay Main street. Nothing distinguished it from any country road, except that perhaps it was a little better worked. In those days, voters worked out their poll-tax on the roads. Only well-to-do men planked down round silver dollars to pay their poll-tax. Their thrift was respected; undoubtedly the time of such men was worth more than a dollar a day. But ordinary men assembled with their teams and tools to repair winter's ravages on their roads.

They were proud of the amount of good work they could do between sunrise and sunset, and contemptuous of a shiftless road-district where rotting planks remained in bridges and wagons mired down in mud at the same spot for successive years.

Board walks began to be built in town during the early years of the new century. They were built partly at public expense if the town's treasury had a surplus of cash in hand. But lumber cost money, and for the most part we were content with gravel held in place by an edge of board. Gravel wore thin and held mud-puddles when it rained, but on the other hand the board sidewalk was more slippery with ice in winter. Hard-trodden paths wandered past vacant lots, and on them in summer the ladies must hold their flounces carefully away from the weeds' yellow pollen.

The heart of town was business blocks surrounding the depot on the north. Often they formed a Square, with the railroad and depot on its fourth side. Here there were trees, perhaps a bandstand, and in summer the trees were decked with candles in Chinese lanterns on those evenings when the Ladies' Aid gave an ice-cream social in the Square. The business buildings, of frame and of brick, were one- and two-storied, the lower ones with tall false fronts, and straggling wooden awnings of various shapes and heights overhung the high board-sidewalks.

Several general stores were on the Square; there was the hotel, the drug-store, the Feed and Produce House, the barber shop, the poolroom, and in towns where the Woman's Christian Temperance Union did not prevail, the corners were saloons. The blacksmith shop and the livery stable were just off the Square; the lumber yard and the flour mill might even be on the south side of the tracks.

Upstairs, above one of the stores, was the G.A.R. Hall. Above another store was the Opera House, where at long intervals townspeople had the treat of hearing a lecture illustrated with magic lantern slides, or of seeing trained dogs and listening to tunes played on the musical glasses. When Blind Boone came to town, he played a piano in the Opera House, and every winter the Ladies' Aid gave oyster-suppers there. In the summers we saw Uncle Tom's Cabin and East Lynne, played by traveling troupes in tents set up in some vacant lot.

There was a feeling that this center of town was masculine. Ladies went there, but with a certain circumspection. Usually they went in couples and a ladylike reserve was expressed in the propriety of their manner and in the care with which they held their skirts high enough to escape contamination from the sidewalk but not so high as to reveal an instep. It was most embarrassing to be obliged to go uptown on a windy day.

Ladies went uptown only for some definite purpose. They might pass through those business streets on their way to call on a lady who lived on the other side of town. They might enter the general store, the postoffice, the grocery store and the drug-store, but they did not linger in these places, and on the streets they passed the livery-stable, the barber shop, the pool-room and above all the saloon with a manner so haughtily oblivious that it all but denied the existence of these places of doubtful virtue or all-too-certain vice. If a lady chanced to meet on one of these business streets a gentleman she knew well, perhaps the husband of her dearest friend, her step became slightly hurried while her eyelids modestly dropped, a reserved smile faintly touched her lips and she murmured, "Good afternoon." He had thrown away his cigar, or hidden it, on perceiving her approach; he lifted his hat high in air, bowed, and also hastening slightly he replied to her greeting. The encounter was over in an instant, leaving both a little flurried but with the sense of having carried off a difficult situation in a perfectly proper manner. Unmarried girls usually found it simpler to pretend not to see the boys they knew when passing them on the street.

There were of course a few shameless women and girls from south of the tracks who could be seen gadding the streets; it was as much as a nice woman's reputation was worth, to speak to one of them. It was said that the most wanton of them even met the trains. All the men in town naturally went to the depot to see the trains come in, so the depot at train-time was the last place where a decent woman would be seen. Whether any two of the lost girls in our town were actually so brazen as to meet the trains, I don't know; it was a rumor. But there were two clear ways to flaunt one's loss of modesty and virtue; one was to wear red, the other was to be seen needlessly gadding around uptown.

Men got the mail at the postoffice and bought the groceries; there was no reason why a decent woman, with her housework, her sewing and mending and gardening and preserving to do, should go uptown.

When necessity or some definite pleasure dictated

such an excursion into public places, a lady prepared herself for it. She took her hair out of curlpapers or curled it with an iron heated in the lamp-chimney, she changed her shoes, adjusted hat and veil and put on at least her second-best dress, and gloves. An hour or more was often consumed in getting ready to go uptown.

It was only thirty years ago that we first heard that woman's place was in the home. We are never aware of the present; each instant of living becomes perceptible only when it is past, so that in a sense we do not live at all, but only remember living. And we are blind to conditions forming our lives, until those conditions are becoming part of the past. It was not seen that woman's place was in the home until she began to go out of it; the statement was a reply to an unspoken challenge, it was attempted resistance to irresistible change.

Until that time, woman's place had been in the home as a fish's place is in water. It is true there are flying fishes. Woman's Rights had been laughed at; Dr. Mary Walker had, we heard, been permitted by a special act of Congress to wear pants, and Mrs. Bloomer had given her name to a garment not mentioned in mixed company. (Though at that time bloomers were not underwear; beneath our layers of petticoats, winter and summer, we wore unionsuits. Bloomers were a shameless form of divided skirts, worn by creatures unworthy the sacred name of woman, astride on bicycles.) And in defence of the home Mrs. Carrie Nation with her hatchet was smashing saloons in Kansas. But it did not occur to us to think that woman's place was in the home; it was there.

In summer we were out of bed at dawn; in winter, since the sun was late, we rose before dawn. There was unquestioned virtue in early rising and this virtue was rewarded by the freshness of summer mornings. In winter, with the fire to make in a cold kitchen stove and the dining-room heater not yet warming the icy chill, with the well-bucket frozen and stars still in the black sky, virtue was grimly sustaining. We had of course slept in our flannel unionsuits. Still we shivered while we stripped off the long-sleeved, high-necked cotton-flannel nightgown, hurriedly tugged at corset strings and tied on petticoats.

A full pitcher stood in the washbowl and the water in it was filmed with ice, but it is not true that we broke the ice. Men simply didn't wash. Women snatched up stockings, shoes, button-hook, corset cover and woolen dress, blew out the bedroom lamp, and scurried to the dining-room to dress by the heater. Father had opened its drafts, stirred the banked fire, put wood on it and gone with a lighted lantern to do the chores at the barn.

We did break the ice on the rain-water barrel, tugging loose the hatchet frozen to it and crashing into water that rose swiftly through the hole. In winter there were no wigglers in the rain-water. The soft water heated more quickly in the tin wash-basin on the kitchen stove than it did in the reservoir that was

part of the stove. When it was warm, we washed
face and hands and dried them on the roller towel by
the kitchen door. A comb hastily smoothed the hair,
but usually the knot or the dangling braid was neat
enough to leave untouched until after breakfast.

There was yesterday's milk to skim, the morning's
milk to strain and set away, milk-pail and strainer to
wash, the fires to stoke, and breakfast to cook and set
on the table. It was a substantial meal. Oatmeal,
ham and eggs or fat cakes of sausage, pancakes with
butter and molasses, fried potatoes and perhaps left-
over baked beans warmed up, with the usual jams and
jellies, and coffee, were routine. Naturally a company breakfast would be more substantial. And
men's requirements varied. A southern husband must
have hot biscuits every morning; a New Englander
demanded pie. Some men wouldn't call it breakfast
without beefsteak. A man must have food that
would stick to his ribs.

Often in the winters we spoke of how good it
would be to have fresh vegetables again. Winter
thickened the blood, so that every spring, to thin it,
we took doses of sulphur in molasses. Through those
first warm days we watched the dandelions, lambs'
quarter, dock and wild mustard growing large enough
to pick for greens. Then from our gardens we got
young onions, radishes, and lettuce leaves to be served
in vinegar and sugar. Strawberries came in May;
peas and new potatoes followed; then string beans,
beets, turnips, carrots, sweet corn, tomatoes, and the
full tide of summer's fruits. Apples lasted into the

winter, and for a treat at Christmas there might be an orange. But from fall frosts until next spring's first mess of greens boiled with salt pork, the food on our tables three times a day was potatoes, meat, bread, baked beans and fruits richly preserved with sugar.

This was not because of poverty, but simply because each neighborhood consumed what it produced. Our gardens were frozen in winter; therefore, naturally, there were no fresh vegetables to be had in the winter-time. Carrots and turnips would last for a little while, but soon grew withered and tough, and onions sprouted and rotted.

Housework began as soon as the men had eaten breakfast and gone uptown. Dishwashing always brought up the question of keeping a pig. It was downright waste to throw away all that good dishwater, the scraps from the plates and the sour milk too old to use in cooking. Butchering made a solid week of hard, disagreeable work, yet there was nothing like home-made sausage and home-cured hams and bacon; it was pleasant to have all the lard you could use, and you couldn't buy headcheese. Still, some folks objected to the smell of pigpens in town; the subject was often brought up at meetings of the town council. Whether we kept a pig or not, the question was vexing. We were used to saying, "Yes," or "No," decisively, knowing where we stood. But the question of keeping a pig was never quite settled; there was something to say on both sides.

Then we swept the carpets, dusted, and made the beds. Feather-beds were encased in stout ticking;

you know what feathers are, once they get loose in the air. It was impossible, shaking and pummeling, to spread feathers smoothly inside the heavy stuff; feather-beds always had a soft, wobbly look, best you could do. Straw-ticks were neater. They were buttoned down the middle; we unbuttoned them and thrust an arm into the crackling straw, stirring it and pulling it from the corners into the hollow where we had slept. A clean, wheaty odor came from the opened straw-ticks when they'd been newly filled at housecleaning time, but before the next fall the dust from the broken straw made us sneeze. Still, there was more satisfaction in making up a neat straw-tick bed than in trying to smooth a feather bed. There was little difference in cost; we kept a few geese or saved the feathers when we killed a hen, and straw was cheap.

The sheets were in various stages of bleaching. We made them of unbleached muslin, for why should we let factories take all that good wear out of cloth by bleaching it? In time, with washing and sunning on the clothes-line, the sheets became white. If meantime they grew thin in the middle, we had only to rip the center seam and sew the outside selvedges together. Then the sheet would be good for several more years before it came to quilt-patches and carpet-rags. We had never thought of muslin so wide that sheets need not be seamed down the middle.

We had, of course, a few sheets of bleached muslin laid away for company. These were often edged with crocheted lace a finger's length wide, and pillow cases were made to match. Some women trimmed even their everyday sheets with knitted or crocheted lace, to make a proud display on Monday morning's clothes-line.

Our bedclothes were quilts and comforters — old-fashioned women called these comfortables, and they were more luxurious than quilts, costing as they did less in labor and more in money. Whole new lengths of goods were used for them, tied to the cotton batting at intervals by knots of colored yarn. After many washings, however, the cotton in them grew more lumpy than in quilts. And quilts were thriftier because they did not require new cloth.

Every house had a scrap-bag and every scrap of cloth was treasured. Nothing was more pleasant than sitting down, in the satisfaction of knowing that all the work was done, to spread out those bits of cloth, lay the pattern on them at various angles to determine how to cut without waste, and then with sharp shears to cut out the squares and triangles. Women looked forward to this for days, saying, "As soon as I get this job out of the way, I'm going to get at the scrap-bag!" They said to neighbors, "What are you doing tomorrow afternoon? Bring over your scrap-bag and let's just spend the whole afternoon cutting out quilt patches."

Scrap-bags were always interesting. "My, isn't that the Turkey red that Ethel wore that time she recited, 'Curfew Shall Not Ring Tonight'?" Yes, and how cute she was. And this is the last of that dress that grandma hated so, but wore every summer because grandfather bought the goods to surprise her. "She never could bear plaids." And here was the pink-and-white check Susan wore the summer before she was married. "I wore this sage green with the chocolate stripes when I was a girl. It's kind of old-fashioned now, but John always admired it." And, "My land, I thought the last of this was in the bed-room carpet! The dress I wore to Fourth of July, that time the horses ran away."

Our quilts were more than useful, they had the faint sentimentality of a pressed flower. And no more beauty. We did not value them for their appearance, but for the memories in them, for their good wearing qualities and the thrift they represented. Pride in the neat stitches had waned; hand-sewing was no longer admired. On dresses and underwear it was a confession that one could not afford a sewing machine.

Mothers, striving against poverty to give their daughters the best, put those difficult slanting tucks into Gibson Girl shirtwaists with such laboriously careful back-stitching that at a glance you would take it for real machine-work.

After the day's routine housework was done, came the week's routine. Only grave sickness or sudden calamity broke that proper routine: washing on Monday, ironing on Tuesday, mending on Wednesday, sewing on Thursday, extra cleaning on Friday, baking on Saturday. Self-respecting women did the housework first. But there was such rivalry in getting the washing out early that some women were suspected of giving their housework only a lick and a promise on Monday mornings; snoopy neighbors ran in on some trumped-up errand, just to see.

Sunday was called a day of rest. It was really the day on which the smooth, bland surface of living became thicker than enamel. It was the only day, except Thanksgiving, when we were dressed-up at home. We woke clean from the previous night's bath; fresh underwear felt strange against the skin; by nine o'clock we were getting into Sunday clothes. Men and boys looked unfamiliar in their best suits with boiled shirts and stiff collars, knotted four-in-hands and polished shoes. The church bells rang a sweeter but no less imperative summons than the school bell, accelerating the last-minute scurry of thrusting in hat-pins, tying veils not unbearably tight over the nose, pinning the watch to the bosom and smoothing black kid down compressed fingers. Petticoats rustled feverishly and voices grew sharp. "Have you a handkerchief? Did you put out the cat? Have you locked the back door, are you sure?" "Hurry, we'll be late." "Well, it's not my fault if we are, I was ready —" "Oh my goodness, don't stand there *talking!*" Then the key turned in the front door, and decorum encased us.

Even the street, the sunshine, the very air had a special Sunday quality. We walked differently on Sundays, with greater propriety and stateliness. Greetings were more formal, more subdued, voices more meticulously polite. Everything was smooth, bland, polished. And genuinely so, because this was

Sunday. In church the rustling and the stillness were alike pervaded with the knowledge that all was for the best. Propriety ruled the universe. God was in His Heaven, and we were in our Sunday clothes.

The rich and heavy Sunday dinner increased this sense of well-being. Sunday afternoons had the mellowness of an over-ripe apple. In winter the heater's drowsy warmth enveloped us, we sank into a lethargy of woolly underwear, of serge dresses and black broadcloth. In summer we sat on the shady front porch. Flounced lawns and dimities grew slightly limp in spite of our care for their freshness. Parents nodded and roused to fan themselves with the folded church weekly and to crush a yawn. They spoke sleepily in the Sunday stillness. "I don't know but I've got a notion to go into the house where folks can't see me and take off this coat. Seems like it's smothering me." "Well, why don't you? I could take a nap myself, only it's too much trouble dressing for church again. Don't know's I ever saw such weather for the time of year." "Yes, be hard on the farmers if we don't get rain. Well, I don't know but I will." "Yes, I would. Why don't you?"

We, in our teens, read the funny papers. Elsie Dinsmore, Jo March and her sisters, and The Five Little Peppers, had been replaced by the Katzenjammer Kids, Buster Brown, Maud the Mule, and the Newly Weds. All through the week we discussed them, they gave us our nicknames and our slang. Their freshly renewed images hung about us in those long, lazy Sunday afternoons while with our chums we lounged in the hammock under the appletree, or dreamily went walking out the long board walk and back.

Boys in their Sunday clothes were walking in couples, too. We passed them with downcast eyes, or boldly, flippantly said, "Hello!" They answered, "Hello," politely or — the fresh thing! "Oh, you kid!" A girl with *savoir faire* would reply smartly, "Skidoo for you!" But few girls had such poise and daring. Our retreating steps sounded unnaturally loud on the board walk, and a truly shameless boy might sing, not loudly, "Just because you made them goo-goo eyes—"

We would encounter those boys again after church that night. When services were ended, they would be first out of church because they sat on the back seats. They waited on the steps, a nudging, half-jeering mass reluctantly parting to let us through. A boy might step out of it to mutter, "M'I see you home tonight?"

Our hearts beat dreadfully. To answer, "No," was final. A blushing yes, or a choked and silent taking of the offered arm, might lead to saucers of ice-cream bought at the Ladies' Aid socials, to the more definite attention of buggy rides on Sunday afternoons, perhaps to the Christmas gift of comb-and-brush set in a silk-lined box that was almost an avowal, and at last to the final bliss of the Newly Weds, with their darling baby that had never been younger and never grew older than the enchanting age of one tooth.

I have written so far, and suddenly everything I

have set down with scrupulous accuracy seems incredible even to me. These are my memories, the memories of most middle-aged Americans today; these are facts of the life we knew. The essence of that life, its inner meaning, was still the meaning of American life only thirty years ago.

It was a hard, narrow, relentless life. It was not comfortable. Nothing was made easy for us. We did not like work and we were not supposed to like it; we were supposed to work, and we did. We did not like discipline, so we suffered until we disciplined ourselves. We saw many things and many opportunities that we ardently wanted and could not pay for, so we did not get them, or got them only after stupendous, heartbreaking effort and self-denial, for debt was much harder to bear than deprivations. We were honest, not because sinful human nature wanted to be, but because the consequences of dishonesty were excessively painful. It was clear that if your word were not as good as your bond, your bond was no good and you were worthless. Not only by precept but by cruel experience we learned that it is impossible to get something for nothing; that he who does not work can not long continue to eat; that the sins of the fathers are visited upon the children even unto the fourth generation; that chickens come home to roost and the way of the transgressor is hard.

And we did not like that way of life. We rebelled against it because we did not like it. We wanted a land overflowing with milk and honey, where everyone would be free and good and happy. I do not know what had become of that concept, good. No one mentions it any more. It seemed to become increasingly incompatible with the overflowing milk and honey, with the freedom and the easy grasp of immediate pleasures.

That way of life against which my generation rebelled had given us grim courage, fortitude, self-discipline, a sense of individual responsibility, and a capacity for relentless hard work. These qualities had been ingrained in the American character from the first. These were the qualities with which the millions of Americans, men and women of thirty years ago or so, set out to get what they wanted, and got it, and lavished it on their children; freedom, ease, comforts, luxuries, in a quarter of a century transforming the whole of American life.

Now some of us seem to see, in our country's most recent experiences, an unexpected proof that our parents knew what they were talking about. We suspect that, after all, man's life in this hostile universe is not easy and can not be made so; that facts are seldom pleasant and must be faced; that the only freedom is to be found within the slavery of self-discipline; that everything must be paid for and that putting off the day of reckoning only increases the inexorable bill.

This may be an old-fashioned, middle-class, small-town point of view. All that can be said for it is that it created America.

The small town itself has vanished. Nothing but external aspects now distinguish our small towns from the cities. In New York, Chicago, San Francisco, in sedate New England villages, sleepy southern towns, brisk little ganglions of the middle-west, in the bland small towns of California's irrigated valleys and the little towns in hollows between the mountains of Oregon and Washington, accents vary and customs differ, but not thought. Today the small-town point of view is not only in the small towns, and the city's point of view, formed by experience with machines and viewing masses of men as mechanisms, is to be met far from the cities. When I found the American small town interesting me as material for fiction, I had to return to the small town of about thirty years ago.

It is necessary to say this, because when some of these stories appeared in *The Saturday Evening Post,* otherwise well-informed persons startled me by supposing that I wrote about today's small town. This was a city man's thought unconsciously remaining in the days when small-town Americans truly were rubes, hicks. Nowadays the small towns do not make the obverse error of despising city men as dudes. Small-town people today, unlike those intellectuals observed by Dorothy Parker, do get around a great deal.

The stories in this book deal with a time and place so remote and so fantastic to us now, that this sketch of yesterday's small town may make them more intelligible to readers under thirty. Writing fiction is an endless and always defeated effort to capture some quality of life without killing it, but in writing these stories I have got a writer's brief and scanty pleasure, partly from remembering and partly from the fun of telling young people what living was like in those ancient days before the war.

II

OLD MAID

MY MOTHER had always told me that it was cruel to make fun of old maids. "Poor things, they can't help it," she said. "People ought to be sorry for them."

So I was sorry for Miss Sarah, and I thought it was mean to send her comic Valentines, with their hideously funny pictures and their verses:

> Red and yeller, red and yeller,
> Ugly old maid,
> You can't ketch a feller.

Miss Sarah did not look like those pictures. She had a great deal of fair hair, coiled in thick braids; she had blue eyes and a heavily curved, firm mouth, and she moved with a kind of pleasing awkwardness. There was an air of capability about her.

My mother said she must have been pretty as a girl. "Why nobody ever took a shine to her beats me."

Mrs. Rogers agreed. "Well, now you point it out— She's thrifty and capable, too, and a good cook. Yes, she'd 've made a real helpmeet for some good man."

"I declare," my mother said, "when you see the

27

girls that do get married; seems to me men haven't got the sense that God gave little apples."

Everybody knew that Miss Sarah would never see twenty-three again. But she was neat and, in a proper, modest way, stylish. Whenever the fashions changed she made over her best black cashmere, with a bit of jet trimming or a new velvet ribbon. She made over her hats, too, and with her bangs curled and her gold watch-chain around her neck, she looked as well as anybody.

She had never had a beau. Since she was sixteen she had taught school, at first in country schools and later in town. She gave good satisfaction and everybody felt that she could go right on teaching Primer and First and Second Readers as long as she lived. Her wages were thirty dollars a month, eight months of every year, so she was provided for and could save something for her old age.

Her parents were dead, and having no relatives to take her in she boarded with old Mrs. Cleaver. It was a good arrangement for them both. With the board money and her pension old Mrs. Cleaver made both ends meet, and Miss Sarah, living under the wing of a respectable widow, could not be talked about.

Miss Sarah made no bones about being an old maid. She did not dress in a kittenish way nor pretend to be younger than she was. And whenever she was with the married women, working at a quilting or at a Ladies' Aid social, she always said right out that she was an old maid.

"Of course, I couldn't pretend to know about that, I'm only an old maid," she'd say, in the gossip across the quilting frames. Or when her cooking was praised, "I guess it's as good as can be expected from an old maid with no husband to practice on." Or if someone said how well her cashmere was wearing, five years old and still good as new, she'd answer, "Well, I try to look as well as the Lord'll let me, for all I'm an old maid."

She flushed a little and her voice had a hard cheeriness. Her eyes fascinated me. They were cheerful and hard, too, but they widened a little, and waited, as if they were determined to be cheerful no matter what happened.

"Oh, well, Miss Sarah," some married woman would respond awkwardly, "I guess if truth was known, you've had chances." Or, with false archness, "We all know you're only waiting for Mr. Right to come along!"

Miss Sarah would toss her head and make a sound like a laugh. "Oh, I'm not one to take the first that offers," she'd say, red spots burning on her cheekbones. "Just to have 'Mrs.' carved on my tombstone!" Everyone felt uncomfortable.

I couldn't understand why she was always saying she was an old maid. Everybody knew she was. If she'd say nothing about it, the others could gloss it over, they could pretend it made no difference. She didn't seem to enjoy speaking about it, either. But she always did.

Like my mother, I was truly sorry that no one had ever wanted to marry her, but I made only one attempt to condole with her.

I was a little girl then, in the Third Reader. One day after school my mother sent me to return a crochet pattern she had borrowed from old Mrs. Cleaver. It was a soft autumn evening; the air was so still that the cowbells coming nearer from the pastures sounded clearly. There was a scent of late roses and second-blooming phlox, and airy balls of dandelions made a fairyland all along the sidewalks. The sunlight was dusty gold, slanting between Mrs. Cleaver's tall lilac bushes. Softly I went up the steps to her narrow front porch.

The two front rooms opened from this porch and one of them was Miss Sarah's. Her door was open, and beyond the dusk of the bitter-sweet vines I saw her in her green hickory rocker. Little Myrtle Sims was cuddled against her breast. They were not saying anything. Miss Sarah's arms held Myrtle tenderly and there was a strange, melting look on her face; she seemed far away in a vague happiness.

Myrtle's curls were tumbled on Miss Sarah's shoulder. They fell across Myrtle's face; I saw only her dreamily parted lips and a curve of cheek. One of her arms fondly clasped Miss Sarah's neck; with the other hand she was stealthily chipping, bit by bit, flakes of green paint from the back of Miss Sarah's rocker.

Suddenly an eye gleamed through the curls; Myrtle saw me, she saw my horror at what she was doing, and before my opened mouth could cry out against it she had flung both arms around Miss Sarah's neck.

"Oh darling Miss Sarah!" she cooed, "Why didn't anybody ever want to marry you? If I was a man, I don't care if you're an old maid, I love you, I'd marry you, poor Miss Sarah!"

All my own pity rushed into my throat. I wanted Miss Sarah to know that I was sorry, too; I was really sorry, sorrier than Myrtle. "I'm sorry for you, too, Miss Sarah," I said earnestly. "I'm awf'ly sorry and so is mama. Mama says, if men had the sense God gave little ap —"

I was stunned as though a tiger had appeared.

"Oh!" Miss Sarah cried. It was a cry of anguish, of outrage, of accusation. It was a terrible cry. She plucked Myrtle from her shoulder and thrust her away with loathing. She sprang up, the rocker lurching almost over backwards.

"Don't you dare!" she cried at us. "I won't have it! I won't stand it! I tell you I don't want to get married! I could have, I could! I could! I tell you!" Tears gushed from her eyes. Her eyes were blazing with anger, and tears poured down her face. We stared at her, fascinated.

"*Liars!*" she said. "Horrid, horrid children! Go away. Get out of here. *Go! Get out!*"

We fled, dumb. Some distance down the sidewalk we stood and looked at each other. We looked at Mrs. Cleaver's house. It was not changed. We looked at each other again. Myrtle whispered, "Did you hear what she said?"

I nodded.

"But how could she ever?   Nobody ever asked her. Mama says so."

"That's what makes old maids.   Nobody ever asks them."

"Miss Sarah," Myrtle whispered, incredulous, awed. "Miss Sarah — told — a — lie." She clapped a hand to her mouth, as if it had committed the sin.

We parted in a wordless understanding that we mustn't tell what had happened. When I timidly stole again to Mrs. Cleaver's porch, Miss Sarah's door was closed.

I was troubled. I felt that something was wrong; my mother told me to be sorry for Miss Sarah, but when I was sorry, this was what happened. Yet I felt that somehow I had been at fault, though I didn't quite know how, and I said nothing to my mother, being sure that she would know only too well. Myrtle and I marveled and puzzled for awhile, and then forgot the matter.

Years passed. I was twelve; Miss Sarah must have been all of twenty six, on the Sunday night when Jay Willard saw her home from church.

Nothing had prepared us. It was a Sunday night like any other. Mrs. Cleaver was ailing, and Miss Sarah had asked if she might go to church with us. She couldn't, of course, go alone. My father and mother in their Sunday clothes walked ahead while Miss Sarah and I, in ours, sedately followed them, past the livery barn, along the block of closed stores that faced the Square, across the railroad tracks and up the slope to the church.

We sat, as usual, midway between pulpit and door. The bald heads and old-fashioned bonnets of the old, devout and deaf, were massed in front of us. In the seats behind the organ the young ladies of the choir were demure. Behind us were young ladies with their beaux, and boys made a stealthy disturbance in the back seats.

Church was always interesting, because there we saw everyone's best clothes, and if any young lady came with a new beau or without an old one, we saw that. Sunday nights always gave us something to talk about through the next week.

That evening the young doctor was there. He was the old doctor's nephew, but nobody knew him. He had worked on his father's farm, ten miles away, till he was twenty-four years old. One day the old doctor, driving by to call on a patient, stopped his buggy by the cornfield, and young Adam Wright laid down his hoe. "I'll never hoe another row of this dodblasted corn," he said. "I'm going to be a doctor. God knows how I'll get the schooling, but I'm going to."

Somehow he had done it, and now here he was. Everybody looked at him. He still had a country air; his sleeves were too short and his collar uncomfortable. But he looked honest and capable, and some day he would have all of old Dr. Wright's practice. It made church interesting to look at him, and to see all the young ladies pretending they did not notice him at all.

But the exciting moment was after church, when we came out and walked down the steps between masses of young men and boys. Then I craned and pushed and hung back to see the big boys stepping up to ask the girls, "Can I see you home?"

Everything was confused in the crowded darkness. From the door came a shaft of dim light; in the shadows boys were jostling and jeering; men stopped to light lanterns; women nudged and murmured. I did not see Jay Willard step up to Miss Sarah.

All at once I felt the sensation, I knew something was happening. Then in a gleam from a lantern I saw Miss Sarah's face. It was all discomposed, startled, embarrassed, almost frightened. Her gloved hand was on Jay Willard's arm.

I stood in their way, staring up at them, too shocked to move, till my mother's hand jerked me aside. In the silence Miss Sarah walked down the steps with Jay Willard.

Everybody began to talk at once, pretending nothing had happened. Mrs. Rogers breathed, "Did you ever?"

"Jay Willard, of all people!" my mother gasped.

He was an old bachelor, all of thirty years old. He had been a great flirt, but he had always bragged that no girl could out-smart him. And no girl ever had.

There was a dash and glitter about him. He wore boiled shirts and stiff collars every day, and a diamond horse-shoe pin in his tie. He smoked two-for-a-quarter cigars. His stories and jokes were the life of the barber shop. And he drove such a wild team — in ivory-trimmed harness, on a red-wheeled buggy — that all the men said admiringly that he'd kill himself yet.

Old Mr. Willard was dead; he had been a saloon keeper and had left Mrs. Willard and Jay well provided for. They lived in a tall gray house near the church, with scroll-saw work on eaves and ridge, and five sharp lightning rods. All the front window shades were always down.

Mrs. Willard was like her house; tall, reserved, precise, with iron-gray hair and sharp eyes. She once told Mrs. Rogers that all she asked in life was to live down the disgrace of Mr. Willard's selling liquor. "I never forgave him for it while he lived," she said, setting her lips in a way she had. "And I see no reason to do so now. It isn't as if we're likely to meet in the hereafter."

"But if I was her," Mrs. Rogers said, "I'd give thought to Jay's hereafter. He playing cards and dancing and I don't know what all. Telling the kind of stories he does in the barber shop and up to some prank or other the whole time."

"Well, I don't know's I ever heard he drank," my mother murmured as though she thought she ought to. "They say give the devil his due."

"He won't get it," said Mrs. Rogers, "till he gets Jay Willard."

And now Jay Willard was seeing Miss Sarah home from church.

We made a little procession of groups and couples, down the slope, across the railroad tracks and along the sidewalk by the Square. Here and there men's legs cast long shadow-scissors snipping across a lantern's patch of light. Usually there was a murmur of talk, but tonight there was a buzz. Little boys kept racing ahead, waiting in front of Miss Sarah and Jay Willard, then falling back with yells.

"I'd think their mothers'd make them behave!" my mother said angrily.

It was a mild night of early spring; there was a smell of dewy grass and tansy beds and plowed gardens. In the starlight we could see the tilt of Jay's hat, his jaunty shoulders, and sometimes a blur of his face turned toward Miss Sarah. We could see her straight back and the bunch of her held-up skirts. He was doing most of the talking but we could not hear what he said.

We passed them at Mrs. Cleaver's gate. Jay lifted his hat with a flourish and my father lifted his, but no one spoke. Miss Sarah's face was turned a little aside, looking down. After we passed we heard her say, breathless, "Well, I— Well, goodnight, Mr. Willard." Jay's answer sounded confident and as if he were laughing a little. After a moment we all looked back; they were still at the gate.

I had that bit to tell at school next day. All the girls were talking about Jay Willard and Miss Sarah, and at recess Elsie Miller and I went into her classroom to look at her. She was at her desk, surrounded by little girls, and she did not seem changed to me. But she was looking everywhere for her pencil and she flushed when Elsie told her it was stuck in her back hair.

Elsie said pertly, "I guess you've got something on your mind, Miss Sarah."

Miss Sarah gave her an odd, hard look. "You might have something on yours, miss, if —" But Elsie's father was on the school board, and Miss Sarah said, "if you were teaching sixty young ones."

Outside, Elsie reported, "She's gone on Jay Willard, anybody can see she is. But she'll never land him, never in this world."

"Well, but he took her home from church."

"I don't care!" Elsie insisted. "Mama says there are just as good fish in the sea as ever were caught and she says Jay Willard's one of 'em and he always will be."

"Then what did he see her home for?" I protested. I was so sorry for Miss Sarah that I clung to hope for her.

My father destroyed the hope that day at dinner. He couldn't keep an ashamed grin from his face. "Well, I can tell you why Jay Willard saw Miss Sarah home last night."

"Well, why?" my mother asked sharply, apprehensive.

"Bob Inman dared him to. And he bet Bob five dollars he'd do it, and kiss her into the bargain."

My mother flushed hotly. "I never *heard* of anything so *outrageous!* Be ashamed of yourself, sitting there grinning at it!"

"I'm not grinning," my father said with indignation. "I know it's a low-down mean trick much as
you do." But the grin kept struggling back to his
face. "Only it was kind of funny," he muttered,
ashamed. "The way Jay got to talking, in the barber
shop."

"I'd like to see him tarred and feathered and
drummed out of town!" My mother's eyes were
furiously blue. "Low-down mean, contemptible
trash! How you men can sit around listening to
him and guffawing! Don't you repeat to *me* what
he said! Did he say he kissed her?"

"Well, not exactly."

"What do you mean, not exactly. He either did
or he didn't, didn't he? Well, what are you keeping
back, now?"

"Seems Bob Inman and a couple others went down
across lots and listened behind the lilac bushes. And
Bob claims Jay lost the bet. But Jay says, he never
bet when he'd kiss her." My father's grin was gone.
"It's downright mean, for a fact. But Jay raised the
bet to twenty five, and he says he'll kiss her, all right."

My mother said slowly, "Killing's too good for
him."

"Well, I guess it is."

"Poor Miss Sarah. Oh, somebody ought to tell
her!"

"It's not your affair," my father said drily. "You
keep out of it."

My mother looked as she did the time the dog bit
her and she thought she ought to burn out the wound;

she heated the poker red hot and stood holding it, looking like that. Then she thought perhaps turpentine would do. And it turned out that the dog wasn't mad, after all.

"Well," she said weakly, "Miss Sarah's got good sense."

She said the same thing later to Mrs. Rogers. "Yes," Mrs. Rogers agreed doubtfully. "She's got sense. But for all that, she's an old maid. And Jay is a good catch."

"Money isn't everything," my mother replied. "She couldn't possibly respect him. Besides, she'll never let him kiss her unless they're engaged, and if he goes that far he'll have to —"

"Not Jay Willard. He'll jilt her, that's what he'll do."

"Oh no! not *that!*" my mother cried. But she knew he would; her horror showed that she knew it.

"She'll never stay here and face it," Mrs. Rogers said, grimly prophetic. "She's got too much pride. It's bad enough being an old maid, she tries to carry that off. But if he makes such a laughing-stock of her — Only she hasn't got anybody or anyone to go to, that I ever heard of."

It was frightening to see Miss Sarah's unawareness. Wherever she appeared there was an awkward silence and it seemed impossible that she didn't know that people had been talking about her. But she did not know, or else she didn't mind it. She laughed and talked more than before, and with a kind of happy assurance; she seemed shyly gay.

After Jay Willard took her home from church again, she went to Miller's store and bought fourteen yards of foulard. She sewed on the new dress till all hours, and wore it next Sunday. The foulard was blue-black, with an all-over pattern in shaded grays; she had made it up with mousequetaire sleeves and three graduated flounces trimmed with double ruffles. White ruching edged the boned collar. Perhaps it was that white ruching curved under her chin and fitting snugly behind her ears that gave her face a clear, transparent look. Her eyes seemed bluer and her smile more vivid.

Jay Willard had not brought her to church and no one knew whether he would see her home. When she went down the aisle, most of the young men and all the boys at the back of the church were waiting to see what would happen. Jay stood between the ends of the seats, letting people go past him. Just as Miss Sarah reached him, he threw back his head and let a laugh silently appear on his shrewd face, for everyone to see except Miss Sarah. Her eyes were downcast; she was pretending she didn't know he was there.

Then jauntily he stepped out beside her, and she glanced at him and took his arm.

I saw her eyes. She didn't seem to be seeing him at all; she seemed to be aware of everybody but him. She took his arm with a kind of avid triumph. I was bewildered; it was almost as if Jay were the one to be sorry for.

That wasn't true, of course. He was mean and

cruel, making fun of a poor old maid that couldn't help herself. When I came home from school the next noon my father was telling my mother what Jay said. They were abruptly silent when I came in, but that didn't matter; Elsie would tell us all about it.

"He called her 'Sweetness,'" Elsie told us. "And he called her 'Cutie.' And she just lapped it up. Bob Inman and the barber liked to died laughing. And she let him hold her hand."

"She didn't!" I cried. "I don't believe it!"

"They saw her. And he tried to kiss her and she said, 'Oh, Mr. Willard! You mustn't!'"

Elsie somehow made it as funny as the hideous comic Valentines. "I don't think it's funny!" Leila Barbrook exclaimed, horrified, laughing.

"You'd ought to be ashamed, Elsie Miller!" Lois Estes said.

"Well, she ought to have better sense. She ought to know nobody's going to fall for her at this late date. My goodness, she's twenty-six! But mama says an old maid'll just believe what a man tells her. If you don't have sense enough to get married, she says, why, then you don't have any better sense than that."

Next Sunday Miss Sarah wore a new hat. She had sent to a mail-order house for it. It was a turban of purple pansies, with a purple bow and a bunch of wheat standing up at one side, and a chenille-dotted veil that came just over the tip of her nose. Her cheeks were flushed all through the service. Jay Willard took her home again.

I came home from school next day to find my

mother and Mrs. Rogers at the side fence. They had
been taking in the washing. My mother said, "It's
going too far. It's got to be put a stop to."

"Well, she says herself the purple's brighter than
she thought it would be, from the catalogue," Mrs.
Rogers murmured. "And now she's got it of course
she's got to wear it out. But Mr. Rogers says Jay
says —"

My mother caught sight of me. "Ernestine, you
go in the house and take that school-dress off, this
minute!"

When she came in with the clean clothes her eyes
were dangerous and her mouth was set. She took
off her apron, smoothed her hair and put on her
second-best hat. Her afternoon calico was clean and
neat.

"You peel the potatoes and put them to boil," she
said to me.

"Mama, where are you going?"

"I'll be back in a few minutes."

Behind the parlor curtains I watched her going to
old Mrs. Cleaver's. The last of the schoolchildren
had passed; no one else was in sight. My mother
marched up Mrs. Cleaver's steps and disappeared behind the bitter-sweet vines. I had to peel the potatoes,
but I was so excited I could hardly make thin parings.

Only three potatoes were peeled when the screen
door slammed. My mother was angry. She jerked
out the hatpins and thrust them into the hat as though
she were stabbing it.

"Mama," I ventured. "Mama, did you — tell her?"

"No!" she exclaimed. "She's gone buggy-riding. Buggy-riding! On Monday! At this hour!"

At supper my father said mildly, "That team he drives, she'll be lucky if she don't get back with a broken neck." He was thoughtful for a moment. "Well, Jay's cute; he hasn't got any witnesses."

"She ought to have better sense!" My mother seemed to be crying out against some injustice done to herself.

"Well, it's none of your business, I told you to keep out of it," my father said.

Next day everybody knew that Bob Inman was trying to get out of paying that bet. Jay claimed he'd kissed Miss Sarah, but he couldn't prove it. My mother said it was one of his low-down lies; Miss Sarah wouldn't allow such a thing. In the livery barn one of the men said to Jay, "If you tried handling that team with one hand, you're more of a fool than I give you credit for."

"Or maybe a better driver," Jay said, grinning. "Oh, I was driving with one arm, all right!"

The men on the school board were uneasy. A good many parents thought they should take some notice of the scandal. Not this year; school was out that week. But there was the question of hiring Miss Sarah for the next term. It was too bad, and in a way it wasn't her fault, and maybe it wasn't true that she had allowed Jay to take liberties, but after all, there it was: A teacher who was talked about wasn't setting a right example to the children.

Warm May days had come, and now on Sundays

the big girls went walking with their beaux. We younger girls followed them in couples. All in our summer Sunday clothes, we strolled along the railroad tracks, out to the trestle and back, then out to the cut. Violets and buttercups were in bloom. Peach trees were still pink with blossoms and wild plums let fall a snow of petals. If you could walk eleven railroad rails without losing your balance, then make a wish and the wish would come true.

From the other end of the cut the country road came back past the graveyard, where old headstones slanted above the graves and the breeze made a mournful sound in the pines, and then there was the long board walk stretching all the way to the Square and the end of Sunday afternoon.

We were scattered along this road, strolling slowly in the warm dust, when a racketing clatter and terror came upon us. Jay Willard's black team came charging, running away. The mad horses seemed gigantic, their great shoulders and steel-shod hoofs plunging at us. We ran, shrieking. One of the big boys dashed toward the horses; he was going to jump and grab at the bridles; he would be struck down, mangled, killed. But he faltered, shrank back; death lunged past.

There was a glimpse of Jay Willard, off the seat, feet braced, his weight and strength on the lines, fighting. His hat was gone. Miss Sarah, white and still, gripped the edge of the seat.

The air swirled and dust hid them. Nobody saw what happened; we heard only the rending crash.

Afterward men examined the wreckage and said that one of the lines had broken.

What was left of the buggy lay smashed against a tree. Miss Sarah lay flat on the ground and the big boys, running, paused and swerved aside; we could see her black-cotton legs almost to the knees, in a swirl of petticoats. But before we girls reached her she had stirred and was pulling her skirts down. Jay Willard was in a queer huddle by the tree. The big boys ran to him.

Miss Sarah got to her feet. There was blood on her face, the pansy turban hung crooked on her loosened hair, she was trembling all over. But she spoke as she did in the schoolroom. "Don't touch him. You girls keep back. Ewing, run for the doctor, quick!"

She knelt down by Jay Willard and took hold of his wrist. A queer look came over her face, her hand jerked away. Then she felt his wrist again, and again let it go. She kept on doing that, while we stood not knowing what to do, and her hair kept shivering and slipping down her shoulder. We heard men shouting downtown, heading off the horses.

The young doctor came hurrying up the long board walk, carrying his medicine case. Miss Sarah looked at him as though she didn't see him. "Get the doctor," she said.

"I'm a doctor," he told her. He began to examine Jay Willard. "Uncle Dave's out on a case," he said. Men and women were running toward us; a buggy had stopped. One of the big girls took off Miss

Sarah's crushed turban and began to mop at the blood; there was only a shallow cut on Miss Sarah's dead-white cheek.

The young doctor stood up, slowly shaking his head. A man asked, "Is he hurt bad, Doc?"

The doctor looked at him, then frowned warningly toward Miss Sarah. The man slowly took off his hat. All the men took their hats off. A woman said, "Oh, his poor mother!" and began to cry excitedly.

"Is he —?" Miss Sarah said, staring up at the doctor. "He isn't —" She seemed to see all the bare heads. "Oh, no!" she cried out.

"Come, come," the doctor said, speaking like the old doctor. "Now we don't want *you* on our hands! We'll do everything that can be done for your husband, madam. Now you just —"

He looked around at the faces, and suddenly he seemed awkward, embarrassed.

"He wasn't my husband," Miss Sarah said. The young doctor turned red. Elsie Miller began to laugh hysterically; she couldn't stop. Miss Sarah straightened up on her knees. "But I was engaged to him," she said, and cried at Elsie, "So don't you laugh at me! Don't you laugh at me! Don't you laugh —" She broke into wild sobs.

There had never been such a sensation.

Many women didn't go to church that night; they were sitting with Miss Sarah, or with Mrs. Willard in Jay's bedroom. He had been carried carefully home on a bedsprings. It was only a matter of time now;

he was still breathing, but his neck was broken; there was no hope.

After church everyone went in to condole with his mother and to look at him, lying under the still counterpane as though he had already passed away. The old doctor had come and done things to him; only his closed eyes, sharp nose and thin mouth emerged from the bandages. His jaw was broken, too; the doctors had set it, and given him morphine.

The ladies murmured sadly to Mrs. Willard, telling her of their own bereavements, and the minister was there, saying, "The Lord hath given, Sister Willard, and the Lord hath taken away." People could never say again what they really thought of Jay Willard. Now they must only speak good of him.

Outside the Willard house, all the talk was about Miss Sarah. There was relish in the women's sad voices. What had happened was like something in a book. It was so amazing to think that Miss Sarah had done what none of the girls, when Jay was younger, had been able to do. It was so sad to think of her, widowed before she was wed. She couldn't have been engaged more than an hour or two. Maybe only a matter of minutes. To think that it was all over, so soon.

"Do you think she'll wear mourning for him?" they asked each other. They thought not. Well, black, of course. "She can't hardly go into widow's weeds; it isn't as if she'd been married to him."

But it wasn't her fault, any more, that she hadn't been.

She was in bed; the young doctor had said she must rest. He called next morning, and the next. "She's a sick woman, she must have rest," he kept repeating to all the neighbors who were there sympathizing with her. "It's the shock," he said.

When they offered to help her dress and go with her to Jay's bedside, she turned her head on the pillow. "No," she said. "Thank you, I— No."

"Seems like you ought to make the effort," old Mrs. Cleaver said to her. "If he's conscious at the last, and you not there, you'll be sorry after he's gone." It wasn't like Miss Sarah, not to make an effort. Though she didn't have a broken bone, nor so much as a sprain, she stayed in bed. And she talked hardly at all. Nobody learned anything more.

When someone came in with broth or jelly, she said thank you. When they said how sad it was and how mysterious of Providence to take her intended, and they so newly engaged, she said, "Yes."

"My, my, and it all over so soon," Mrs. Miller sighed. "It must have happened that very afternoon, didn't it? You couldn't 've been engaged to him more than an hour or two. Were you?"

"No," Miss Sarah said. So he must have popped the question just before the runaway, and maybe that was why the team bolted. He couldn't control those high-spirited horses with one hand.

My mother confided to Mrs. Rogers, "You could 've knocked me over with a feather."

"Me too," Mrs. Rogers said. "The way he was talking — and all — But if she says so — Anyway I guess he must have asked her, even if he —"

"Yes, even if — Well," my mother said delicately, "maybe it's all turned out for the best."

Incredibly, Jay Willard was still living, that day, and the next day, and the next. And the next. It never seemed possible that he could last through the night, but in the morning he had done it. The women were taking turns sitting up with him, now.

Miss Sarah was still in bed. It was the young doctor's orders. Every morning he said more sharply, "She must get some rest."

The whole atmosphere was sharpening, in the suspense. The women looked more keenly at Miss Sarah. Suspicion didn't quite come to words, but there were glances.

"It's wonderful how he's holding out," Mrs. Miller said to Miss Sarah. "It would be Providential if he got well. Wouldn't it?"

"Yes," Miss Sarah said weakly. Then she roused. "Yes, of course! I hope he does."

My mother bristled. "Well, of course you do!" Afterward she said to Mrs. Rogers, "That Mrs. Miller! I'd like to wring her neck!"

Mrs. Rogers sat up with Jay that night, and next morning she came hurrying in while we were doing the breakfast dishes. My mother took her hands out of the dishwater at once. "When did he go?" she asked gravely.

"No," Mrs. Rogers answered, excitedly. "No,

but — Oh, poor Miss Sarah! And his mother —"

Mrs. Willard had said right out that Miss Sarah was a liar. "It's a bare-faced lie!" Those were her very words. "My poor boy never thought for one minute of marrying that old maid. The very idea!"

My mother was indignant. "Everybody knows Miss Sarah's never told a lie in her life. If she says they were engaged, then they *were* engaged. And I don't know what good it'll do Mrs. Willard to —"

"But that's not all!"

The old doctor said he'd seen men survive worse things than a broken neck. "It all depends on whether the spinal cord's injured," he had told Mrs. Rogers. "There's no way of finding that out, now. But the way he's mending, I wouldn't be surprised," he said, "if we had him up and around again as good as ever, one of these days."

"Good — *land!*" my mother said. She and Mrs. Rogers gazed at each other, and slowly a kind of cold rage rose in my mother. "I'll never believe him, never. Not on a stack of Bibles. He had no business starting it in the first place. And if you don't believe he proposed to her, I'll never forgive you."

"So do I!" Mrs. Rogers exclaimed. "She's had too much to bear and I don't care! I don't blame her. And it's all that young doctor's fault. If he hadn't jumped to conclusions —"

"But my goodness!" my mother cried. "A broken neck!"

"I mean, if he hadn't said Jay was her husband —"

"Well, of course! That's what I mean. But what

can we do? Oh, poor Miss Sarah! It'll be all over town."

She was untying her apron strings and I knew well enough what would happen; I would have to finish the housework by myself. "And don't you give it a lick and a promise, either," my mother said viciously, departing.

She had forgotten to mention the woodbox. I left it empty, escaping to Miss Sarah's as soon as I could. Her room was crowded, and the porch; dishes must have been left unwashed and beds unmade, all over town. In the kitchen Mrs. Cleaver was saying to somebody, "Well, that's real nice of you. Crab-apple, too! I was saying to Miss Sarah, 'What you'll ever do with all this jelly—'"

On the porch Mrs. Miller murmured "She looks like death. And no wonder."

But from the doorway Miss Sarah didn't look like death. She was sitting up in bed, in a snow-white nightgown with a tucked and lace-edged collar buttoned to her chin. Her face was so thin that the cheeks were faintly hollowed. The tawny braids of her hair hung straight down either shoulder, and her eyes were enormous. The thin cheeks, the firm curves of her pale lips and those heavy-lidded eyes gave me a strange sensation. I knew she was old, and no one thought her pretty, but I could not take my gaze away from her.

My mother was remonstrating, "No, Miss Sarah. You stay right where you are until the doctor comes."

Miss Miller pushed past me. "I don't know's there's

so much the matter with her," she said. "Seems to me she might as well get up now as later."

Unexpectedly Elsie spoke up. She had got there before I did, and was standing in the corner by the washstand. "Yes," she said with a competent air. "Either she's engaged to him or she isn't, and I guess he knows. Hiding here in bed won't make any difference."

In the shock everyone looked at Miss Sarah. A thin flush ran up her transparent cheeks and her lips parted. But my mother spoke first; she looked like a mule ready to kick.

"That's enough from you, miss!" she said. "Children should be seen and not heard." She had made an enemy of Mrs. Miller, but she didn't care.

Mrs. Miller gave her one look, and turned to Miss Sarah. "You are engaged to him," she said smoothly. "Aren't you?"

"It's disgraceful!" Mrs. Rogers exclaimed. "You leave her alone, the doctor says she's a sick —"

Miss Sarah said firmly, "I certainly am engaged to him."

Everyone was staggered. Mrs. Miller gasped, "Why, but he's getting well!"

Miss Sarah leaned forward, those heavy braids swayed and hung straight. Her hands were clenched on the counterpane. "I'm glad he's getting better, I hope he gets well. I'd never 've let the whole town know what's only our business, if I'd been myself at the time. I wish him well, only I've changed my mind, since. I've had time to think it over. And if

I want to break my engagement, I don't see it's any of your business."

She was magnificent.

Mrs. Miller gasped, but there was nothing she could say. She was routed.

"And now I'll be obliged to you," said Miss Sarah, "if you'll all step out for a minute, so I can get up and dress."

But she didn't get up; the young doctor was already at the gate, and there was barely time to hide her nightgown under a dressing-sacque.

He wasn't used to being a doctor yet; he tried to act like the old doctor, but he was nervous with so many women watching him. He gripped the medicine case and was awkward about lifting his hat. Someone near the gate asked him, "How is he, doctor?"

"He's improving," he said. "He's conscious, and taking nourishment."

"Oh doctor," Mrs. Miller pounced at him. "Has he talked yet? What did he say?"

"He can't speak," he told her. "His jaw's broken. And we are keeping him perfectly quiet. Nobody can see him." He repeated with emphasis, "Nobody."

When he had gone, stiff-backed, up the steps and into Miss Sarah's room, Mrs. Miller snorted, "Well!" Mr. Miller owned the store, the Millers were as important as the banker's family; she wasn't used to being spoken to like that. And the idea of keeping people out of Jay's room, when he was sick! "The very idea!" Mrs. Miller said.

My mother and Mrs. Rogers came out of Miss Sarah's room with the young doctor; they walked through the gate with him, and I ran with a skip to join them. My mother was saying, "And I for one believe every word of it."

"Miss Sarah wouldn't lie," Mrs. Rogers said firmly. "She couldn't do such a thing to save her life. And besides, it serves him right!"

The young doctor had a gaunt, raw-boned, country face, but when he smiled it lighted up surprisingly.

When he had gone, they walked slowly up the gravel walk. "How old is he?" my mother asked.

"Twenty-nine last February," Mrs. Rogers said.

"Well, that's a good three years."

"Yes," Mrs. Rogers agreed. "I thought you'd noticed. You think she did?"

"No, not yet," my mother replied. "She's had too much else on her mind. Goodness, it seems almost too much to hope for, with all the girls setting their caps for him the way they —"

I was making nothing of this, but suddenly my mother saw my eager attention and instantly she thought of the empty woodbox.

So I was astonished when one Sunday afternoon we saw Miss Sarah and the young doctor going buggy-riding. Miss Sarah was wearing her cashmere and her old hat. She sat stiffly, knowing everyone was watching. The young doctor stared straight ahead, driving the gentle livery-stable team as if it required all his attention. The buggy went past the schoolhouse and out on the Mill Creek road, where all the apple-orchards were now in blossom.

"That young man's got nerve," said my father. "The way you womenfolks gossip in this town, I'd as soon face a den of lions as walk right up in the face and eyes of everybody and start sparking Miss Sarah."

"She's the salt of the earth, and thank goodness some man's got the sense to realize it," my mother said indignantly. Her rocker creaked for a moment, then she said, "I only wish she didn't have to tell him —"

"Tell him what?" My father looked at her curiously.

"Oh well, honesty's the best policy. But I must say I'm glad of one thing; Jay Willard's got his come-uppance. He can say anything he wants to, he'll never convince *me* that Miss Sarah didn't jilt him. And serve him right, too!"

"That's the truth," my father said. He said it as those words were always said, as if at last and with great relief hearing something that was true.

The odd thing was that Jay didn't say much. Miss Sarah didn't marry the young doctor until the next year, but they were already keeping steady company while Jay was still under the old doctor's care. My father was in the barber shop when Jay first came down town, pale, and walking as if he still felt cautious about his neck. When he came in, Bob Inman asked him how it felt to be jilted.

"That's all right," Jay said, grinning. "There's no woman living smart enough to out-smart me, and don't you think she did it!"

"Well, looks like the young Doc's beat your time, anyhow," Bob Inman said. "And what about that bet? You owe me twenty-five."

"Not on your life I don't!" Jay said.

"That why your team ran away?" the barber chimed in. "Takes a pretty good driver to handle 'em with one hand, I guess."

"Oh, go to hell!" Jay said, and walked out of the barber shop.

III

HIRED GIRL

MY MOTHER often said she wouldn't have a hired girl, not if you paid her for it. "The idea!" she said. "Paying out a dollar and a half a week, not to mention what she'd eat, just to have another woman around underfoot till you can't call your soul your own. When I want to speak to my husband for his own good, I'll not have a hired girl sitting there gawping. My land, I don't know how Mrs. Boles stands it."

Mrs. Rogers agreed complacently. "I never had a hired girl myself was worth her salt."

"That's so, you did have Minty Bates at days' work, that time you were sick," my mother said quickly. "But I mean a real hired girl."

"Yes, yes of course," Mrs. Rogers murmured, collapsing.

It was true that my mother didn't want a hired girl, but it was also true that she couldn't afford one. And neither could Mrs. Rogers. Mrs. Miller sometimes had a hired girl and so did Mrs. Mason, the banker's son's extravagant wife; at those times they said, "the hired girl" as often old maids, if anyone ever married them, said "my husband." Nobody liked hired girls; Mrs. Miller and Mrs. Mason always complained about theirs, and everyone except Mrs. Boles listened enviously. Mrs. Boles had a hired girl to complain about all the time.

"It don't seem reasonable to me it's Mr. Boles insists on keeping Almantha," Mrs. Rogers said. "I guess if truth was told he'd as lief have a wife who'd pitch in and do a day's work like anybody else. But no, she must be smearing on grease for her complexion, and dolling up and gadding downtown after him. Hanging on his arm and looking at him like a sick calf — and she an old married woman who'll never see thirty again!"

Almantha must have had a surname, but nobody ever heard it. She was an orphan from the country when she came to the Boles. Mrs. Boles always said that Mr. Boles had hired Almantha during their honeymoon. She said she hadn't even thought of such a thing as having a hired girl till Almantha came lugging an old carpet-bag onto the back porch and said that Mr. Boles had hired her.

"He wouldn't let me spoil my hands," she said, proudly laughing and preening to show off her rings. "Mr. Boles always brags so on my little white hands, I tell him he's downright silly. 'Now, Lester,' I say, 'It's just downright silly to be so crazy about an old married woman like me!'" Her laugh would tinkle while she glanced eagerly at the other women's faces around the quilting frame, but they'd watch their needles and sew hurriedly.

Without thinking about it, I always felt that Almantha was more a part of the tall livered-colored house than Mrs. Boles. Mrs. Boles was a thin, nervously bright little woman, all curls and ruffles and beads and dangling ribbons, and she was afflicted with a mysterious pain in her side that held her white and quivering for moments together. "I've always been frail, from a child," she'd gasp. Almantha was big, angular, ungainly and solid, like the house. She would listen respectfully to Mrs. Boles, saying, "Yes'm," and "No'm," and then she would unwrap her red, bony hands from her apron and do as she pleased. Mrs. Boles just couldn't do one thing with that girl.

Still, Almantha was clean and willing. She kept the house so scrubbed and polished that a fly'd have slipped and broken his neck. The parlor was always rigidly neat; Almantha dusted behind the pictures and never left the shades up to fade the carpet. On Mondays she did the washing, on Tuesdays the ironing, on Wednesdays the mending. Thursday and Friday she gave the house an extra cleaning, aired the beds, churned, and worked in the garden. Saturday was the big baking day, and on Sunday there was the Sunday dinner to get and the best china to wash afterward.

Naturally Almantha did the usual housework and cooking every day, and fed the pig and milked the cow. Twice a year she pitched into the housecleaning, all summer she put up fruit, and at butchering-time she tried out the lard, made mince-meat, headcheese and sausage; the hams and bacons that Almantha cured and smoked were the best in town. In her idle time she sewed carpet-rags; all the upstairs carpets were made from rags she had sewed.

Sometimes a hired girl at the Millers' tried to boss Elsie, but Almantha never quarreled with Mary and Gertrude Boles. She'd comb their hair and press out hair-ribbons; she made their dresses and underwear and kept their shoes blacked, but she never ordered them to wash their hands or to behave themselves. "Now get out of my kitchen!" she'd say sometimes, or, almost resentfully, "You go ask your ma; they're not my cookies to give anybody."

She slept in the kitchen lean-to. It had been the woodshed, but was nicely ceiled inside to make a room for Almantha, heated summer and winter by the kitchen stove. There she had a warped bureau and an iron bedstead. When the white paint chipped off the iron, Almantha with her own money bought paint and painted that bedstead a violent raspberry pink. She had an old sheet for a bedspread and kept the floor scrubbed bone-white.

"That's my room; you keep out!" she'd say fiercely if we started to go in. But we could see it all; the door was always open, in winter for heat and in summer for air. Almantha had only a little unbleached muslin underwear and a change of calico dresses. She was too big to wear Mrs. Boles' old clothes, but she had a pair of Mr. Boles' worn-out shoes to wear in the barnyard.

At meal-times, when she had set the last dish on the table, dealt out the napkins in their rings and filled the water-glasses, she hurriedly washed her face at the kitchen washbasin and smoothed her carroty hair. It was strained back so tightly that it seemed to pull her eyebrows, and her big, homely face stuck out, shiny with soap. She'd bawl, "Dinner's ready!" and sit down at table. She would never touch a thing that Mr. or Mrs. Boles didn't pass to her, but if she had to wait for them to come she'd say, "A pity you spoil good vittles, lettin' 'em get cold with your dawdling!"

Mrs. Boles would flutter helplessly, but Mr. Boles could always pacify Almantha with some careless remark.

Sometimes I stayed all night with Mary Boles, to help her with her lessons. Mary was like her mother, fair and delicate and rather dull, and I was always generously willing to show her how smart I was. At the supper table I never could forget that Almantha was there. And when she had washed the dishes, blown out the kitchen lamp and brought her basket of carpet-rags or mending into the dining-room, there until bedtime she solidly was. Of course she was only the hired girl, but I understood what my mother meant. Mrs. Boles couldn't have spoken to her husband for his own good, if she had wanted to.

There was something oddly baffling about Mr. Boles. Mrs. Boles was always fluttering at him and somehow being baffled. Looking at him, I'd think, "Like water off a duck's back." A duck's feathers look so soft, you'd think any drop of water would sink into them, but it can't penetrate them at all.

Mr. Boles was a smiling, easy-going man who got

along well with everybody, and didn't care. Though
he had been postmaster for years, he never argued
about politics and on election nights he was the only
unexcited man in town. "It'll be all the same a hundred years from now," he'd say, as if that thought
were comforting.

On summer afternoons we girls went to the post
office. We did not expect any letters but we wanted
to go somewhere and there was nowhere else to go,
unless we had an errand to buy something. From
the street we heard Mr. Boles softly whistling to
himself. One popular song he whistled for years
after everyone else was singing newer tunes.

Life's a funny proposition after all,
Just why we're here and what it's all about
Is a question that has puzzled many brainy men
*   to solve,*
It's a problem that they've never figured out.

Through the General Delivery grating we could
see his plump back with the suspenders crossed upon
it, his head bent over some report or ledger. Behind him Mrs. Boles was usually perched in a chair,
crocheting.

"Oh, Lester! Lester, look!" she'd wail eagerly.
"Look, I've made a mistake. Now I've got to ravel
out the whole row!"

"That's too bad," he'd say politely.

When he came to the window she'd come, too.
She was as pretty as anyone could be after thirty

and she took care of her looks as if she were a girl. It was whispered that she used face-powder. Her fair hair was always beautifully curled and puffed and coiled and held with rhinestone combs and barette, and she dressed as stylishly on weekdays as on Sundays. Her light voice was always eager.

"My, what a pretty dress!" she'd say. "Lester, look, isn't that a pretty dress?"

"Sure is," he'd say, watching the letters flip through his fingers.

"Looking for a letter from your sweetheart?" she'd tease, and exclaim, "Look, Lester, she's blushing! Yes you are, too, Ernestine! Isn't she, Lester, look. Isn't she blushing?"

"But, Mrs. Boles, honest I haven't any sweetheart. Mama says I'm too young."

"Sixteen, aren't you? Well, never mind, there's time enough. I was nineteen when Mr. Boles first laid eyes on me and wouldn't take no for an answer. Wasn't I, Lester?" She'd sparkle archly at him. "Nothing would do him but we'd elope right away, would it, Lester? remember, mm? I was so popular, mama always said I'd go through the woods and pick up a crooked stick at last. My goodness, what a time you had getting me, didn't you, you poor thing? Oh my goodness, of course I didn't mean — Why, you know I didn't mean you're a crooked stick, don't you, Lester? Why, I've never been sorry one minute I waited for Mr. Right! And you've never been sorry either, have you, Lester? Have you?"

"Not so you'd notice it," he'd respond gallantly,

and with her hand fondly on his arm and her eyes tugging at him, he'd smile and glance toward her eager face. "Nothing for you today, girls; sorry."

His smile always said that nothing would matter a hundred years from now. Then he went back to his ledger and his whistling would cross the threshold with us;

Just why we're here and what it's all about —

"Listen, Ernestine," Elsie Miller said one day, taking my arm and speaking low. "I don't believe he loves her."

"Who? Mr. Boles?" I was startled. "Why, but they're married!"

"Just the same, I don't believe he does. I bet he's sick to death of her."

"Well, he better not be!" I was indignant. "His own wife! Why, Elsie Miller, of course husbands love their wives. They promise. They have to."

Of course wives had to hold their husband's love; they did it by never wearing mother hubbards or curl-papers in the afternoons, by dressing up and always being just as sweet and smiling as if they hadn't got the man yet. But Mrs. Boles did all that.

"I guess I know they have to!" Elsie retorted. "But maybe they don't, sometimes." She continued hardily, "I bet wives don't always, either. I bet if I was married to that grouchy old mean Mr. Hutton, I'd just hate him."

"Elsie!"

Across the dusty cross-roads we could see Mr. Hutton sitting behind the patent medicines in his drug-store window. He always sat there, bowed over the swollen hands on the head of his cane. He was rheumatic and he had the asthma. Mrs. Hutton did the clerking and he snarled at everyone until she couldn't have kept a customer if there had been another drug-store. She was a soft, gentle woman. Her dark hair fell softly in natural waves from its parting and her cheek dimpled when she smiled, but her smile and her eyes were always anxiously trying to please Mr. Hutton and not offend anyone else.

"If you'd married him, you'd love him, all right," I said stoutly. "You don't marry anyone you don't love, do you? Well, then!"

"She married him to get to go to the World's Fair," said Elsie. "She gave Mr. Boles the mitten because he couldn't afford to take her to the World's Fair, and that's —"

"Why Elsie Miller, how can you say such awf —"

"That's how Mrs. Boles caught him, on the rebound," Elsie declared. "And at the Fair, Mr. Hutton got rheumatism floating around in lagoons — they're a kind of boat. That's the way the Lord punished her, and I bet she's repenting like anything."

"It's gondolas," I murmured, overcome.

This was not a subject to mention to one's mother, but one night I spoke before I thought. We were sitting on the porch, my mother comfortably rocking and I on the top step with my chin in my hands. We had said nothing for some time. There was a dewy smell of clover. Katydids were shrilling in the maples and fireflies twinkling everywhere. Lonely steps sounded on the board walk and a wandering little whistled air floated by in the shadowy night.

Life's a funny proposition after all —

When it was quite gone I said suddenly, "A married man wouldn't love anybody but his wife, would he?"

My mother's chair abruptly stopped. "What put such an idea in your head?" she asked sharply.

"Nothing. I was just thinking."

"Well, don't!" she snapped. Her chair went on rocking, but there was agitation in its creaks. At length she asked, "Who were you thinking of?"

"Nobody," I said promptly. But I was no match for her; in two minutes she pinned me down.

"I'd like to slap that Elsie Miller!" she said angrily. "Putting such thoughts in your head, the very idea!" I said nothing, and after some time she said she guessed she might as well tell me the rights of it; maybe it would be a lesson to me.

It was true that Mr. Boles and Mrs. Hutton, then Dorothy Brown, had once seemed smitten on each other. They were keeping steady company when Daisy Bell came to visit her cousin and made a dead set at him. Any visiting girl has an advantage, but she didn't make any headway till one night her cousin gave a hay-ride for her, and the only chaperon they took was Mrs. Sims.

"We all knew better than to go, when the wagon came around and we saw who was chaperoning," my mother said. "True, Mrs. Sims was married, but she wasn't fifteen, and giddy at that. We knew better, but there we'd been looking forward to the hayride for days, and we were all dressed up to go, and everybody dared everybody else — I blame the parents. So if sometimes I seem strict to you, Ernestine, you'll know the reason why."

They drove to a farmhouse three miles in the country and pulled candy and popped corn and ate apples and altogether had such a good time that it was ten o'clock before they started home. It was a frosty night with a full moon, and they'd gone hardly a mile when the boys began complaining that they were cold, and daring the girls to get out of the wagon and walk with them. Some of the bolder girls did; Daisy Bell was one of them, but Lester Boles couldn't get Dorothy out of the wagon. Mrs. Sims should have stopped it, but she was younger than any of the others, for all she was married and should have known better, and she didn't say anything.

The wagon jogged on slowly, couples straggling behind it in the moonlight, and they were all singing and shouting back and forth to each other. It was some time before they missed Lester Boles and Daisy Bell.

My mother said then that the wagon should go back for them at once. But Mrs. Sims only laughed and said, "Oh, we'll go slower and they'll catch up." The others climbed into the wagon at once and they went on singing and joking, but growing sober underneath.

Mrs. Sims didn't stop the wagon until they had almost reached town. They waited in it until nearly midnight, and Mrs. Sims was frightened enough when the girls insisted on being driven home. She and Mr. Sims drove back to look for those two.

Next day of course there was an uproar. Daisy Bell said she'd sprained her ankle, and Lester Boles said he'd carried her for miles. He said he'd yelled his lungs out for help, but nobody paid any attention. The girls said they didn't believe Daisy Bell, and that Lester Boles was lying like a gentleman. Dorothy Brown told him that nobody'd compelled him to get out of the wagon with Daisy Bell in the first place, nor to lag so far behind with her that nobody could hear him if he yelled, and now he'd ruined her reputation he'd better marry her. Next day Dorothy married Arthur Hutton and they went to the Chicago World's Fair on their honeymoon.

Naturally everyone cut Daisy Bell. And with good reason, for she had no more sprained ankle than a rabbit. She pretended she had, she kept it bandaged, and Lester Boles carried her to the buggy when they eloped, the day before Mr. and Mrs. Hutton came home. But next Sunday she came walking into church on her husband's arm, as chipper as you please.

"For all she's turned out a good, respectable woman and there's never been another breath of scandal against her, so far as I know," my mother said.

"You don't suppose he'd — maybe kind of go on caring for —"

"No, I don't suppose anything of the kind! You

get such notions right out of your head," my mother said sharply. "The thing for you to remember's the trouble that comes of going on such parties without a proper chaperon."

"Yes, mama."

For some reason I felt an awed respect for Mrs. Boles. Yet I was sorry for her, too. After that, I felt something piteous in her fluttering eagerness, the arch glances she was always giving Mr. Boles, her constantly appealing to him, her way of pretending to pick a speck from his sleeve so that she could pat it. I cried from an overwhelming pity when she died.

One night the pain in her side was so bad that at midnight Mr. Boles came for my mother. He and Almantha had done everything they knew, and his face was anxious and bewildered in the lantern light. My mother dressed hurriedly, and taking the bottle of liniment on which she relied she told my father to send Mrs. Rogers. Together they worked over Mrs. Boles and toward morning the pain stopped. But my mother was worried when she came home.

"I hated to tell Mr. Boles he better get the doctor," she said. "But I felt it my duty to. If it turns to inflammation of the bowels —"

Mrs. Rogers was grave and hushed, too. "You did exactly right. If it's that, it will be a comfort to him later that he did everything he could. What's that new-fangled name they call it now?"

"Appendix-something."

"But I don't know's it makes any difference what you call it."

"No."

That day the Boles house was still and frightening and full of women. Mrs. Boles lay in bed, red-cheeked and bright-eyed and talking. They kept every breath of air from her, changed the wet clothes on her forehead and brewed snake-root for her, but nothing kept down her fever. The snake-root had no more effect than the doctor's medicine. Mary and Gertrude were scared and I couldn't think what to say to them. Almantha went clumping about, more awkward and ugly and heavy-footed than ever.

During the night my mother came home to get some sleep. She was kindling the kitchen fire and I was washing my face next morning when Mrs. Rogers came in. The sun was rising and all the birds were chirping. My mother stood holding the stove-lid on the lifter and looked at Mrs. Rogers. Mrs. Rogers nodded.

"Poor soul," she said, and tears ran out of her eyes. She mopped at them with her apron. "She's not gone yet, but as good as. The most pitiful thing I ever — Let me have a handkerchief."

She blew her nose and tried to tell us about it. About two o'clock that morning Mrs. Boles roused herself and looked at Mr. Boles. He'd fallen asleep in a chair with his mouth open and was snoring. Mrs. Boles motioned to Mrs. Rogers to keep quiet and to give her the hand-mirror ; she looked into it and whispered, "He mustn't see me like this." She was burning like a coal, and weak as a kitten. The curl had come out of her hair, but she did the best she could with it, and powdered her red face. Mrs. Rogers brought the face-powder from where it was hidden in the closet. "I know it's awful," Mrs. Rogers sobbed. "And her thoughts should have been on higher things, but — but I couldn't deny her — "

"You mean she — knew?" my mother asked.

"Yes. Yes, she knew. Sitting up there and — in the face of death — And she wanted her ruffled pink dressing sacque on. I helped her into it." Mrs. Rogers couldn't go on for a minute.

When she had fixed herself as pretty as she could, Mrs. Boles called, "Lester! Lester, dear!" He jumped and struck out at something; then he realized where he was and came over to the bed. Mrs. Boles asked him to keep the children with him, not to let anyone else have them, and he promised. Then she said, "Oh Lester, you do love me, don't you? Don't you, really, just a little bit?"

Mrs. Rogers sobbed, "He broke down crying like — crying like — I never want to hear such a thing again. He kind of choked out, 'Yes,' but I don't know's she heard him. She was out of her head. Talking all kinds of things. Not a rational word since. The doctor says it won't be long now. Oh I wish — I wish things were different in this world!"

My mother was crying, too. "It don't do any good — " she wept. "I'll make you a hot cup of coffee. You're worn out, and no wonder."

Mr. Boles spared no expense. He sent for a satin-

lined coffin, and four black horses drew the livery-
stable's hearse. But even while the buggies were coming back from the graveyard, people felt a little odd
about Almantha.

"Of course he don't mean to keep her, and anyway
she wouldn't stay," my mother said. "It's natural
she'd stay to straighten up the house, but she's a good,
respectable girl."

"You heard me offer her a place to stay tonight,
yourself," said Mrs. Rogers.

"Well, just for tonight— And after all, the girls
are there, poor motherless things. I'm going to take
them baked beans; folks always fill up a house with
fried chicken and cakes after a funeral."

The Boles house had the chill emptiness of all be-
reaved houses. Neighbors never stayed long; they
brought their gifts of food and went away to leave
the family with its grief. Almantha was busy in the
kitchen as usual.

"You'll be looking for another place now, won't
you, Almantha," Mrs. Miniver said. "Or will you go
back to your folks?"

Almantha looked at her doggedly. "I got no folks
to go to."

"Well, you just come right over to my house," Mrs.
Miniver said generously. "You can stay with me just
like one of the family and work for board and room
as long as you've a mind to."

"Thanks," said Almantha.

All the way home my mother and Mrs. Rogers sput-
tered and fumed because Mrs. Miniver's Christian

charity was getting a hired girl for nothing but her keep.

The next day was Thursday. Early in the morning the Boles' clothesline was full of quilts and comforts hung out to air, and neighbors heard from the Boles kitchen the steady thumping of the dasher in a churn full of cream. That afternoon Almantha took in the bedding. That evening she called and fed the hens, and milked the cow as usual. That night a lamp burned in the Boles kitchen and the faint clatter of dishwashing could be heard there, while on the porch Mary and Gertrude, in their black dresses, sat with their father.

Still it took time to realize that Almantha was not going to Mrs. Miniver's. It took time to believe that she actually meant to stay in that house with Mr. Boles. Women were first incredulous, then aghast.

"Why yes, I guess Almantha's staying," Mary or Gertrude answered when questioned. "No, she doesn't say anything about going away. She does the work same as usual, and papa hands her her wages on Saturdays, like he always did. Why, she's always been there. What would she go away for?"

"Poor innocent children, isn't it awful?" Mrs. Miniver went around saying. "Somebody ought to stop it."

Mr. Boles was in the post office as usual. The lines were deeper around his mouth and the wide black band was on his sleeve. Sometimes he began to whistle, and stopped abruptly. He had always been quiet, in his good-natured, uncaring way. There was still that indefinable baffling quality in him. It kept even the men from saying anything to him about Almantha.

"Well, Mary's not strong enough to do all that work, and Gerty's only ten," my mother said. "I know it don't look right, but so far as it's being really downright wrong —"

"Well, I must say!" Mrs. Rogers interrupted, unexpectedly standing up to my mother. "If you think it's an example for young folks, a man and a woman living in the same house without being married! Right in the face and eyes of everybody, and you with a girl of your own. I must say I wonder at you."

"Oh, of course I don't stand up for anything like that —" I was astounded to see my mother scuttling before Mrs. Rogers' indignation. But if even Mrs. Rogers was wondering at her, we had to think of our own reputations. My mother, a respectable married woman with a husband to take her part, might have stood firmly for her opinions. But I was a young girl; nothing was more fragile, more perishable, than a young girl's character; a breath of talk about me would have smirched mine forever.

My mother told me not to go to the Boles' house any more. "I don't say there's anything wrong there," she said. "But we must avoid the appearance of evil." And to my fancy that house did have a sinister appearance, now that only Mr. Boles used the front door and the parlor shades were never raised.

My mother was silent when all the other ladies were working each other up about Almantha's scandalous behavior. Mrs. Miniver felt it most, living right across the street from the house where that girl was flying in the face of decency. At last one day she undertook to speak right out to Almantha, if all the others would come with her. My mother refused. "Not that I take up for her, but I won't mix into what's none of my business."

Mrs. Miniver flared up. "I'd have you know I mind my own business as much as anybody and if you don't care what goes on in this town with your own girl growing up, all I have to say is, I hope and pray you don't live to repent it!"

My mother flushed red, too, but glancing at the others she shut her lips tight together. A day was set when the Ladies' Aid would call on Almantha. My mother was the only one who wouldn't go.

But when the day came, for one reason or another most of the ladies failed to arrive at Mrs. Miniver's. Only Mrs. Miller, Mrs. Rogers and Mrs. Miniver went to speak to Almantha. Behind our parlor curtains my mother and I watched them solemnly crossing the street, holding up the skirts of their second-best dresses. They knocked for awhile on the Boles' front door and then went single file around the house.

Half an hour later Mrs. Rogers came rushing breathless to my mother. "I never in all my life!" she gasped.

They had found Almantha making apple-butter, Mary and Gertrude helping and licking spoons. Mrs. Miniver put the girls out and shut the door, and then she told Almantha in plain words what was thought of her goings-on, and the sooner she left that house the better. And Almantha turned on them.

"I'll have you know I'm an honest girl making an honest living!" she said. "I been here fifteen years come September, I got no other place to go and I'm not going no other place if I had one and you can lump it. Low-down, sneaking, mean liars is what you are and you can say what you please, Mr. Boles is a gentleman if there ever was one and I'm going on working for him. I'm not going to leave him in the lurch and you can just get out of here. Get out! You hear me!" she shouted, coming at them with the apple-butter ladle. "Get out of here and I hope you choke on your stinking mean lies about a decent girl's never done anybody any harm!"

"I declare I'm shaking yet," Mrs. Rogers said. "That Mrs. Miniver squawked like a hen. I believe that girl'd 've done us harm in another minute. My land, I never was so scared!"

"Well, there, you've done your duty, you just forget about it," my mother soothed her.

"We heard her boo-hooing like she wanted to die when we come by the kitchen window," Mrs. Rogers remembered. "So maybe she is taking to heart what we said."

"And maybe the poor girl's not so much to blame," my mother suggested. "Of course it don't look right, what's she's doing, but I don't believe there's been any — well, downright sin. And I don't know why the girl always has to bear the whole brunt, anyway. Mr. Boles is full as much blame and everybody treats him same as ever, so I don't know why we can't leave Almantha alone."

Mrs. Rogers seemed struck by a thought. "That's so, he is," she said. "And he a lodge member. And postmaster."

"So the best thing's to think no more about it," my mother said with emphasis. "It's none of our business."

"You're right," Mrs. Rogers agreed. "I don't know why it's always the women that have to do everything."

It is hard to say how I knew, while summer mellowed to autumn, that the scandal was becoming more serious. My father and mother came gravely home from lodge meetings, my father gruff and my mother's worry puckering her forehead. Lodge members called and I was sent out of hearing. As if from the air, I gathered that there was talk about preferring charges against Mr. Boles in the lodge. We whispered about it at school, and Mary Boles cried because we kept secrets from her.

Then somehow the matter became a wholly masculine one of politics. Elections were coming on. One week day evening my father in his Sunday clothes met the train bringing an important politician, and he did not come home until eleven o'clock. I heard the lantern click shut after he blew it out, and my mother asking from bed, "Well?"

"Miniver put it to him strong," my father answered. "He said he'll tend to it, he'll see Boles tomorrow."

"Well, he's been a widower almost the full year

and it isn't as if he was taking notice of anybody else."
My mother said this doubtfully, but as if it might jus-
tify something.

Next Thursday Mary and Gertrude Boles didn't
come to school, and Elsie Miller knew why. They
had a stepmother. On his way to the post office that
morning, Mr. Boles had married Almantha at the minister's. "And high time, too!" Elsie said.

That Saturday afternoon I went up the street to see
Mary Boles. It was a chill October day; cold rain
was falling in gusts and the dead leaves were sodden
underfoot. The Boles' front porch had been recently
scrubbed, so I took off my rubbers on the steps.
Gerty opened the door when I knocked. At the end
of the hall the dining-room was warm and Mary sat
at the window, watching the street. The new Mrs.
Boles was kneading bread in the kitchen.

I suggested a game of crockinole and Mary shook
her head. "I can't. I've got to watch, so if I see any
ladies coming to call we can light the heater in the
parlor."

"Let Gerty watch awhile," I said. "Ask — ask your
mama to make her."

"Almantha's not our mama," Gerty declared. "We
don't have to do what she says. Do we, Almantha?"

Almantha put the cover on the bread-pan and lifting it in her big, floury hands she turned around.
"No," she said. "Just as your pa told you, you mind
him, same as always. I'm nothing but the hired girl,
same as always. That's the bargain." She turned to
me and I stared at the red splotches widening on her

ugly cheek-bones. "You can go tell everybody that's the bargain, and I hope they're satisfied, with their hounding him!"

She slammed the oven door open, slammed a chair in front of it, and gently set the bread in the warmth.

Mary nodded solemnly to me. "Everything's just the same as ever," she whispered. "Only she's kind of — funny, somehow." There was indeed something strange about Almantha. She went on vigorously working, there in the kitchen, peeling apples and rolling out pie-crust, setting the black kettle of lard to heat for doughnuts. But her ugly face reminded me of the way my mother had looked when she went on doing her work the same as usual after the telegram came saying that grandma was dead.

Subdued, we watched for awhile at the window, but nobody came, and as soon as I could I said I had to go home.

The ladies' perplexity was ended; they didn't have to call. A few of them did; my mother took Mrs. Rogers to sit fifteen minutes in the parlor with Almantha and leave cards. But Almantha did not return these few calls. That winter Mr. Boles took his demit from the lodge; a married man could hardly go to the social meetings without his wife, and Almantha would have been out of place.

Mr. Boles rarely whistled now. He borrowed heavy, dull-looking books from Mr. Sherwood and sat in an armchair behind the letter-boxes, reading them. His smile was the same only more so, but his eyes changed. There was a glint in them as though he were laughing scornfully at himself. He was always good-natured and kind, but more and more remote. If he lived anywhere, it was at the post office. His house felt like a hotel, where no one lived, but people ate and slept.

Spring and summer and autumn went by, snow and cold came again, and one night Mr. Hutton's rheumatism suddenly settled in his heart.

"I guess you heard the news?" my father said, going into the post office next morning. He was earlier than he intended; no one was there but Mr. Boles, sweeping out. No one had heard the news yet; Mrs. Hutton had run for the doctor and the doctor had stopped for my mother.

"Hutton's gone," my father said. "Mrs. Hutton woke up in the night, and there he was beside her, stark stone cold and —" Mr. Boles looked so queer that he stopped.

"What?" Mr. Boles said, bearing down on the broom so hard that the broomstraws buckled. "Not—" He laughed out one hard, cracking laugh.

"Sounded plumb crazy," my father told us. "Must have been a shock, the way I put it."

An odd look came over my mother's face. "Enough to shock anybody," she said. "I'm surprised you had no better sense, and if I was you I'd say no more about it."

At the funeral everybody said it was wonderful how Mrs. Hutton bore up. Mr. Hutton left no insurance; there was only the mortgaged house and the rented drug-store. She'd have to sell for what little she could

get and go to live on her married sister's husband.
The ladies sincerely wept for her. But afterward,
while they were all condoling with her, Mrs. Hutton
startled them all.

"I ran the store while he was living," she said,
pale and desperate in her widow's weeds. "And I can
run it now. And not be beholden to anybody."
Her hands clenched together under the folds of crepe
veil in her lap. "If only you'll all stand by me —"

There was a moment of panic in her small parlor.
The ladies looked at one another and didn't know what
to say. Then my mother spoke up. "Yes, Mrs. Hutton, we'll stand by you," she said, rising and putting
an arm around the widow's shoulders. "It isn't as if
you were a young girl. I guess if a good, respectable,
Christian woman we've known all her days can't run
her own departed husband's business in this town
without making talk — ! You go right ahead, Dorothy Hutton, and if you have any trouble you just
call on me and I'll see to it my husband settles it.
We'll all stand by you," she said, so forcefully that
the others murmuringly agreed.

Mrs. Rogers demurred on the way home. "A public store's no place for a lone, unprotected woman.
Meeting strange men coming in, and dealing with
traveling men, and all. Oh, I know Mrs. Hutton's
a good woman and a lady through and through, but
still. There's no telling what such things'll lead to."

"If they lead to any harm, it'll be nobody's fault but
ours," my mother said. "I'm glad I spoke up like I
did and I mean every word I said. There's times I

wish I'd done it sooner. I'm sick and tired of the old hens' cackling goes on in this town. If folks 'd mind their own business for once!"

"Well, of course I'm not one to gossip, myself," Mrs. Rogers replied. "You know I don't go around talking about anybody behind their back, like that meddling, snoopy Mrs. Miniver does. But I must say I don't know what the world would come to if there wasn't any gossiping. You know yourself this town is full of folks that are leading good steady honest moral lives, just because they're scared of being talked about if they did what they wanted to."

"Well, yes, that's so," my mother had to admit.

Any flutter of talk about Mrs. Hutton soon died down. She was propriety itself. Though she was a widow, even the traveling men didn't tell jokes about her. That summer we girls spent long afternoons in the drug-store. It was nice to have somewhere to go, where we could stand around talking and seeing through the big glass windows all that went on around the Square. When Mrs. Hutton began to emerge from deepest mourning she was warmly friendly, almost gay with us. We'd lean for hours on the glass-topped counters full of pills and toothbrushes and writing tablets, talking to her; her brown eyes listened wisely and merrily. When she closed the store at supper time we liked to walk home with her.

Elsie Miller and I were with her one evening when we almost collided with Mr. Boles. He came suddenly from the butcher shop, with the brown-paper package of meat he was taking home for Almantha to cook. Our steps faltered. And this faltering embarrassed us; it looked almost as if we were stopping to talk to him on the street. I felt Mrs. Hutton recoil and quiver. Mr. Boles hurriedly stepped aside, lifting his hat and muttering, "Good evening."

"Good evening, Mr. Boles," Mrs. Hutton murmured primly, bending her black-veiled head with the narrow white band of half-mourning smooth across her dark hair. His gaze was on her face. I had never before seen his eyes without their tired, half-mocking smile. He was gone in an instant, but I kept remembering those wide-open eyes with the bewildered pain in them; the look of a child who's whipped without understanding why.

I think that nothing more would have happened if I hadn't pried inside Mr. Boles' old watch. In those days we said of married couples that they were "in double harness," and thus bound together they went on living without complaint till death parted them. There was nothing else to do.

Mary unearthed the fat old watch from one of the little drawers on top of her father's bureau. I had come to see her about practicing for the Easter cantata and found her helping Almantha clean Mr. Boles' bedroom. Almantha would never go into it without one of the girls, even when he wasn't in the house. It was a big corner room upstairs; Mr. Boles had a parlor lamp and an armchair in it and spent his evenings there.

Now the carpet was up, the curtains down, the bedstead had been taken apart and put in the hall. Mary was carrying out the bureau drawers and Almantha was on her knees in a corner, beginning to scrub the six-months' dust-grime from the floor. The smell of lye and soap and wet wood mixed with the scent of spring that came through the open windows. House-cleaning was always a vaguely exciting time; it seemed to mean change, though it never did.

"My goodness, what's this old thing doing stuck in among papa's handkerchiefs!" Mary exclaimed. She turned the heavy, old-fashioned watch in her hand. We looked at the stopped hands under thick glass and at the steaming locomotive engraved on its plump back.

"Look, I believe it'll open," I said, and took it out of Mary's hands and pried. The back flew open with a tiny click.

"Oh, it's mama's pic—" Mary's eager exclamation broke in two. Brown eyes looked sweetly out of the faded little picture and dark hair waved softly from its parting. I hadn't known that Mrs. Hutton had been so charming a girl. Behind us Almantha lumbered to her feet and said, "I don't know's your pa'd want you meddling with his things." And in hot, blind embarrassment I said, "Why, how did water get into it?"

The blister on the picture was damp; I touched it. A little, round blister. We stared at it, Almantha's head between ours. Then my glance fled from Mary's, I gazed at Almantha's stricken, ugly face. And a staggering clap of noise violently struck my cheek. Through chaos I saw Almantha plunge into the closet; its slammed door cut short a kind of howl.

There wasn't another sound till I clicked the watch shut. Trembling, I laid it carefully on the bureau top and wiped suds from my tingling cheek. I said politely, "I must be going now."

"Your hat's crooked," Mary quavered. "Oh, Ernestine, please don't be mad at me. I wouldn't for anything have had such an awful — I don't know what made Almantha do such a —"

"I'm not mad," I said. "Only I must be going now. Come see me sometime, won't you? Because," I cried out suddenly, "I'm never going to set foot inside this house again with Almantha in it, never as long as I live!"

Perhaps a week later the thing happened. It was Thursday, and my mother and I were weeding the onion bed when we heard the screams. Gerty Boles came tearing down the street, screaming horribly and running as if she were crazy. My mother rushed into the street and caught her; she struggled and kept on screaming. I hardly recognized her wild face; she'd fallen, the palms of her hands were skinned and dented with gravel. Women came scurrying. My mother shook Gerty, slapped her, and Gerty shrieked, "Almantha — in the well. Almantha's gone and — something's in the —"

She dropped in the dust; Mrs. Rogers picked her up. My mother was cutting the rope from our well-bucket. Men ran shouting. Two men carried a ladder. Everything went past rapidly and unreal and looking down the round, dark cavern of the well I saw water glinting around a floating something. My mother said sharply, "Ernestine! Keep away!"

The well-bucket hung overhead, pulled up high, the rope jammed in the pulley. Someone threw in all the rope's coils and the splash hollowly echoed. Someone ordered, "Get that ladder away, it's too short." Another man said, "Hold the rope and I'll shin down it." Voices objected, "It won't hold the weight." My mother gripped my arm and Mrs. Miniver was saying, "Poor soul, see how the bucket's caught. She tried to jerk it loose and slipped, it's plain as day and fell in—how awful. How awful and no one home to hear her—"

"You come with me," my mother said to me grimly; she thought this was no place for a young girl. "I'll get a sheet to cover her with," she said.

The kitchen was spotlessly neat. The order in Almantha's little room was somehow frightening. In the middle of the sheet on the raspberry-pink bed lay a pile of banknotes, and on them a wedding ring.

My mother shut the door and put her back against it. The shut door muffled shouts at the well; there was an enormous silence in that cramped space under the sloping roof. When I tried to speak my mother said harshly, "Shut up!"

Her sunbonnet was askew and there was a smudge of garden-earth on her cheek. I watched her white face harden. Her mouth set. She took the banknotes and put them under the mattress. The ring she dropped into her apron pocket. Heavy steps were slowly coming across the back porch; my mother snatched the sheet from the bed and said to me, "If you ever breathe one word of this, I'll —" The threat was more terrible because she didn't say what it was. She opened the door.

They had covered Almantha with some woman's apron and through the crowd of legs and skirts as they laid her on the bed I saw only a big, soaked hand limply swinging. It was the left hand, with no ring on it. My mother's hand closed over it and she put it under the sheet, saying, "What a terrible, terrible accident." The doctor was making everyone leave the room; only my mother and Mrs. Rogers stayed to help him, and after he had gone they stayed on to lay Almantha out.

"Did you notice how her poor hand was swelled up around her wedding ring?" Mrs. Rogers asked my mother. "Seemed like that ring was just cutting into the flesh."

As Mrs. Miniver had said at once, it was plain how the accident had happened. Women had always complained that dug wells were dangerous and now everyone agreed that drilled wells were worth the extra cost. The surprising thing was the money Almantha had saved. Mr. Boles inherited it, of course, and a dollar and a half a week for nearly seventeen years was quite a sum.

"But then she had nothing to spend it for," Mrs. Rogers said. "'Tisn't as if she'd had a family, or even a beau to dress up for. So far's I know, no man ever looked at her twice. Being a hired girl, of course, and not much to look at, either, for all she was a good soul and hardworking."

I never dared speak to my mother about what she had done. Only once I came near doing so. It was another evening when we were sitting on the porch. A full moon was rising, the maple boughs spread dark against a creamy sky and frogs were croaking at the mill pond. The moonlight was so clear that we recognized Mr. Boles, going home. His steps had a springy sound on the board walk and he was whistling.

You're as welcome as the flowers in May,
And I love you in the same old way...

It was pleasant to hear the pretty, new tune swinging up and up and falling liquidly in the soft brightness of the moonlight.

"Well, his year's almost up," my mother remarked, rocking placidly. "Like enough he's been calling on her a second time, and a good thing if they make a match of it. A store's no place for an unprotected woman, and Mary'll be glad enough to get that big house off her hands."

I drew a deep breath and said it. "And mama, if Almantha looks down and sees them, probably she's glad now they don't know what she —"

My mother's chair thumped as she got up. "I declare it's bedtime and past! And us sitting out here in the night air!"

IV

IMMORAL WOMAN

MY INTEREST in Mrs. Sims began when my mother told me about the disastrous hay-ride she had chaperoned at the age of fifteen. Mrs. Sims had been married when she was fourteen. I was going on sixteen and already felt the shadowy approaching dread of being an old maid. "Sweet sixteen, and never been kissed," our elders teased, and girls laughed coquettishly between hope and fear.

My mother said that fourteen was too young; she had married at nineteen.

"I want Ernestine to take her time," she often said. "I tell her I'd just as soon she don't get married till she's twenty, even. A girl's only a girl once, and she'll be a long time married. Better be safe than sorry, I tell her." Hoping that such defences would not be needed, my mother was nevertheless prudently preparing them.

I felt an intense interest in Mrs. Sims. Myrtle was only ten and Pearl was nine, but although I was so much older I often went home with them after school, just to talk to their mother.

At that hour, four o'clock in the afternoon, it was all right to go into her house. It wasn't polite to em-

barrass a woman by calling in the morning. Women
wore old clothes in the mornings, going about with
their hair in curl-papers and buttons missing from
their shoes ; some even went without corsets. It didn't
matter how they looked while they were scrubbing,
washing, cleaning and filling lamps, carrying out ashes
and blacking stoves, and it would have been wasteful
to make carpet rags of garments with any wear left in
them. But after dinner a lady washed her face,
combed her hair, and put on clean shoes and a fresh
dress. Young married women must do this to hold
their husbands' love ; older ones did it because someone might call.

At that time not a word had ever been said against
Mrs. Sims. Her house was well kept, her children
well-behaved, her husband contented. But even then
she was different. There was an energy in her, an
almost disturbing warmth and spontaneity.

Myrtle and Pearl rushed into the house and ran to
her as if they were glad to see her. She'd nod to me,
laughing, while she hugged them ; she tweaked their
braids, tickled their ribs, even kissed them. The scene
embarrassed me. One knew of course that mothers
loved their children, but not like that, not with such
gaiety and unrestraint and lack of dignity. I did not
know where to look.

Then we would settle down and talk. Indeed, we
chatted. Myrtle and Pearl had no reserves at all and
I told things I would never had dared tell my mother.
Mrs. Sims knew all about the notes passed in school,

the picture of teacher that Ewing Adams had drawn on his slate, and why I slapped Elsie Nichols at recess. We both knew I shouldn't have done it, but Mrs. Sims felt, too, that Elsie shouldn't have snatched the note Ewing had written me.

When I got home my mother would look up, her face reddened by the heat of the cook-stove. "I've had to bring in wood. What makes you so late home from school?"

"I just stopped a minute at Mrs. Sims'," I said defensively.

"Did she ask you to?"

"Yes'm, she did. Honest she did."

"Well, you stop making a nuisance of yourself just because she's too polite to send you home. Put away your books now and pull up a pail of fresh water, supper's almost ready."

Mrs. Sims told us all about her romance. I knew the lazy, good-natured Mr. Sims who lounged in Miller's store, his vest hanging open and his shirt wrinkled across his fat middle. Mrs. Miller was his sister, so Jim Miller had given him this job clerking and paid him good money; thirty-five dollars a month. I knew him, but I never connected him in my mind with the masterful young man who had courted and married Mrs. Sims.

She flushed shyly, proudly, when she told us the climax. "So that night when he saw me home from church, we were standing at the gate and he said, right out, 'Ella, will you marry me?' Well, I didn't say anything. I didn't know if I wanted to marry him or not. I was just standing there not saying anything and a little kitten came purring around my feet so I picked it up, I cuddled it up under my chin and I said, 'Isn't this a darling kitten?'

"Well, Mr. Sims just reached right out and took that kitten away from me and dropped it on the ground and he said, 'Don't talk to me about kittens,' he said. 'I'm not asking you anything about kittens,' he said. 'Now you answer me; are you going to marry me, or aren't you?'"

We were thrilled. "Yes, mama, go on, go on! Then you said—"

"Well, I just kind of whispered, 'I don't care if I do.'"

So they were married and lived happy ever after. Mrs. Sims' romance seemed to me ideal.

There was only one thing she wanted. She wanted another room built on her house. It was a small house, though no smaller than many in town; only the banker's family and the Millers lived in mansions with double parlors and an upstairs. Mrs. Sims' house was a nice little house in a good neighborhood. It had three rooms; front room, bedroom, and kitchen. She wanted to build on another bedroom.

She told my mother about it, one afternoon when she was calling.

"My girls are growing up," she said. "They'll be having beaux before I know it, and I'd like to fix up a real nice parlor for them. If we could build on a bedroom for Mr. Sims and me, then I could move our bed out of the front room and fix it up for a parlor. I've been at Mr. Sims and *been* at him about it, but— I don't know—"

She was wearing her best dress, a black cashmere trimmed with bands of black velvet. She sat primly upright, her gloved hands holding handkerchief and card-case in her lap. Her face was surprisingly fresh and vivacious; she seemed almost girlish, though she was twenty-five.

My mother smiled with a little complacency. We were sitting in our own new parlor. We had had it only two years, so our pride in it had not begun to wane. It was a beautiful parlor, with an ingrain carpet and machine-made lace curtains. The wallpaper was dark red and gilt, with large figures which always seemed to me like cut-off, grinning and gory heads in spiked helmets. The three chairs were all rockers; one was a spring-rocker. Across a corner stood our parlor-organ, with three books on one of its jutting little shelves. Another book lay on the center-table. And from the ceiling hung a lamp glittering in pendent crystals; it could be pulled down on its brass chains to be lighted if we had company in the evenings, and the kerosene in its glass bowl was colored red. My mother would not have been human if she hadn't felt complacent.

"Well, likely Mr. Sims will get around to it in his own good time, Mrs. Sims," she said. "It does take managing and contriving, to get ahead."

"Yes," Mrs. Sims said hesitantly. She seemed to retreat from the verge of saying more. "Are you putting up much apple-butter this year?"

When the fifteen minutes were up and she had gone, my mother stood looking after her. Mrs. Sims had a good figure and a stylish air; her slim back was straight as a ramrod and her skirts were gracefully gathered up in one hand. But she had worn that dress three years and now she had turned and sponged the goods and was making it do for best another year.

"It's a shame!" my mother said in her everyday voice. "Saving and doing without, the way she does, and Mr. Sims making all that good money. What he does with it all— Well, that's another call I've got to make."

We did not doubt that Mrs. Sims would get her parlor. Wives were always scheming to get something out of their husbands, and we girls were naturally our mothers' allies. Some men yielded to good food and flattery, others must be teased or even nagged, sometimes the struggle came to tears and quarrels. But Mr. Sims, a fat man, easy-going and good-natured, didn't seem difficult to manage.

He was not mean, he did not drink, he did not run after other women. Every afternoon at sunset we saw him strolling homeward, carrying the meat for supper. He was a hearty eater; meat three times a day, pie and cake always on the table, hot biscuits every morning for breakfast. And Mrs. Sims was a very good cook. It was strange that she did not get her parlor.

Her longing for it became part of our thought of her, like her expressive brown eyes, her curled hair, her active hands. She pored over the furniture pages in catalogues; she made Mr. Sims talk to the owner of the lumber-yard. The new room would cost fifty dollars; furnishing the parlor as she wanted it would cost about sixty. She would paint the woodwork herself, but she did want Nottingham curtains, an ingrain carpet, and a parlor suite.

Naturally other women sympathized with her, but as Mrs. Rogers said, "It does seem as if she ought to 've found some way to get it out of him. My land, she's been at him a year and more."

"Well," my mother said, "I'm glad I haven't got one of those lazy, easy-going fat men to contend with."

Mrs. Rogers agreed. "Mr. Rogers has his faults, but I must say he is a good provider."

Every evening when we sat down to supper my mother asked, "Well, what did you hear in town today?" and my father replied, "Oh, nothing much. Everything same as usual." The words were a habit. My mother asked without expectation, my father answered mechanically, I heard without hearing. Later he might contribute some item to the flagging talk. "Dave Hoover's painting his livery-barn."

"Is he?" my mother would say. "What color?"

"Same color. Red."

"Well, it's a good serviceable color."

"Yes, Dave's got good sense. Red's the cheapest color you can get and it wears as well as any."

"Yes, that's so. It does."

But one evening my father did not make his usual reply. He said, "Jim Miller's putting in a milliner shop."

We were startled, shocked. "A what?" my mother exclaimed as though she doubted her ears. I stopped eating.

"A milliner shop. Yes, and that's not all. Guess who's going to be the milliner."

We simply gazed at him. He was enjoying this immensely; he prolonged the moment, getting its full savor. "Mrs. Sims."

"*No!*" my mother cried. "Why—but— Why, but she's married! You don't mean Mrs. Henry Sims?"

My father had it straight from Jim Miller himself.

"Well!" My mother was aghast. "Well of all things! I never in my— Mr. Sims is *letting* her?"

Supper had never been so animated. In the end, my mother said of course it wasn't as if Mrs. Sims was going out among strangers. Mr. Sims would be right there in the store and Jim Miller was a relative by marriage; it was kind of a family affair. "How much is Mr. Miller paying her, you know?"

My father didn't. He didn't know how Mrs. Sims had got Mr. Sims to allow such a thing, either. My mother did the supper dishes that night, while I hurried up the street to Mrs. Sims' house.

Thrifty with kerosene, the neighbors had not lighted lamps; they were sitting on their porches in the dusk. There were no wagons on the shadowy street, where little boys raced and shouted. The tansy beds smelled sweet and Roses of Sharon were in bloom. The windows of Mrs. Sims' front room were yellow with lamplight.

She was hurriedly making over a dress. Her cheeks were flushed and her eyes sparkling; she sewed with quick runs of the needle and bit off the thread decisively. Myrtle and Pearl were excited and jubilant. "We're going to get the parlor!" they shouted as soon as they saw me.

I went home rich with news. Mrs. Sims was going to St. Louis with Jim Miller, on his fall buying trip. (It was all right; Mrs. Miller was going with them.)

My mother gasped. Not even Mrs. Miller had ever been to St. Louis; it was an over-night trip on the train. St. Louis was two hundred miles away, too far even for imagination to go.

The millinery company had a free school in St. Louis, where Mrs. Sims was going to learn how to make hats. It was a traveling man's idea. He had talked it up to Jim Miller in the store one afternoon; Mrs. Sims happened to go in and heard them talking, and right away she offered to be the milliner. It was all settled before Mr. Sims knew anything about it, and he didn't make much fuss, because how could he? Mr. Miller was his boss.

"What traveling man was it?" my mother asked.

"His name's Mr. Harris."

"Mmm. I wonder if that's the good-looking one, in the gray suit?"

I didn't know. Mrs. Sims hadn't said. Jim Miller

was going to pay her six dollars a week for seventeen weeks; a hundred and two dollars. She'd have to get a hired girl to do the housework and stay with the children after school and Saturdays; at a dollar and a half a week that was $25.50, and she'd have more than enough left to build the parlor.

"Then, mama, if she sells enough hats Mr. Miller's going to hire her again in the spring, and she'll earn the rest of the money for the furniture. She's going to get her parlor, mama, she really is."

My mother said, "She'll be talked about if she isn't careful. All those traveling men around."

"Well, but anyway she's going to get the parlor. She isn't going to work any more after that. That's all she wants in the world is just a real nice home and then, she says, she's going to stay home and enjoy it; just *try* to get her out of it!"

Dozens of times my mother repeated this first-hand information. The whole town was stirred, and excitement was hardly lulled during the two weeks that Mrs. Sims was gone, with the Millers. It rose to a fever when they returned, Mrs. Sims quite unchanged to the eye, but Mrs. Miller with new clothes from head to toe, and an ostrich-feather boa, and a thousand things to say about the city. All that week, while Mrs. Sims was busily stacking packing-cases around a cleared space at the rear end of the dry-goods counter, and scrubbing it and washing the window and unpacking sample hats and hat-materials, all the ladies were making appointments with each other to go downtown on the afternoon of the Grand Opening Day.

The town was changed that winter. Ladies had always dressed up and gone in couples to make formal afternoon calls, and of course there had been church, and lodge, and Ladies' Aid. But now there was somewhere to go, every afternoon. A few women even went gadding downtown to the milliner shop in the mornings. (Giving their houses no more than a lick and a promise.) Every afternoon the narrow space inside the walls of packing-boxes was crowded. After school we girls always went there.

A long mirror hung beside the window, and all the shelves along the store's wall displayed hats. Deliriously we tried them on, hat after hat, all the hats except the sacrosanct five-dollar one. We looked at that, but didn't touch it. Mrs. Sims hardly expected to sell a hat so expensive, but it gave tone to the shop.

Married women began to call each other by their first names. In the milliner shop they chattered like girls, laughed, and spoke without thinking. At home there was always something exciting to talk about, for all over town there were family struggles. We were all getting hats. And more than one woman tried to get the five-dollar one.

"You women've got the bit in your teeth," my father grumbled. But he grumbled only because he liked to feel powerful and generous. There was no serious trouble at our house.

Mrs. Sims worked from seven in the morning until

the store closed at nine. When she wasn't on her feet selling hats, she was making them. Often she took velvets and trimmings home and worked almost all night. She wore her old second-best dress every day and her rusty best one on Sundays; the hired girl let down last year's dresses for Myrtle and Pearl and patched their flannels. Mrs. Sims wasn't spending one penny. Jim Miller kept her wages for her, except enough to pay the hired girl. Every week meant $4.50 saved for the parlor.

Everyone was pleased when she said the shop would open again in the spring. Jim Miller was more than satisfied; she had sold all the hats but three, and the store had never done such a rushing business.

A few days before Christmas the milliner shop closed, and that day I waited to walk home with Mrs. Sims. It was almost supper-time; everyone else had gone. Mrs. Sims sat close to the window in the last daylight, ripping up the five-dollar hat to save the velvet. The shelves were empty, the floor littered with snippings of thread and a dribble of ashes from the heating stove. The dreariness of the alley, with its rubbish heaps partly covered by dingy snow, seemed to have come into the shop.

"We're going to have our parlor, aren't we, mama," Myrtle bragged.

"Yes, duckling, we are," Mrs. Sims said. She was thinner and there were shadows under her eyes, but she smiled happily. Her fingers were so rough from sewing that the velvet caught on them. She worked quickly because the light was failing and now and then a sigh came from her constricted chest.

She put one hand to the back of her neck and pressed her head hard against it, in that fierce gesture that rests a woman tired from sewing, and suddenly she said to me,

"Ernestine, you get some money of your own! Don't you marry anybody, not anybody, till you've got a hundred dollars of your very own money. Remember what I say; *don't you do it!*"

I stared at her. Myrtle laughed aloud; she had put on a hat-frame and the buckram brim had slipped down over her nose. "Lookee! Lookee! Mama, look at me!" she shouted, laughing. She hadn't heard. I was so uncomfortable that I stayed only long enough to pretend that I wasn't uncomfortable; then I went home by myself.

What she had said didn't make sense. How could a girl get any money of her own? She couldn't, of course. We had to get along as best we could, till we got married. Without thinking about it, we always took it for granted that we would have everything we wanted, when we were married. Yet of course we'd never marry for money.

I was profoundly disturbed, but all I thought or felt was that I didn't want to see Mrs. Sims any more.

Not an hour later I had to go to her house on some errand. I even pleaded to do the dishes first; I did not want to go, though I hardly knew why, and my mother sharply told me to obey her. "The sooner you do as you're told, the sooner it'll be over with."

The stars were out, but all the light seemed to come from the snow, which was piled in drifts along the sidewalks and gleamed icy in the paths and the wheel-ruts. Boys were out with their sleds on Mullins' hill, I could hear their shouts. Snug in my mother's old shawl, I enjoyed the frosty air; there was a feeling of Christmas in it.

I was walking cautiously on the slippery path to Mrs. Sims' porch, when a sound terrified me. I stood petrified with fear. Again, then again, I heard the low sound. I did not know what it was; it sounded like something dying. Some animal, horribly mangled, dying under the porch or in the shadow of the house. I could not move.

Then I heard Myrtle whimper, "Mama, mama, don't!"

Somehow, without caution or thought, I'd rushed into that front room. The lamplight dazzled my eyes; I heard after it had happened the slam of the door behind me. Mrs. Sims was on the bed. She had been lying face down, she was struggling up. Her corseted body moved stiffly and her legs were hampered by her skirts. The hired girl stood holding the camphor bottle and watching avidly.

Mrs. Sims sat on the edge of the bed and I saw her face. I hardly recognized it. "Don't cry, Myrtle," she said in a harsh voice. Her mouth twisted as if it were a separate thing, writhing on her face.

Myrtle stared, terrified; she was not crying.

"My land what's the matter with you, Mis' Sims?"

the hired girl demanded. "Bawling like I don't know what." The most frightening thing was that there were no tears on Mrs. Sims' cheeks or in her eyes. Her hat was grotesquely askew and the collar of her dress was wrenched open; her union suit showed.

"We aren't going to get the parlor," she said. "My poor girls—" Her hands twisted together; a seam in one glove ripped slowly.

The hired girl said with eager relish, "She acts to me like she's out of her head. She come in just the same as usual and no sooner shut the door behind her when all of a sudden—"

Pearl asked why they couldn't have the parlor. Mrs. Sims put up her arms stiffly and took out hatpins. She pushed her hair back from her forehead. Pearl asked again, "Mama, why can't we—" "Oh, be quiet!" Mrs. Sims cried.

We were quiet. The hired girl brought a glass of water and she swallowed a little. Then she said, "I might as well tell you. The whole town'll know it."

They could not have the parlor because Mr. Sims owed Jim Miller almost five hundred dollars. When she asked for her wages Jim said he'd just let them apply on the debt. "What debt?" she asked; she didn't know there was any debt. Then Jim Miller told her that Henry Sims had been running big grocery bills all these years, and owed him something around five hundred dollars. There was no money for Mrs. Sims.

"But mama, it's your money," Pearl argued. Myrtle was huddled against her mother, crying terribly; Mrs. Sims was trying to hush her. "Mama, you earned all that money, didn't you?" Pearl insisted. "Didn't you? It's your money, isn't it? Mama, isn't it?"

"No it isn't!" Mrs. Sims said fiercely. "Not according to law it isn't."

"But why isn't it?"

"Myrtle, darling, don't, you mustn't. Myrtle, stop it! You'll make yourself sick."

I wanted to go away, but I didn't know what to say, how to get away politely.

Pearl kept on. "But mama, why isn't it? Mama, *why?*"

"Oh, shut up, Pearl!" Mrs. Sims cried out. "It's not my money because I'm married, that's why! That's the law!"

I decided to go away without saying anything, but before I could do it, we heard Mr. Sims' steps on the porch. He opened the door slowly, and carefully shut it behind him. Myrtle's sobs diminished. Nobody spoke while he got out of his overcoat.

Here was authority, power. He would do something — something violently unreasonable, perhaps, but decisive. The air was electric and heavy with waiting for it.

"Supper ready?" he asked loudly. He did not look at anyone and the loudness sounded hollow.

"Della's taking it up," Mrs. Sims said.

Still glancing aside, he cleared his throat. He ventured, "It's some colder out. Looks like we might have snow." He was like a cowering dog, timidly wagging. Mrs. Sims sat looking at him with hard, bright eyes.

Somehow I passed him, got the door open, and fled.

My mother and Mrs. Sims had become intimate friends that winter. They spent a long afternoon together; I was shut out, but I knew that my mother was consoling her, pointing out that many wives had heavier crosses to bear. It wasn't as if Mr. Sims drank, or beat her, or ran after other women.

In public, of course, no one so much as mentioned a parlor in Mrs. Sims' presence. Nothing else was discussed when she wasn't there, and everyone was regretful. "I'm going to miss the milliner shop," someone always said, and all the other ladies sighed and said they would miss it, too.

But next spring Mrs. Sims went to St. Louis again with Mr. and Mrs. Miller. She was re-opening the milliner shop. No one had imagined that she would carry so far the decent pretense that nothing had happened. Certainly she could get no money for her work, and Mrs. Rogers and my mother agreed that they wouldn't be caught dead, slaving to pay off that debt. On Opening Day every lady in town tried to crowd into the milliner shop.

Mrs. Sims was wearing a new black silk grenadine dress cut in the very latest style. Her hair was elaborately arranged in braids and puffs held by glittering combs, and there was powder on her face. She moved about confidently, showing us the new hats, chattering about new styles in dress, and every step was accompanied by a rich swishing of silk petticoats and a delicate wave of perfume. The sensation was enormous.

The whole town buzzed with one question, "How is she getting the money?"

"She isn't getting any money," my mother told me. "She's taking things out of the store, and charging them."

I was bewildered, then shocked. "Charging — why — But it isn't honest!"

"Well, what she says is, she works as hard as Mr. Sims does, and if he can charge things, she can. She says she's worth more to Jim Miller than he is. And that's true."

"You mean because he runs in debt, she's going to be as bad?"

My mother was shocked, too, and more confused than I. "Well, but if she's earning —" There was no precedent to guide us. What Mrs. Sims was doing couldn't be honest, and it was horrifying to think of a woman's deliberately being as bad as a man. Yet somehow she seemed, in a way, justified. We were bewildered.

I asked why Jim Miller didn't stop it, and my mother said in an odd tone, "He can't. He can't, without letting her go, and she's making him money."

Suddenly we burst out laughing, laughed till we cried. We were ashamed of our laughter but we couldn't control it. There was something triumphant in it.

A delirium swept the town that summer. After

the activity of spring housecleaning, living did not subside into its usual drowsiness. Every woman was sewing. An appalling thing was that mothers were seized by a madness for clothes, for themselves. Shirt waists were coming in, and lace boleros and pulley-belts and dangling, tinkling chatelaines; monstrously, our mothers sometimes got these new styles before we did. Mrs. Sims had them all; she was first to appear in them.

Nobody but Mrs. Miller could afford to keep up with Mrs. Sims, and she was a half-step behind. Mrs. Sims' black mousseline de soie was made up over all-silk. Mrs. Sims had a black silk parasol with chiffon ruffles half a yard wide. Nobody could say which was her best dress, her best hat; she had so many. It was rumored that she wore silk stockings.

Myrtle and Pearl had countless new hair-ribbons; they had organdy dresses worn over sky-blue and pink silk; they had leghorn hats smothered in roses, and pale blue and pink parasols, lace-ruffled. Their everyday underwear was made of Swiss embroidery, and riotously they wore out their shoes.

Every afternoon women overflowed the millinery shop; the whole dry-goods side of the store was a-chatter with them; groups lingered talking even on the sidewalk, heedless of the men loafing there. Some ladies even went downtown after supper and were seen in the store. Some, always in groups of course, even talked with the traveling men.

My mother stoutly maintained that there was no real harm in this. A change, a kind of giddiness, had

come over my mother. She and Mrs. Sims were together every day; they never tired of talking to each
other; if they had been girls one would have called
them chums. Often Mrs. Sims stopped by for my
mother after supper.

"Gadding around all hours of day and night!" my
father stormed. His grumbling was no longer good-
natured. Indeed, all the men in town were sharper
with their wives.

"You can't say I neglect my home," my mother retorted with spirit. Though she dressed in proper
dark brown and black and wore her heavy wedding
ring, she no longer looked like an old married woman.
She was well on in her thirties and of course could not
look young, but her eyes were alight and her face
alive with changing expressions.

It was as though Mrs. Sims made everyone about
her more alive. She came in impetuously, calling
gaily from the porch. No one else wore clothes as
she did, subordinating their elegance to something
vital in herself. She was all sparkle and shadow, like
running water, yet somehow, incredibly, she was still
a lady.

My mother went downtown with her, and what
could my father do? That was the astounding discovery; he could not do anything. No wonder my
mother lost her head a little.

Otherwise she would have withdrawn, at least
slightly, from Mrs. Sims. Something intangible was
in the air. Mrs. Sims was not actually talked about,
but glances were exchanged. And attention was fo-

cusing upon her and Mr. Harris, the traveling man. Nothing could be definitely said; it was known that she never saw him alone. Yet, there was something —

I had never spoken to Mr. Harris, but I had often observed him intently. He was not handsome, but he was pleasant-looking. His shoulders and his way of walking suggested reliability and common sense. Unlike most traveling men, he did not flirt with girls from south of the tracks. Men said he was making money and saving it; ladies said he was a perfect gentleman.

One day Mrs. Sims was at the front counter, displaying a fresh assortment of Persian lawns while several of us admired them wistfully, when Mr. Harris came in with his sample cases. He took off his straw hat and said good afternoon. "How are you, Mrs. Sims?"

We all looked quickly at her; she smiled. "Very well, thank you, Mr. Harris."

"I see you're busy."

"I'm sorry, I am, just now."

"Jim in?"

"He's in back, getting out a barrel of molasses. Bring him over in half an hour, I have an order for you."

"Good!" he said. "Good for you! That's what I like to hear!" There was something sturdy and reliable in his smile, too. His glance met hers. He turned away and she went on showing the lawns and laces, but we were inattentive.

There was some strange quality in that glance. It

was open and frank ; his eyes were not bold and hers
not coquettish, yet they weren't veiled by a decorous
reserve.   It was not a flirtatious glance ; it didn't hide
any slyly secret understanding.   But it expressed
something mutually understood.   I had never before
seen such a glance exchanged between a man and a
woman.   It was disturbing because I did not know
what it meant.

I wished to believe the best of Mrs. Sims, but I
did not forget that odd glance.   The catastrophe,
when it came, did not surprise me.

Mrs. Miller could not go to St. Louis that fall.
Of course Mrs. Sims could not go with Mr. Miller,
and she could not travel alone at night.   Jim Miller
grumbled that that was the nuisance of women's meddling in business affairs where they didn't belong ;
they were more trouble than they were worth.   But
he insisted that Mrs. Sims must get the new styles.
He had to delay his trip so that she could go and
come back before he left ; otherwise there might have
been talk.   By traveling on local trains she could
make the trip in daylight, and in the city she could
stay with some distant relatives and not be alone in
a boarding house.

She confessed to my mother that she was scared to
death, but to everyone else she said she wasn't afraid
at all.   All her friends accompanied her to the depot
and Jim introduced her to the conductor, a respectable
and elderly married man, who promised to look out
for her.   The relatives would meet her train in St.

Louis. Next day a telegram came, reporting her safe arrival.

Rain fell steadily all the two weeks she was gone, and on the day she was expected home my father brought us news of the flood. People still recall it. Bridges and roads were washed out; whole towns and valleys inundated. Seven passenger trains were stalled in the little town of Lyndon; telegraph wires were down. Our meager news came from train-men. When at last the old newspapers came, there was no mention in them of Mrs. Sims.

Three days later she arrived, tired and disheveled and excited. She had endless stories of the floods and the crowds, of escapes and rescues, of frantic men and hysterical women and babies crying from hunger, of the work of the train crews. "I never worked so hard in my life." She laughed. "Honestly, I enjoyed it!"

The milliner shop would open on Saturday, but before that, on Friday afternoon, she was going to give a Reception. "This town needs waking up," she told my mother. "I'm going to start some social life." In St. Louis she had been to a Reception. Of course she could not equal that, with what she had to do with, but she knew how a Reception should be given and she'd planned how to do with what she had.

She brought a box of stationery and my mother helped her write the invitations; all the ladies in town were invited, from three o'clock to five. She made new curtains and hung them in her front room; Friday morning she would take the bed out; chairs and cups, spoons and plates were borrowed; the hired girl was baking bread and killing hens; my mother offered to make one of her famous gingerbreads. Everyone was sewing frantically. My mother was making a green nun's veiling trimmed with black lace appliqué.

"It isn't a light green," she said anxiously, "and the black tones it down. You don't think it's too young for my age?" I assured her that it wasn't; the excitement had infected even me, though I was too young to be invited to the Reception.

We saw that something was wrong when my father came home to supper on Wednesday. My mother asked no questions; she felt guilty about the dress. We ate almost in silence for some time; then he told her, drily. Mrs. Sims and Mr. Harris had been seen together in Lyndon. They had stayed at the same hotel.

Bright spots of red appeared on my mother's cheeks. "I don't believe it!"

Larry Shipp, the stockbuyer, had been there. He had seen them.

"Well, if it's true, there wasn't any harm in it," my mother said, trembling. "I'll never believe that Ella Sims would —"

My father pushed back his plate. He looked straight at her, a hard look. "You think there's no harm in it? A married woman staying at a strange hotel with another man?"

"But — it wasn't — I mean with the flood, and only

the one hotel, what else could she —" Suddenly her eyes were as hard as his. "No!" she said strongly. "Not if it was Ella Sims."

My father got up. He put on his coat and hat and walked out. We heard his steps cross the porch, crunch on the gravelled walk; the gate slammed. I was terrified. Women were deserted if they did not hold their husbands' love. My mother began to gather up the dishes and I helped her, not daring to say a word. She had the look of a horse with ears laid back, ready to bite.

Next day everybody was talking. Nevertheless, my mother stoutly defended Mrs. Sims' character. "What would you expect her to do, sleep out in the rain with the trainmen? There was only the one hotel. I guess plenty of others were there, too. Larry Shipp stayed there himself, didn't he? Well, then. He don't say there was any harm in that, does he? It's all stuff and fiddlesticks. She was sleeping in a room with three other women and their children."

"I know that's what she said," women murmured. "Well, I think myself it was probably all right, except for the looks of —"

"Of course it was all right! I never heard such nonsense!"

She would, I think, have saved the situation but for Mr. Sims. Nobody had paid any attention to him for a long time. His fat no longer expressed content- ment; it seemed to hang upon him listlessly, and his mouth had begun to have a trick of turning down its corners as if to say, weakly and bitterly, "Do as you please, I don't care!"

Rain had begun again and the sidewalks were slippery with thin mire; my mother made me put on overshoes when she sent me for soda to make the gingerbread. It was Friday morning. All the loafers had come in out of the rain and were gathered on the men's side of the store. Mr. Sims gave me the soda and took the nickel without a word, and I went across to the milliner shop, just for a minute.

Mrs. Sims was hurriedly unpacking new hats and several of the girls were there. We did not hear the trouble begin. An outbreak of men's voices struck us silent, and then we heard Mr. Harris. "If you want to insult your wife it's none of my business, but I'll tell you right now —"

There was another outcry and a scuffle. All the girls were crowding and pushing to see what was happening. Mrs. Sims stood still; her hands crushed a bright blue velvet hat against her breast and her face was the color of ashes, even her mouth was gray.

We did not see clearly what happened. The men were in a crowd between the pickle kegs and the plows. Mr. Sims swore. Some men were holding him and Mr. Harris shook off others and stepped through the doorway. He turned and said, "I wouldn't fight you, you lump of lard. But any man who says what you've said about Mrs. Sims is a goddam liar."

Some said that Mr. Sims knocked him down. It wasn't true. He slipped on the sidewalk. He went down with a crash, jumped up and leaped down into the muddy street to pick up his hat. He walked rapidly toward the hotel. In a minute Mrs. Sims went straight out of the store without looking at anybody, and went home.

Whatever my father said to my mother was said privately. At dinner they were constrained and miserable. They did not look at each other and said hardly a word. My mother's mouth was grim. My father hesitated before he went out, looking into his hat as though he might say something; then he put it on and left. As soon as he was out of hearing I asked, hushed, "Mama, are you going to the Reception?"

Tears came into her eyes; she brushed them angrily away with her hand. "Oh, I don't know. I like her so much, and it isn't true. It isn't! But what can I do? He won't let me." She broke down and cried. "I did send her the gingerbread, I gave Tommy Webb a nickel to take it to her. Oh, surely somebody'll go!"

The only room from which we could watch was the parlor. Fall housecleaning time had not yet come and the heater was still in the woodshed; rain fell drearily and the air was chill and damp. Huddled in shawls, we watched through the lace curtains. "She can't be expecting everybody," my mother said, "on account of the rain."

We watched till five o'clock. No one, not even Mrs. Miller, went to the Reception.

It was the end of the milliner shop, the end of

everything. Mrs. Sims would never be able to hold up her head again. Ladies would not speak to her on the street. Looking at my mother's face, I didn't know whether even she would have the courage to.

I felt that I hated my father. When he came home I was getting supper; I told him curtly that my mother was lying down, and he went into the bedroom. The door was ajar and for a long time I heard their voices murmuring in the thickening dusk. Then the lamp was lighted and I saw my mother standing before the bureau, combing her hair. My father stood close to her, admiring its shining length, and they were wholly absorbed in each other.

After supper my father went downtown almost reluctantly, saying he wouldn't be gone long. We put the red cloth on the table and my mother settled down to her mending. I got a plate of apples and spread open a book. The clock ticked, the lamp's wick drank the oil with a cosy tiny purring, and looking up when I turned a page I saw my mother's face serenely quiet and intent upon some inner beatitude.

There was a step, a light knock, then the door opened and Mrs. Sims stood there. She was windblown and wet, covered from head to foot in a ragged shawl. Her eyes were bright with anger. Looking fiercely at my mother, she thrust out a gloved hand holding teaspoons.

"I'm returning these, thank you so much." Her mouth had a curl like the tone of her voice. "And good-by! I'm leaving for good." She was holding her hat under the shawl, she was wearing her black traveling suit.

My mother got up. "Ernestine!" she said.

I knew that tone; protest, delay, were useless. I stalked into the kitchen and slammed the door. And instantly I ran out into the windy dark and rain, sped around the dining-room and crouched under the parlor window. My mother would take Mrs. Sims there, where they could not be heard from the kitchen.

She had done that. I heard her say, "But you *can't.*"

"Well, I am," replied Mrs. Sims' voice. "The girls are at the depot now. I'm going to flag the Cannonball."

"Ella! You're out of your mind, you mustn't. You don't know what you're doing. Oh Ella, *please.* You don't realize. What ever'll become of you, all alone with nobody to take care of you?"

"Who's taking care of me now?"

"I know it's hard. But you've got a home, you've got a husband. It's better to put up with anything than — Think of the children. Think —"

"I thought all afternoon."

"Oh, I didn't want to treat you so mean, I didn't want to! But —"

"And who got me into this? *He* did. Taking care of me!"

"He meant well, Ella. Men are like that. He was protecting your good na —"

"Protecting fiddlesticks! I can take better care of myself. Yes, and the children too. Let him divorce me if he —"

"*Ella!*"

"Why's it any worse disgrace for a woman to be divorced than for a man?"

My mother was right; I shouldn't listen to such things. Why were they silent? What would they say next?

"You haven't got any money. You can't live, how can you?"

"I'm going to borrow money."

"Borrow —?" There was a pause. My mother said, "So it's true."

"No it isn't true. But he'll lend me money till I get work. I know he will. I'm going to the hotel to ask him, now."

"No man lends a woman money for nothing."

"Think what you please." Mrs. Sims' silk petticoats rustled. "Good-by."

"Good-by," my mother said coldly.

The door opened. Lamplight shone out through the slant of the rain and Mrs. Sims appeared briefly in it. Wrapped in the ragged shawl, her head bent to the gusts of wind, she went down the path and through the gate. It shut behind her. Then the door closed too and she was only a sound of steps going away in the dark.

So she remained in my mind, a figure piteous and terrible, the cast-out woman against whom doors are closed. She had gone out of our known world, was somewhere in St. Louis. In time Mr. Sims divorced her. Mr. Harris did not marry her. She was forgotten.

Twenty years passed swiftly before I saw her again. We met at a dinner in New York and liked each other at once. For a month or so we saw a great deal of each other; then she went to Bermuda, I to the Balkans. The next year we missed each other by a few hours in Buda-Pesth, but the following spring we met by chance in the Louvre and went to tea.

Meantime the magazines had begun to print articles about her. It was a good story, the career of Ella Maybry Sims, creator of the Mary-Marie (trademark) Frocks. American women from Canada to Mexico were wearing those cleverly designed fadeless cottons, at $1.49, $1.98 and $2.74. The biographies of her briefly mentioned an early marriage, leaving the inference that Mrs. Sims is a widow, and they did not exaggerate her fortune; the truth is staggering enough.

We ate incomparable strawberry tarts, in that twittering French atmosphere so like that of an aviary, while she told me she was going to put out a line of daytime pajamas, and I reflected how perfectly she is the type of American woman who is at home everywhere — and nowhere. Her hair is gray now, almost excessively becoming with her clear contours and dark young eyes, and she is one of the reasons why French women envy American *chic*.

"How is your mother?" she asked, and this re-

minded me that my parents were planning to cele-
brate their silver wedding anniversary.

"Think of it," I said. "Think of a man and a
woman, living forty years together in a little town,
making a — yes, a truly happy marriage."

"I rather envy them, too," she said.

We smiled at each other. "Tell me, are we sacri-
fices to the feminist movement? No, really, why do
we never meet men who are stronger than we are?"

"I think it's the wifely art to create them," she
said.

Struck by a sudden memory I asked, "Why didn't
you ever marry — what was his name? the traveling
salesman."

"Mr. Harris? What did they say when I didn't?"

"That naturally he wouldn't."

Laughter bubbled from her throat and made her
whole face merry. "Of course! They thought I
was a fallen woman! It's amazing how one forgets.
Oh, we weren't in love, not at first, in the hard days.
Later — Well, I was a better salesman than he was,
I was making more money — I'm glad I didn't. It
wouldn't have been a success. You know. He
couldn't have stood it."

Her vivid face, not quite regretfully smiling, was
blurred by musing. "He married, of course; a
charming woman, and they have three children. I'm
terribly fond of him still. He's a good customer of
ours — has a shop in Des Moines; splendid credit rat-
ing."

We finished tea a little hurriedly; she had an appointment, and we walked up the rue de Rivoli to her hotel. The springtime gaiety of Paris, intangible and pervasive as the thin sunshine, filled us with a light happiness. "I wish I were an Italian," she said, "singing O sole mio." She was flying to London next day and I was going to Tirana, but we knew that we would meet somewhere again, and parted casually.

V

LONG SKIRTS

MY MOTHER became, that spring, an almost unbearable irritation to me. I had never thought much about her, before; she had always been there, like the weather, or Providence, incalculable and governing but on the whole benign. Now she seemed to exist only to annoy, exasperate and thwart me.

"Ernestine's at the awkward age," she said patiently to Mrs. Rogers, and my scowl did not begin to express the resentment I felt at her talking about me as if I were a mere child.

"Yes, but my land, you never can tell what they'll turn into, it's too soon to lose hope yet," Mrs. Rogers consoled her. And turning to me she added, "I wonder at you, Ernestine. It's a real pretty dimity, and if your mother says mutton-leg sleeves, it's mutton-leg sleeves, and I don't know why she stands any of your lip."

"I don't want mutton-leg sleeves!" I all but yelled.

"Ernestine!" My mother's tone quelled me, but still I muttered, "Well, I don't." I hadn't the courage to add aloud, "And I won't have them!" Inwardly I argued, "It's my dress, isn't it? I got to wear it, don't I? I guess if I want mousquetaire sleeves I got a right —"

Mousquetaire sleeves would take two more yards of dimity, and that was ten cents. But the real difficulty was that the only woman in town who had a mousquetaire sleeve pattern was Mrs. Miller. We were poor; my father was the drayman; and long ago when I was little, before we moved to town, we had been country folks. The Millers were as rich as the banker's family; Mrs. Miller's house and her clothes were the finest in town, and she had been so kind to the poor drayman's wife that my mother would have died of hunger, politely refusing food from Mrs. Miller.

But I felt that I had enough to bear, without looking like a freak. All the other girls would be wearing the latest style in sleeves. Elsie Miller's best summer dress was to be China silk. Lois Estes was having organdy made up over pink silkaleen, and Blanche Anderson had a pale green silk mousseline. Day after day I pleaded, argued, coaxed, and at last broke down and cried.

"Oh, why can't I ever have anything like other girls? It isn't my fault we're poor! It's only a horrid old five-cent dimity but I'd try to bear it if only you'd make it up in style. I don't know why you won't ever do one teeny weeny little thing to keep me from being utterly miserable!"

My mother said, "I don't think you ought to talk to me like that, Ernestine. Someday you'll have a girl of your own, and if you're poor —" She bent

over the skirt-gores in her lap and went on hurriedly
basting them together with an empty needle. "Well,
go. Go ask Mrs. Miller."

"Oh, mama!" I flew to change my dress and
shoes and put on my felt hat with the polka-dot band.

Springtime was in the air; the muddy street
steamed, all the yards were filmed with green and
only scraps of dirty snow remained on the shady side
of woodpiles and under the edge of the board sidewalk. I was so happy I could hardly bear it, but in
my happiness I vowed never to forget my sufferings.
When I was married, all my children should always
be beautifully dressed. "Darlings, you shall want for
nothing," I murmured tenderly in my thoughts,
"Mother remembers, mother knows how you feel."

From our gate I waved to old Mrs. Bates, watching me from her sitting-room window. She was an
invalid and sat all day watching people go by. Last
year all the girls had been kind to her day after day,
but this year nobody read the Elsie books. Now it
was the thing to know all the characters in the funny-
papers.

The sunshine was warm, the network of tree-tops
was knobby with swollen buds. Mares browsed in
the livery-stable pasture, their gangling colts beside
them. Walking haughtily past the boys scuffling in
front of the livery-stable, I saw that new spring dress-
goods were still coming to Miller's store.

The dray was backed up to the sidewalk; my father
had wound the lines around the whip and was un-
loading boxes, while inside the doorway Mr. Sims

and Ben Herrick pried off the tops. "Hello, kid!"
Ben said. "Come in and have a look at 'em!"

Everybody liked Ben Herrick. He had worked
his way up from south of the tracks; he was a steady,
dependable young man who worked hard and saved
his money and always had a cheerful word for anyone. There was something warm and hearty about
him. You didn't mind his clumsily patched shirts
and the nail that fastened one suspender to his
trousers. His hair was ginger-colored, his nose was
pug, and in summer he always freckled. He ripped
the last board off a case, and began lifting bolts of
goods to the counter.

"Pretty, ain't they?" he said, enjoying them. All
along the counter, organdies and muslins and Persian
lawns were piled high; the whole place bloomed with
their freshness. My hands were clean, and with a
finger tip I touched a sheer white sprinkled with
flowers. Ben said, "Spring's here, all right."

I knew what he meant. Something was there that
couldn't be said. There was no way to say it, but it
was there — in the delicately colored and snowy stuffs,
in the air that smelled of grass and damp earth, in
the jingle of bits when the horses shook their heads,
and in the lilt of someone's whistling. The ham-
mering at the blacksmith shop was like bells.
There was a shimmer, just in being alive. Ben felt
it, too.

He was old; he must have been nearly thirty years
old. But for a startled instant, I knew that he knew
it was springtime.

"What're you doing uptown?" my father asked me then. He spoke kindly, but we both knew there was plenty of work I could be doing at home, and that nice girls didn't hang around the store.

The Miller's house was somewhat intimidating. It stood back from the street in a big yard. There were two iron deer on the lawn, always looking startled and a little rusty, and the house was two-storied, with bay windows and a tall eight-sided cupola. Colored glass panes surrounded the bay windows and the heavy front door, which had a ground-glass scene of deer and trees set into it, and a round-bellied doorbell on it.

I did not have to twist the handle of the bell; the door stood ajar to the long hall and a sewing-machine hummed in the dining-room. The sound was hurried and harassed; Mrs. Miller, with five girls and herself to dress, had to do more sewing than any other woman in town. Bolts of longcloth and Swiss embroidery lay in the dining-room chairs; patterns and fashion-plates, whalebones, cards of laces and buttons and hooks-and-eyes were everywhere. Elsie was turning and preening before the tall pier-glass.

"Hello, kiddo!" she sang out, triumphant. Her hair was done up. The flounces of her new plaid gingham dress almost touched the floor.

"Why, Elsie Miller!" I gasped before, ashamed of my impoliteness, I turned to her mother and murmured, "Good morning, Mrs. Miller."

Elsie didn't give her mother time to reply. "Like it?" she said airily. She pulled the belt down smartly

in front, smoothed her hips, set her skirts swinging.
"Mama, I'm *going* to have rhinestone combs and a
barrette to match." And she was only two months
older than I.

I thought of saying virtuously, "I don't think we're
old enough for long skirts yet. We'll be grown-up
a long time, and we're only little girls once." But
Elsie's mother spoke first, louder than the noise of
the driven machine. "It's ridiculous! You're not
old enough."

With no effort at all, I told the lie. "My mother's
putting me into long skirts."

Elsie glanced at me suspiciously, and I saw that I'd
stepped into a trap. Now I'd have to make my
mother do it, or I could never hold up my head
again.

"Seems to me you're rushing your age." Mrs.
Miller snapped the thread, then let her hands rest on
the heap of petticoat ruffles. Some change came over
her; she sighed. "My, my, the way you young ones
grow up."

"Well, I guess you'd be sorry if we didn't!" Elsie
retorted pertly. No other girl was so quick, so smart
as Elsie. No wonder her mother just couldn't do a
thing with that girl. I envied her with all my heart,
while Mrs. Miller hunted for the mousquetaire sleeve
pattern and I politely answered her questions. Yes,
my mother was well, thank you. Mrs. Bates was
about the same, I guessed. Yes ma'am, the new goods
came; Ben Herrick was unpacking them when I came
by.

"Ben's taking a shine to Minty Bates," Mrs. Miller remarked.

"What?" Elsie cried, shocked. "Not Minty Bates! Why—why, I don't believe it! As if our Ben'd take other men's leavings!"

Her mother said sharply, "Don't talk like that, Elsie. You don't know what you're saying."

Elsie would not be silenced. "I guess I do so! That Minty Bates is an old maid if ever there was one, and if that's not men's leavings, what is? And wasn't she engaged twice, and neither of 'em took her? Jilted once is scandal enough, but jilted *twice* — My goodness, I don't know what more you'd *want* against a girl — two broken engagements!"

"She's good as gold to her poor old widowed mother," said Mrs. Miller. "And whatever happened, you can't tell me there was ever a true word said against poor Minty. And I'll thank you, miss, to speak more respect— Elsie, you come right back here! Elsie!" she called, "Where are you going?"

Elsie had swept me into the hall with her. She called over her shoulder, "I'm only going's far's the store with Ernestine." She said yes, she'd be right back. Yes, she'd do the dishes when she got back. "My goodness, mama, don't nag so!" she shouted impatiently. And nothing happened. Nothing except that we were free. We were free in the soft sunshine and the breeze that seemed somehow wild and gay.

Elsie tucked her arm comfortably into mine. "That's one thing I'm never, never going to do when

I'm married," she confided. "I'm never going to nag my children."

Then she offered to tell me a secret. Dizzily I asked myself if it could be possible that Elsie Miller was choosing me for a chum. I crossed my heart solemnly and promised never to tell, never as long as I lived to breathe one word to any living soul, and never, never, not if I were dying, to let my mother even suspect. And after that, I had to coax her. But at last she told. She had met a traveling man.

I was shocked to the marrow. I didn't know what to say. The pickets in Mrs. Sherwood's fence seemed to wobble before my eyes.

There was more. His name was Mr. Andrews. "Call me Andy," he said. He worked out of St. Louis, he wore a real diamond ring, and he said that Elsie was the prettiest girl in his whole territory. He was mad about her, simply mad about her. "And Ernestine," Elsie dreamily murmured in my ear, "Oh, Ernestine, it's true love at last! I know it is, because — don't ever tell —" She whispered, "I love him."

My feet could hardly find the sidewalk. "Elsie!" I gasped. "What — what does it feel like?"

She said it was wonderful, just wonderful. Slowly we walked around the Square. She told me what he said, what she said, what she thought, and what she thought he thought because he'd said — The sleeve pattern was crumpled in my feverish clasp, I knew my mother was expecting me, but I couldn't tear myself away. "Elsie, he didn't! And then what did you say?" We kept on walking, around and around the Square. And it was incredible that Elsie Miller, of all girls, was confiding such a secret to me.

I ran all the way home. My mother was taking up the dinner and my father, already washed, was combing his hair before the little mirror on the kitchen wall. He looked at me sternly. "You see to it, young lady, you help get dinner after this. Your mother slaving away her time for your fol-de-rols; you know she hates sewing. Now fill up those water glasses and be quick about it."

My mother protested, "Don't be hard on her, Joe. She just forgot. Ernestine's a good girl."

"Well, I'm not going to have her gadding the streets with that girl of Miller's." He drew his chair to the table and took his napkin out of the ring. "Don't you let me catch you making such a spectacle of yourself again," he said to me.

"No, papa," I said.

They talked about setting out tomatoes, then about taking down the heating stove. The door was open and the sweet air came in. There would be violets soon along the country roads, and buttercups and dandelions in the vacant lots. My serge dress felt stuffy on me, but I had outgrown last summer's dresses. My mother would want to let down their hems again, but I knew desperately that I must have long skirts.

As soon as my father had gone, I began. My mother was firm at first. It made no difference to her that Elsie Miller was going into long skirts.

Frantically I spoke of modesty, and she blushed as hotly as I. Looking aside I muttered, "I'm too big, mama. I can't let people—boys—see my lower limbs." I cried passionately, "It just isn't decent! If you won't let me have decent clothes I'll just have to— I can't go anywhere! I'll just have to stay home and hide. Oh mama, please, *please!*"

"But I don't know how on earth I can!" she said in desperation. "It means all new goods—" She sighed. "Well, maybe I can inset gores and put a scalloped flounce on your pique. And I can get along with my last summer's lawn, I suppose."

I hardly heard that. The sigh meant that she yielded, and jumping up I began with an industrious clatter to scrape and stack the dishes. Joyously over the dishpan I sang,

When you hear them bells go tinga-linga-ling,
All join hands and joyfully we will sing,
There'll be a hot time, in the old —

"Ernestine!" My mother was no more shocked than I. I knew that wasn't a nice song. But I hadn't thought. Indeed, I didn't really know what awful thing that song meant, and I was speechless in guilt and confusion. After a dreadful pause my mother's voice, slightly blurred by pins, came again from the dining-room. "When you get the dishes done, run over and ask Minty Bates when she'll trade works with me, cleaning house."

Hurriedly I finished the dishes. There was a fascination about Miss Minty Bates. She was the only woman in town who had been jilted, and she had been jilted not once, but twice. No one knew why; she and her mother had never told, and both men had left town, so nothing could be learned from them.

No one could help searching her face for that secret. When she went down the street, walking in her stiffly awkward way, with two red spots on her cheek-bones, the men in the livery-stable and the bar-ber-shop spoke about it, and the loafers turned to watch her. When she came down the aisle in church, we girls looked at her with curiosity. And everyone was always especially polite to her, not wanting to hurt her feelings.

There had been no change in her face, there was no clue, when she answered my knock at the side door. Her complexion was a clear white, her black hair was naturally wavy, and her curved lips were red. She might have been very pretty. But her hair was pulled back as tightly as possible, so that her forehead stared out white and hard from tiny curling wisps, and her red mouth had a hard, set look. Something in her eyes was always trying to get away; I could never look at it long enough to see what it was. The lids drooped, the cherry-red spots came out on her cheek-bones, and she moved a little, awkwardly. "It's Ernestine, mother," she said.

I went in. "Mama wants to know when you can come help houseclean."

Mrs. Bates sat in her rocking-chair by the sitting-room window. She was my ideal of a beautiful old lady. Her soft face was pink and white and her eyes bright blue under lids like tissue paper. A flat cap of black lace lay on the parting of her wavy white hair, and a white knitted shawl was fluffy around her shoulders. Her feet in pale blue knitted slippers rested on a hassock.

The whole room was like her. The window-panes shone, the curtains were fresh, there was not a withered leaf on the house-plants. The very threads of the ingrain carpet showed clean in the oblongs of sunshine. Mrs. Bates was a perfect housekeeper, and though she could do no work herself she saw to it that Minty kept everything just so. Every morning before Minty went to work she scrubbed every floor in the house.

Minty said now, "I'm helping Mrs. Willard this week, and then I thought maybe Mrs. Miller'd want me. Let's see—"

The front gate clicked, and we all saw little Tommy Webb coming up the walk. Minty went to the door, saying, "Maybe that's word from Mrs. Miller, now."

Tommy grinned at me and said, "Hello, Ernestine!" He was much younger than I; he was still in short pants. I said, "Hello," coldly, and turned to Mrs. Bates. She was intent on Minty.

The note was shaking in Miss Minty's hand. A quiver went over her face, then a dark blush surged up from her collar; her face blazed so that it seemed to be heat that brought tears to her eyes. Tommy Webb stared up at her, open-mouthed. She thrust a hand at him as if to push him away, her head turned this way and that, and she almost ran into the kitchen, shutting the door behind her.

"Who's that note from, Tommy?" I demanded.

"I got a nickel not to tell," he said, looking doubtfully at the kitchen door. "Ben said he'd give me another if I brung an answer. What's the matter with her?"

I almost shouted, "He's going to take her buggy-riding, I bet!" And saying hurriedly to Mrs. Bates that I'd come some other time about the housecleaning, I rushed home to tell my mother.

Patterns slithered in the breeze of my entrance. My mother, on her knees on the floor, went on taking pins from her mouth and marking the rows of perforations in that enormous sleeve pattern.

"That's nice," she said absently, when her mouth was empty. "Ernestine, it's going to take four yards more, and I'll have to have fifteen yards of beading and black velvet ribbon to run through it."

Her forehead was grooved with anxiety and she paid no attention at all to my news. It took me a little time to think of an excuse for going to Elsie's. At last it came to me. "Mama, when I go for the goods, I'll take back the sleeve pattern."

"That's my thoughtful girl," she said, pleased. "It does go against the grain to be beholden to that woman a minute longer than I can help. Remember your manners, now, and thank her nicely."

Elsie flatly refused to believe me when I told her. But I was right; Ben Herrick did take Miss Minty buggy-riding the next Sunday.

The dimity wasn't finished; I had to wear my winter best to Sunday School and church. It was a hateful, old, short, navy-blue serge with pink baby-ribbon edging its satin yoke and cuffs. Elsie was lovely in pale blue muslin and a leghorn hat smothered in roses, but she asked me to go walking with her that afternoon. The earth was still moist at the grass-roots and the crossings were muddy, but springtime had come.

All that afternoon we walked slowly up and down the long boardwalk that went toward the cemetery. Trees arched over it. The shadows of their branches quivered on the boards, and looking upward I saw a mist of color against the shimmering sky — the shy color of opening buds and of leaves too small to be seen. The day was still with a Sunday stillness; far away on the farms a dog barked, a hen cackled. The rustle of our petticoats was stylishly loud.

We heard buggy-wheels sucking through mud, and looking up we saw Ben and Minty.

He was all dressed up, and she had let her hair curl under the brim of a new straw sailor. They sat stiff and straight. The red spots were on Minty's cheeks, and when Ben tried to say, "Hello, kids!" as usual, his voice was gruff. We stood watching the buggy till it passed the cemetery and turned into the creek road. Then Elsie said, "If she isn't brassy! Of all the nerve! Well, you mark my words, she'll never land him."

She didn't say why not; she merely repeated firmly that Minty never would. "Why, the very idea!"

she said. "Why, Ben works in our store! He just won't marry Minty Bates, that's all, and there's no three ways about it!" Then she went on talking about her Mr. Andrews, the traveling man.

Our shadows slowly lengthened down the board walk until they melted into twilight. The sun had set, and Elsie shivered in her muslin, but still we walked slowly back and forth. Lamps were lighted in the houses, the faint stars grew bright. My mother had no idea where I was, out after dark and without permission, but just once more we walked to the far end of that long way and there we stood, talking, talking.

At last Elsie walked almost home with me, and I walked home with her; we talked a long time at her gate. From time to time I coaxed, "Oh, Elsie, come just a piece with me!" till she came with me past the closed stores and the livery-stable. Then she coaxed until I walked back with her, as far as Miller's store. There at last, reluctantly, we parted, calling back to each other through the dark, "Good-by! See you tonight at church!" "Good-by, good-by, don't forget what I told you!" "I won't! Good-by! Good-by!"

My worried mother pounced upon me with questions and I answered them dreamily, hardly hearing them and quite oblivious of her scolding. Elsie Miller and I were chums. Elsie Miller, so pretty, so smartly quick-tongued and pert, so popular with the boys, and so richly, stylishly dressed, had chosen me for her very best friend. I could hardly believe such rapture.

All through April and May we were inseparable. We promised that all our lives we would always tell each other everything. I was to be her bridesmaid and she was to be mine, and our first daughters were to be named for each other. Through all the storms and tribulations of life, our friendship would never for one instant falter.

And all this happiness, the happiness of my whole life, my mother tried to take away from me. Elsie had warned me that she would, and she did.

I paid no attention to her first mild resistance, her protests and advice; I was hardly aware of them. My father grumbled and I did not hear him. They had to be polite to Elsie when I brought her home, and I contrived to stay all night with her almost as often as she stayed all night with me. I became quite skillful at trapping my mother into giving me permissions that she didn't want to, and her increasing grimness I ignored, until one June evening when she acted with appalling suddenness.

"Where are you going?" said she.

"Just out," I replied with something of Elsie's airiness. "Out for just a —"

"No you're not."

"Only a minute, mama. I'll do the dishes when I —"

"Not one step." She stood between me and the screen door, the door that led to the soft, wild dusk

under the stars. She was no taller than I had grown
to be, but she seemed to tower.

"But mama !   Only just a minute, I won't stay long,
honest, I—"

"I won't have you running around any more with
that Elsie Miller."

"Why, whatever makes you think I was—" But
my mother's face suggested that that lie might be a
fatal error. I abandoned it. "But mama, why—
why, she's *Elsie Miller !*"

"I know they have money and all that, but money
isn't everything, and—"

"As if it was *money !*" That was disgusting.
"Why, Elsie—Elsie's— Why, if the Millers were
just the lowest dirt, there isn't a girl in the whole
world that wouldn't just *die* to be chums with Elsie!
Why, she's the most—the smartest, the—" But it
was hopeless. Nothing I could say would budge my
mulish mother. She didn't have the mind, the soul,
to appreciate Elsie.

"Just this one more last time, mama," I begged desperately. "Only for five minutes, honest. I got to
go, mama! I got to! It's important."

"No, you don't," she said. And instantly, "What
for ?   What's this, so important ?"

For an instant I felt that her piercing eyes could see
the envelope hidden inside my corset cover, and all
that it meant. The guilty truth, which I would have
died rather than reveal, was that I had met Elsie's
traveling man. And they trusted me. I was getting
his letters to Elsie, under my name at the post office.

If her father found out, he'd ruin her whole life. And I knew very well that if my part in this secret romance were discovered, my life would be ruined.

Blindly, in my terror, I attacked. "Oh, aren't you ever going to let me do anything! Are you always going to drag me down and make me miserable? My goodness, mama, I'm not a child! I'm *sixteen!* I'm almost going on seventeen, and just when I'm beginning to have a little pleasure in my life —" I was crying, wailing, "Oh, why do you always have to spoil everything? Why can't you let me *alone!* Aren't you ever going to stop making me utterly miserable?"

"Ernestine, I only want what's best for you." She was softening! I wept more wildly. Her arm clasped my heaving shoulders, and I couldn't help convulsively stiffening; that sharp-cornered letter was only a few inches from her hand. Her arm fell limply away, and she sighed. Hope leaped in me.

"Then you'll let me! Oh mama, just this once!"

"No," she said implacably. "No, Ernestine. I won't have you running the streets after dark any more, not for Elsie Miller or anybody else."

"But mama, I promised Elsie. She's waiting. I promised, and I've got to keep —"

"I don't care if you did. This is going to stop right now. You can tell her tomorrow I wouldn't let you."

Something in me broke; I felt myself go all to pieces. "Oh no, *you* don't care!" I sobbed at her ferociously. "You don't care what she thinks of me, you don't care if she gets mad, you don't care what

becomes of me! Your own way's all *you* want!
You don't care if it kills me! Nobody cares how
miserable I am. Oh, I wish I was dead, I wish I'd
die!"

"Stop that!" she said with such force that sobs
strangled in my chest. After a moment she added,
"That's better. Now go sit on the porch and be
quiet."

I hated her. Weakly, trembling, I sank on the
porch steps and clutched my knees in my arms. I
felt sick all over, as if I'd been beaten with a stick.
"I hate her, I hate her!" I whispered. Nothing happened. Doubtless God heard me, but He didn't do
anything. Experimentally I repeated, "I hate her,"
and still no lightning struck.

Anyway, I didn't have to do the dishes. Faint
clatters from the kitchen gave me a morose satisfaction. I thought of all the work I did, yet I was never
thanked, never rewarded, never allowed to do the least
little thing I wanted to do.

A sickle moon was descending beyond the maple
trees. It shed a faint light on the street and on the
picket fences. The roses smelled sweet, but the
bushes were vague blobs in the dusk; only the snow-
ball bush showed ghostly blossoms. Steps went farther away on the gravelled walk, mysterious, and a
little whistled tune wandered in the night. The sky
was a crowd of stars.

> *The night has a thousand eyes,*
> *And the day but one,*

Yet the light of the bright world dies
With the dying sun.

Chin in hands I repeated it slowly, luxuriously, with long-drawn sadness. "The mind has a thousand eyes, and the heart but one —" The maple's leaves sighed, a scent of white clover passed. Low voices murmured somewhere. "Yet the light of a whole — life — dies, when Love — is — done —"

Those voices were at Mrs. Bates' gate! I sprang up. Yes! Ben Herrick had seen Miss Minty home from somewhere. They were close together, only the gate between them. Miss Minty laughed, shyly, breathless. Ben said something too low to be heard. Silence. The gate's latch shivered. Ben was leaning across it; he was holding Miss Minty's hand.

All this time he had been going with her, and now maybe he was proposing. She was all in white; that was her new dress with the graduated flounces. Wearing white, at her age! But maybe she had actually landed him.

The silence lengthened. At last she must have made some sign; whispered, or nodded. My straining eyes saw Ben's dark arm make a quick, clasping movement and I quivered. But Miss Minty escaped the arm and — "Minty!" he said. "Darling!"

"Goodnight!" Her voice made it the loveliest word. Then she fled into the house.

"Mama! Mama!" Blinking in the kitchen's lamplight, I poured out the news. "And mama, listen! Listen to him!"

His song rollicked away, masculine, exultant.

When you hear them bells, go tinga-linga-ling!
All join round, and sweetly we will sing,
There'll be a hot-time! in the old town!
Tonight! My ba-by —

"I'm certainly glad for her," my mother said
fervently. "She's good as gold, Minty is, she deserves
to get married if ever a woman did. I wonder if her
mother — Don't laugh, Ernestine; there's nothing
funny about a poor old maid."

"I wasn't," I protested. "I'm not laughing at her.
I'm just — laughing." I didn't know why.

"You better go to bed," my mother said.

But I could not sleep. The curtains whispered,
and beyond them the night sang with mysterious tiny
voices. Elsie said it was wonderful to be kissed.
Also she said, with a toss of her pointed chin and an
inimitable flirt of her skirts, "Pooh, what's a little
kiss?" Impishly, under her breath, when only I
could hear, she'd sing a naughty song:

> *K, that's the way to begin,*
> *I, that's the next letter in,*
> *S, that's an intermission,*
> *S, that's the fillin' in.*

I turned the hot pillow and turned it again, trying
to cool my cheeks. And half upraised on an elbow,
I was frozen by a terrible scream. "Help! Help!

Mrs. Bla-a-ke!" It was Minty Bates, screaming in the night. "Come, quick, quick! Mother's taken bad — Oh, come quick!"

Doors slammed while frantically I got into petticoats and dress, left my shoes unbuttoned. My father was lighting the lantern, he would go for the doctor. I sped across the alley and into Mrs. Bates' kitchen. Lamplight shone into the sitting-room from the bedroom. My mother was working over Mrs. Bates. "I don't believe it's a stroke, Minty, have you any more camphor?" she said.

Mrs. Bates' face was crumpled on the pillow, without teeth. Her white hair straggled thinly, her veined, limp hands and closed lids were piteous. Minty went down on her knees by the bed, frantically rubbing one of those hands. "Mother! Mother! It's Minty, mother. Can't you hear me? Mother! Oh, God forgive me if I've killed her!"

She was still wearing the flounced white dress. The whalebones in the tight net collar held it prim under the lobes of her ears and her pompadour was smoothly wavy. It was strange to see her face so frantic. Mrs. Bates' eyelids quivered. Minty went on pleading with her to speak. My mother stood holding her other wrist and looking oddly grim.

"Minty —" Mrs. Bates whispered.

"Yes, yes, mother! Yes! Minty's here."

The lamp's purr was as loud as that whisper. "Don't — leave — me — Minty."

"No, mother, no. I'll never —"

"Don't say anything you'll wish you hadn't," my

mother said.   Her calm voice was like a shock of cold water.

Minty stared up at her.   My mother's face had its smooth, sick-room look that didn't answer any questions.   She laid Mrs. Bates' hand down and said capably, "I wouldn't wonder 'f she'll come out of it now, her pulse is good.   No harm to have the doctor, now he's sent for, but I doubt if you had to go to that expense."

Indeed, at that moment Mrs. Bates seemed to come to.   She had opened her eyes before the doctor came. He said it was not a stroke.   "Nothing to worry about at all, Miss Minty," he said.   "Digestion's a little upset, maybe; won't do her any harm to stay in bed a day or two if she feels like it.   Your mother's not as young as she was; but then, none of us are." He lifted Mrs. Bates' limp hand.   "Come, come, Mrs. Bates!   You'll live to dance on all our graves!"

Next day everybody knew that Miss Minty and Ben Herrick were engaged.   Downtown, Ben was setting up the cigars.   All the girls came to see Mrs. Bates.   Her bedroom was so crowded that Elsie and I could hardly squeeze into it.

Mrs. Bates looked sweet as a doll, sitting up against the lace-edged, snowy pillows; her teeth were in and her eyes bright again, her cheeks softly blushed. Minty fixed her up prettily, in a fresh nightgown and cap, every morning before she went to work; she couldn't afford to give up fifty cents a day, and there was always someone to stay with her mother.   We filled the bedroom with roses, and all the ladies brought jellies, and chicken, and nourishing broths and custards to tempt her appetite. She ate daintily from her tray set with rosebud china. And nobody dared ask, even now, why the two other men had jilted Minty.

"Anyway, she landed Ben," I told Elsie.

"Oh, I don't know," she replied.

"Ben Herrick wouldn't jilt anybody!" I was indignant.

"Well, they must have had reason to," said Elsie. "And I don't think she's so smart. She hasn't got him married to her yet, but she's just as sure of him as if she had. You can tell it by the way she looks."

It was astonishing to see the change in Miss Minty. She was truly pretty. Her cheeks were rosy and her eyes bright; she had dimples that I'd never seen before. She even walked differently; she wasn't awkward now. Ben had given her a diamond engagement ring, and a set of rhinestone combs that sparkled beautifully in her black hair. He gave her a comb-and-brush set in a hand-painted velvet box. He took her to the ice-cream socials, and to prayer-meetings and to church, and every Sunday afternoon they went buggy-riding.

Ben bought the little square house across the street from Mrs. Bates' rented one; he was building a room on it for Mrs. Bates and repairing the roof. Minty chose wall-paper and furniture from the catalogues and made curtains to fit the windows. She papered the walls herself, without one mistake; every strip matched. Ben put on new window-screens, and two coats of the whitest paint that money could buy; Minty piled and burned the trash in the garden and cut the dead wood out of the rosebushes. In September they were to be married.

"They put me in mind of a pair of birds at nesting time," my mother said.

"Me, too," said Mrs. Rogers. She sighed, "My land, it's a pity it don't last. Those ribbons'll last till about the second washing; she'll never sew them on a second time." A September wedding meant winter nightgowns, but Minty was making hers of white outing flannel trimmed with pink ribbons.

My mother stood up for Minty. "Yes she will; she won't spare pains to fix herself up pretty for him, long as she lives."

She could sympathize with Minty Bates; she'd sympathize with anybody but me. I simply had to have a foulard waist, made up with black lace appliqué simulating a bolero; I begged for it with tears in my eyes, but all she said was, "Your nice clean piqué waists are all you need. And I won't have you aping Elsie Miller."

There was no reason whatever for this cruelty to me; it was pure meanness. Again and again I swore to Elsie that my mother didn't suspect anything. I was still getting Mr. Andrews' letters from the post office for her, but I wasn't allowed to stay all night with her any more.

"But why, mama, why? Can you give me just *one* reason?" I demanded passionately. "I know you don't like Elsie! But why don't you?"

"I don't; that's why!" my mother replied shortly. She'd add, "And I won't have you running around with her, like it or lump it!"

Once, after my father and mother were asleep, when the house, the whole town, slept, I crept noiselessly out into the night and ran, breathless, all the way up the street alone. Everything was still and strange. I was afraid, afraid someone might see me, afraid I'd meet a man, a tramp perhaps, and afraid of the night, of the stealthy strange shadows in the moonlight, but my own daring intoxicated me. The hour must have been eleven, at least. In the shadow of Miller's store I met Elsie, and we stole green apples from the tree in Mrs. Sherwood's back yard.

Then we walked far out the boardwalk and sat on its edge, eating those apples and talking earnestly about life. I felt dissolved in the moonlight. The great trees were alive, mysterious and beautiful. The tree-toads' chanting went up from their branches in an eternal rhythm, the song of the trees, of the moon, of the night. There was a hidden meaning, some secret just beyond my knowing; the night knew it, and the moon, and the trees.

"And when I get married," Elsie said dreamily, "every single piece of furniture in my bedroom's going to be birds'-eye-view maple." She knew so much more about everything than I did. I had never even heard of birds'-eye-view maple.

It was her idea that her Mr. Andrews should bring, the next time he came to town, another traveling man for me. She had, of course, always taken me with her when they met. Now she thought that two couples would be just as proper and kind of more complete than just the three of us.

I was too restless to listen to her; under that midnight moon I wildly wanted something I'd never known, and looking down the white road that went past the cemetery and on to far-away and unimagined places, I said, "Elsie, let's start down that road and walk and walk and keep on walking and never come back."

"You must be crazy," she said. "And who knows, he might be your fate. And we'd have a double wedding!"

"You said you're going to elope," I told her crossly.

In August I got from the post office, for Elsie, the letter that set the time and place for that fateful meeting; next Sunday night, after church, on the boardwalk. In snatched, excited conferences, Elsie and I evolved our plan. I was to tell my mother that I'd stay all night with Blanche; she'd let me do that. Elsie would tell her mother she was staying all night with me. Then we could stay out as late as we liked, and next day we'd tell our mothers that we'd got mad and come home.

Never before had my mother's eye seemed so like the awful eye of God. Every time she glanced at me I quailed; I almost believed she could see the thoughts in my head. From hour to hour, all through Saturday and Sunday, I postponed speaking to her about spending Sunday night with Blanche. Desperately I tried to behave in every way as usual, but I was not quite sure how I usually behaved.

At our cold Sunday supper, my father made some flimsy excuse for not going to church again that day, and my mother accepted it without objection; I didn't know what that meant. Whether she suspected me or not, I couldn't tell. I dreaded our walk to church together. All the way to church I tried to talk brightly; she was almost silent. As we entered the church door, her hand closed on my arm and she said firmly, "You're coming up front with me."

Everything shook before my eyes. But when I dared glance at her face, it was placid. Perhaps she'd meant only that I couldn't sit with the other girls, fluttering and whispering in the middle rows of seats and getting notes from the boys in the back row.

There was the standing up, the sitting down, the hymn, the prayer. The sermon began. Outside the open windows the moonlight waited. Out there, the night was quivering to the tree-toads' drums.

I shut my eyes, trying to be calm. I opened them and forced myself to look at the hats before me. Most of them were faded a little; only Minty Bates' pink cotton roses were fresh. Ben was not with her, and I thought he was waiting outside with the other men who listened to the sermon through the open windows. It was very hot in the church; all the slowly waving fans moved the torrid air without cooling it.

The sermon ended. There was only the benediction now, and my mouth went dry, there was a flut-

tering in my wrists. I must speak now. In the slow
crowd moving down the aisle I couldn't. From the
other aisle Elsie's lively face smiled at me, and I cleared
my throat. My mother was close behind me; I must
speak to her. The crowd's decorously jostling pressure slowly propelled us to the church steps. There
was an eddy in the mass; girls were pairing off with
the waiting boys. I croaked desperately, "Oh mama,
Blanche wants me to spend the night with her."

She wasn't listening. "Mama," I said. "Can I—"

Loudly and cheerfully, my mother spoke the only
downright lie I had ever heard her utter. "Oh,
there you are, Minty Bates!" she said. "We've been
waiting for you."

She tucked an arm into Minty's, the other into
mine. I was walking down the slope, toward home,
with my mother and Minty Bates. My mother continued, "It was a real good sermon, I thought. I
don't know's I ever heard a clearer interpretation—"

When I tried to speak, her hand warned me to be
silent. As in a bad dream, I continued walking beside her and she continued talking. I couldn't think.
Jagged fragments of thought clattered in my mind;
Elsie, Mr. Andrews, the unknown traveling man, were
waiting; I must do something, but a nightmare im-
potence was on me, while my mother quoted Bible
texts and we walked sedately in the straggling procession across the railroad tracks. Where was Ben?

Tommy Webb popped out of the depot's shadow
and stood in our way, staring eagerly at Miss Minty.
"I got a note for you!" He was shrill with excite-

ment. "It's from Ben, he left on Number Five. Jew know he's leaving? Jew know 'f he's coming back?" He was like a little dog jumping up at something out of reach.

"Well, of course we know all about it," my mother said coolly. "You go tend to your own business for a change, Tommy."

Then I knew what had happened, again, to Minty Bates.

In silence we went on past the Square, the blacksmith shop, on down the slope toward home. Our footsteps were loud on the board sidewalk and then on the gravel, though I was walking softly. There didn't seem to be any sound anywhere but that loud sound of our steps. At our gate we stopped. My mother said, hesitating, "Want me to go on home with you, Minty?"

Miss Minty shook her head. The shadow of her hatbrim masked her face. She just stood there, not moving or speaking, till my mother said, "Come in and sit with me awhile, if you'd rather."

Going up the porch steps Miss Minty stepped on the hem of her skirt and stumbled. My mother was holding her up. The moon dimly lighted our parlor. Somehow Miss Minty stumbled to the sofa. My mother pulled down our hanging lamp on its brass chains, and lighted it.

Miss Minty's face was gray. She opened the note in her hand, read it with one glance, and suddenly she was a heap sliding off the sofa.

"Ernestine, get some water!" my mother said. I

didn't want to stay there, but I couldn't go. Miss
Minty hadn't fainted. She squirmed there on the
floor, beating at the sofa with her hands and striking
her head against its wooden arm. My mother gripped
her under the arms and tried to lift her, then pushed
her against the sofa's soft middle. "Minty Bates!
Stop that! You hear me?" she said.

Miss Minty made sounds more horrible than the dog
made after the train ran over it. They ran into something like a laugh. My mother leaned over and
slapped her, hard, twice. "Stop it!"

"Oh, not Ben!" Miss Minty gasped. "He couldn't,
not Ben! How could he? Oh, why, why, why did
he?"

"Don't you know?" my mother asked her.

"No! No! No!" Miss Minty screamed. She
squirmed around, grabbing my mother's skirts and crying out, "No!" It was like a torture. "No, no, not
you! Not you, too! Don't say that—not you! I
didn't let him even kiss me, I never let him kiss me. I
swear it, I swear it before God. I never even let
him— Oh, I wish I had! I wish I had!" Her hat
hung by its pins, all its pink cotton roses lolling
grotesque. "Not even one kiss. I'd rather be a bad
woman; I would! I would! Oh, I don't know
what I'm saying." She began to cry. "Oh, but I
can't understand why—Oh Ben! Ben! Why did
he—and I was so sure he'd never—"

"Ernestine! Water!" My mother added, "Get it
from the pump."

She would think of that. She knew very well that

the pump must be primed. I stumbled against chairs, ran into the table's corner in the dark kitchen, hastily grabbed the jangling pail and dipper. Outdoors the moonlight was calm and cool; anything might happen, and that vast calmness would not care.

Miss Minty was lying on the sofa. My mother took the glass from my dripping fingers and held it to her lips. Minty swallowed a little, obediently. My mother's mouth was set and her eyes had that look of a horse's with its ears laid back. She wiped the wet glass with her handkerchief, put it carefully on the center-table and said briefly, "You stay here." She went out.

I did not know what to do; I could not think of anything to say to Miss Minty. The thing that had happened was like a death; there was nothing to say about it. But the silence couldn't be borne. I cleared my throat. "Miss Minty —"

"Oh please, please let me be."

I went out on the porch, shutting the screen door without a sound. Ben's newly painted house shone white in the moonlight. Minty would have to see it every day. Tears gushed suddenly from my eyes. And somewhere in that moonlight Mr. Andrews and his friend were waiting; somewhere Elsie was waiting, abandoned, and blaming me. In the whole universe, everything was all wrong, nothing was right anywhere, and burying my face in my arms folded against the porchpost I wept luxuriously, with all my heart. After some time I felt that I was crying because I was so lonely; I wanted my mother.

I could hear her voice, speaking low and rapidly. She didn't care what happened to me, I said to myself; she could go to Mrs. Bates' house while I was dying of misery. But there was no conviction in this muttering within me; I knew it wasn't true, and I had crossed our yard before I realized that the dew was wetting the hem of my long skirts. My mother's voice came strong and clear. "You wicked, wicked woman!"

I sped toward it. The lamp burned in Mrs. Bates' sitting room. Panting, I gazed through the screen door. Mrs. Bates leaned forward in her chair, her pointed chin thrust out and her eyes glittering. My mother stood against the wall as if she had backed there, and she looked as she had looked when she killed the snake.

"You lie!" Mrs. Bates said. "He wasn't here."

"I saw him," my mother told her. "I knew you'd sent for him."

"You — you think you're so smart!" Mrs. Bates, who couldn't get out of her chair, had got out of it. "Well, then, I did! I did! It's done, ain't it?"

My mother was terrible. "Be ashamed of yourself! Be ashamed! Your own girl's whole life!"

"Her life! *Her* life! And what about my life? What about me?" Mrs. Bates' shriveled old fist struck her chest. "Six girls I had! Six to your one. And where are they now? All but died in childbed for every one of 'em, and worked my fingers to the bone to do for 'em, and where are they now? Colics and measles and mumps, never one good night's sleep

I had for twenty years, nor an easy mind by day, and then when they're old enough to be some good to you, then tempers and foolishness and worrying you sick day and night, what trouble they'll get into with some no-account fellow, not heeding a word you say but sassing you to your face and sneaking behind your back. And if you manage somehow to keep 'em decent through their fool age, then it's off they go with their husbands and what's it to them, you left in the end of your days with nothing, nothing to show for it all? What about my life? Where's my life gone? I got a right to something myself!"

My mother was shaking all over, but she wasn't afraid. "Don't talk sinful blasphemy to me, you shameless wicked creature! God Himself's made us women and—"

Mrs. Bates wasn't stopped. "Oh, you fool! I saw it coming! I saw what I was coming to! One of 'em, thinks I, one of 'em I'll keep! Minty's the best of the lot, and she's not leaving me, I'll make short shrift of her beaux. Things they wouldn't believe from anybody else they'd swallow down when her mother told 'em. Then thinks I, jilted twice, there's an end. No man'll come around for her now, a girl's been jilted twice. First time in thirty years, I can settle down to comfort. And what's it to you? What're you meddling for? Coming here, trapping me—"

I was slamming through the door, somehow I was between them, screaming, "Don't you touch my mama, don't you talk to mama like that—don't you dare! You leave my mama alone!"

"Come, Ernestine," my mother said quietly, holding me, urging me out of the room. Her arm was firm around me till we got across the yard and were in the alley. "Ernestine, be quiet. Get hold of yourself."

I sobbed on the scratchy lace yoke of her Sunday dress. "Oh mama, mama, it's all lies! Why didn't you tell her it isn't so!"

She fished a handkerchief out of her petticoat pocket. "Here, wipe your face and stop crying. Stop it, I say. You mustn't let yourself go like this."

"I won't, mama. I'm stopping. Oh mama, say it isn't so!"

"You just forget all about it," she told me comfortingly. "There's not many like her. It's safe to say there's not another woman living, so meanly selfish she'd hurt her own girl!" Her voice deepened with abhorrence.

"That's not what I mean!" I cried. "It isn't *so!* It's all lies, just nothing but lies! It's not so, mama, is it! Having—having children isn't like that?" I had not meant the words to turn into a question.

She did not answer. The question hung there between us. I knew she didn't want to answer it. And she said steadily, "That's one of the things you'll understand when you're older, Ernestine."

"I won't go away," I said. "I won't ever go away and leave you all alone when you're old. I don't want to get married, mama; I won't ever marry anybody, honest."

"Nonsense! of course you'll get married," she replied. "I wouldn't want you not to."

We went slowly into our own yard; the gate swung
shut behind us, and we paused.   I didn't want her to
begin thinking about Minty, yet.   I wanted to do
something for her, something important.   It came into
my mind that I might promise to give up Elsie.

"Mama," I said, low.   "Mama, I – I'm sorry I –
talk back to you, ever."

For the first time in my life, I saw my mother at a
loss.   She didn't know what to do, how to deal with
this.   Hurriedly, embarrassed, she muttered, "That's
all right; that's my good girl."

A strange thing happened then; I saw my mother.
I saw her as a person, separate; not as my mother at
all.   There was the feeling that she was just a
woman; and that she had been a girl herself, once,
and had married and had me to bring up, and that she
wasn't quite sure about everything yet, and could be
puzzled and confused and afraid of making mistakes.

She was just a woman, standing there in her last
summer's Sunday lawn, faded a little now but with
every ruffle carefully ironed; she was holding those
ruffles above the dewy grass.   I saw the wavy hair
that she curled with such care, putting on a dressing
sacque over her corset-cover and petticoats, heating
the iron in the lampchimney and testing it with a mois-
tened finger and gazing so anxiously into the glass;
she was a settled married woman but still she wanted
to look nice, and I could have cried over that wavy
hair.   She did look nice; she looked kind and brave
and sensible.   She was really beautiful.

"Ernestine," she said, "I've got to go and tell Minty.

She's got to be told. Maybe we can get Ben back and fix things up without a scandal. Now you listen to me: you mustn't ever tell this. Never. Not to anybody. I want your solemn promise."

"I promise," I said solemnly. "Only I don't know just what — what it was that Mrs. Bates did."

"She told a terrible lie. She told him Minty wasn't a good girl. And then let her go to church expecting he'd bring her home!" It hurt her to think of it.

"Oh," I said. I could not understand why Ben didn't know that Minty was a good girl. I knew that, and I didn't know Minty as well as he did. And she had not let him kiss her; that should have kept his respect. But I knew well enough that this was one of those subjects that one must not ask questions about. "Well, then, mama, while you tell her," I said delicately, "I'll go in the side door."

VI

TRAVELING MAN

I could not have said how I knew that traveling men were bold, bad, and wickedly dangerous. No one had told me so, and though I had seen traveling men I had never spoken to one. There were girls who did, but they were not girls that nice girls knew.

There was a glamour about those city men who came and went without being known. They stayed over night at the Howell House, paying a dollar a day; of course they were not spending their own money, still such extravagance was awesome. We saw them sometimes through the hotel windows, sitting in the shabby chairs among the brass spittoons; we saw legs sprawled with abandon over chair arms, thumbs in the armholes of resplendent vests, derby hats pushed back on heads and fat, gold-banded cigars cocked in the corners of mouths. We hurried past modestly, eyelids lowered.

Fat Mrs. Howells and her fatter, slatternly sister must have known the traveling men, circumspectly. Not a word was ever said against Mrs. Howells and Queenie. But we hardly ever saw them because they did all the work in the hotel and never went anywhere. Jay Willard knew all the traveling men, and dressed almost like them. The storekeepers knew them, of course, in a business way, and my father hauled their heavy sample-cases in his dray and knew their names. But only Jay Willard joined the scandalous card-games they played till all hours, and for money.

Traveling men had been everywhere, they had seen everything. They wore boiled shirts and stiff collars every day; their shoes glittered with polish, and rings glittered on their fingers, and glittering watch-chains looped across their fancy vests. Little wrinkles of knowingness were at the corners of their eyes and their mouths smiled flexibly. They came from cities; they went back to the wicked cities. You couldn't trust traveling men.

When Elsie Miller had confided to me that she knew a traveling man, I had recoiled. When she had whispered in my ear that she loved him, the very air seemed to shake. In that first shock, a doubt almost formed in my mind: Could even Elsie Miller actually land a traveling man?

If anyone could do it, Elsie could. No other girl could even begin to compare to Elsie. It was not only that she was pretty and dressed so stylishly; she had an air. She was never shy or awkward, never at a loss; with the boys she always had something to say, she always knew what to do.

"She's just plain boy-crazy," my mother said. "I wonder she hasn't been talked about before this."

"She isn't either boy-crazy," I defended Elsie too impetuously. "Oh, I'm sorry, mama; honest I didn't mean to contradict. But mama, how can she help it if all the boys are crazy about her?"

It was Elsie's question. "Can I help it if they're all crazy about me?" she asked airily. She had a charmingly pert way of speaking, tilting her chin, switching her skirts. "They can just *be* crazy, for all of me! Twenty three skidoo for them!"

When I saw her glance at a boy I felt excited, embarrassed, and bitter. I couldn't glance at a boy like that. Elsie was capturing boy after boy, and I hadn't yet got even one steady beau.

We were sixteen now, going on seventeen. Already Lois Estes was engaged, and several other girls were keeping steady company. My mother was eager to welcome any beau I could get, and I felt her disappointment in me. I longed to ask how she had got papa, but I couldn't. We both pretended that I wasn't interested in boys.

"I must say I'm thankful Ernestine hasn't got boys on the brain, like some I could mention," my mother told Mrs. Rogers.

Mrs. Rogers agreed. "My land, yes. I don't know what Mrs. Miller's thinking of."

"Oh well," my mother said. "Maybe boys will be silly about a girl like that, but when it comes to marrying they pick out a good, sensible, worthy girl. Elsie Miller's rushing her age now, and you mark my words: One of these day's she'll find herself on the shelf." Her tone was grimly expectant.

Books confirmed her opinion. None of the Five

Little Peppers had been like Elsie, and they all got married. Jo March — who was most like me — had been an old maid, but she consoled herself by praying and thinking, "Be worthy love, and love will come," and in the end she got an old German professor. He wasn't much, but anyway, she did get married.

The trouble was that I didn't want to be a sensible, worthy girl. I wanted to be like Elsie.

"You know, Buster," she said to me one day, "I don't think you know how to manage boys."

Such frankness was a thunderclap. I hesitated, then like Elsie I cast away decency. "How do you manage them?" I asked humbly.

Airily she replied, "Oh, I don't know. It's just a gift, I guess. Some girls have it, and some just don't. It isn't anything you could learn."

My breath halted. I was cold. For the first time it was real to me that I could be an old maid. Of course I had always known that there were old maids, but such a fate had been, like death, a thing that couldn't happen to me. I managed a hardy laugh. "Well, I don't care. I don't want to get married. Why, I wouldn't marry the best man on —"

"When I get married," Elsie continued dreamily, "I'm going to live in the city and have my own carriage and wear silks and diamonds, and I'm just going to be on the go every single minute. I'm going to be the most popular young matron in society." She added generously, "I'll ask you to come visit me sometimes and you'll see how I dress up to go to parties."

She was always so generous that I felt compelled to be grateful. I was ashamed of the bitterness in my gratitude.

"Oh, it's so wonderful, Buster," she went on, rapt. "So wonderful, to be in love at last. The whole world's like a dream. Oh, I'm so happy — I just can't *tell* you. Buster, I'd die for him, I'd just *die*."

She had met her traveling man in the drug-store. His name was Mr. Andrews. ("Call me Andy," he said. But of course Elsie wouldn't do that; not yet.) She had been buying a nickel's worth of sulphur to take for her complexion, and he was just standing there at the counter. It seemed Providential, now. "Honestly, Buster," she asked solemnly, "don't it seem to you as if it was *meant?*" She wasn't thinking about him at all; she wasn't expecting anything, or anything like that. She just kind of happened to glance at him. And he was looking at her! So of course she looked right away from him. But he kept looking and looking at her, and she didn't pay any attention at all. But she must have just kind of glanced that way, or something, and he said, "Hello, Snookums!"

Just like that. "Hello, Snookums!" he said. Wasn't that *strange?* "Honestly, Buster, don't you think that's the *strangest* thing?" Because of course Elsie had been Snookums ever since we began reading the Sunday funny papers. But he didn't know that. And yet he said, "Hello, Snookums!"

"And Buster, I had the queerest feeling. Right that very minute, I knew he was my Fate. Because you know what I believe? I believe that when a girl meets the one man in the whole world that's meant for her, she *knows*. Because I knew. I had the funniest feeling. I knew right then he was my Fate. You know I always believed in love at first sight, but I didn't know if it would happen to me because I always thought probably when I met my Fate, why I'd be engaged to some other man, and — But Oh Buster, to think! To think, only two more days and I'll see him again!" Her thin hand clutched my arm. "Buster, you've *got* to manage it somehow, you've just *got* to!"

Mr. Andrews' regular route would bring him back to town on Number Five, Wednesday night, and somehow Elsie must meet him. I had to go with her, because of course she couldn't meet him alone. Somehow we must elude her parents, and mine, and somehow we must meet him secretly yet the meeting must appear accidental.

"He's got to think I'm surprised when I see him," Elsie explained, "Or he might get the notion that — well, that I'm kind of — well, easy." She tossed her head, saying with spirit, "He needn't think it's going to be any easy job, getting *me!*"

"But Snookums, if he's got any sense at all, how can he help guessing —"

"Oh, don't be a boob!" she snapped.

"Well," I said, "the first thing's to get mama to let me stay all night with you. And you've just got to come with me, to ask her."

In Elsie's presence my mother couldn't say what

she thought about her. For two days I was a model daughter, eagerly helpful at home. I swept and dusted without being told, I didn't leave a single pot to soak when I did the dishes, and I kept the wood-box full. After school on Wednesday Elsie and I took my softened mother by surprise and before she could think of one plausible objection, I had snatched nightgown and toothbrush and we were safely out of the house.

Elsie squeezed my arm jubilantly. "Well, that's done! Oh, I just knew everything's going to be all right! I've got a feeling."

The splendor in which the Millers lived was already less intimidating to me. Elsie and I went past the iron deer and the round beds of cannas and followed the path around the bay-window to the side porch. A chain-bucket pump stood there, and the boards were damp with splashed water.

All the rear part of the house was untidy. Sewing and toys and garments were scattered everywhere, the worn furniture was dusty, and Elsie's little sisters and brothers made a great noise. In the big, unswept kitchen Mrs. Miller was dishing up supper.

"You might get home from school in time to help, once in awhile!" she said to Elsie. "How you expect me to do everything, with this big house and five young ones on my hands!"

"I did the dishes last week!" Elsie retorted. "And you can just make the kids do it tonight! I'm not going to, and there's no three ways about it!"

I would never have dared talk to my mother like

that. Mrs. Miller went on quarreling but did nothing drastic, and I was astounded. In silence I took my turn at the washbasin and the draggled roller towel.

The supper table was loaded with food. My mother set such a table only when company came for Thanksgiving. Elsie didn't even try to eat everything her father put on her plate. Mr. Miller, after he had mumbled grace, did not say another word. We ate in subdued uneasiness. Even Elsie felt a proper awe of her father. At last he pushed back his plate, emptied his coffee cup in one long draught, wiped his mustaches, and rose. He walked out, going back to the store.

A clamor broke out at once, and Elsie sprang up. "Come along, Buster!" Her sisters raised an outcry about the dishes, and she turned on them. "I've got company. I'm not going to do any old dishes, and that's flat and you kids can just lump it!"

Mrs. Miller began, "Elsie, I won't have you speaking to your—"

Elsie slammed the door. We raced the length of the long hall, turned and dashed up the stairs and into Elsie's room. She locked its door, stuffed the keyhole, pulled down the windowshades and lighted the lamp.

"Now," she said generously, "you can watch me dress up."

There were lace curtains at the windows. The wallpaper was covered with large pink roses, the carpet was red and green. Bureau and washstand were only old-fashioned things, but the big bedstead was gleaming brass. Clothes were flung on the floor, hung on doorknobs; tangles hung from the open bureau drawers, the closet bulged with garments hanging on hooks and fallen from them; every chair was full. I perched on the unmade bed and watched Elsie.

She had always sworn to me that she didn't rough her hair. "It's just naturally thick," she'd said. But now I saw her roughing it industriously, strand by strand, with swift comb. She took a rat from under the mattress where it had been hidden, and pinned that on, too. "Mama'd just kill me," she muttered through hairpins. "But I'm not going to look like an old stick-in-the-mud!"

Her pompadour stood up beautifully. Expertly she coiled the ends and thrust large shell hairpins into the knot. She tucked in rhinestone side-combs and clamped a wide tortoise-shell barette. "There!" she said, satisfied. "Now Buster — Pull. Pull *hard*."

I tugged at her corset strings till I couldn't tighten them another breath. Her corset cover was starched and ruffled, but she pinned on several handkerchiefs besides. Then she tied the strings of a changeable taffeta petticoat and got into her best dress, a pale blue silk stylishly flounced and trimmed with yards of black velvet baby-ribbon.

When she had smoothed back the skirt so I could hook the placket, and tugged her belt down in front, I said she was simply perfect. That only showed my ignorance. Elsie inspected her reflection critically, then suddenly she pounced upon a pillow, stripped it, and stuffed the pillow-case into the front of her waist. That was the final touch. With that full, bulging blouse, she looked exactly like a fashion-plate.

"Oh Snookums!" I cried, hardly able to bear my envy. "He'll be wild! You're beautiful, just simply beautiful!"

"Well, but there's no credit to me," she replied, turning and primping before the mirror. "Oh, maybe being stylish is. But being — well, anyway pretty, and popular, and smart, that's only because God made me that way. If He'd made me like you, why then I guess I'd have to be like you, or — well, anyway, God can do anything. But I'm honestly not one bit vain, because I don't think men like a girl that's vain, do you?"

I supposed not. "Elsie Miller, what are you putting on your *face?*"

It was a clear liquid from a small bottle. "Epsom salts and water," she told me. "It takes the shine off. And Buster, when I'm married you know what I'm going to do? I'm going to powder. I am, I don't *care!* I'm going to do it, and if people talk about me after I'm married, why, they just can!" She blew out the lamp. "Now see if you see the kids anywhere."

The stairway was empty, the hall below was dark. Elsie's silks loudly rustled, but we got downstairs before anything happened. Mrs. Miller called, "Elsie? That you?"

The shock stopped me an instant, then I dashed after Elsie. The opening dining-room door let a shaft of lamplight into the hall; Mrs. Miller called sharply, "Elsie! You can't go downtown —"

We escaped. We raced past the iron deer and through the gate. My heart was pounding. "She can't do anything," Elsie said blithely. "What can she do?"

It was true. Elsie was too big to whip. What could her mother do? Stunned, I saw that my mother couldn't actually do anything, either. We were free, and abroad in the wide, wild night.

The stars were out, but trees cast shadows on the long board walk. We strolled to its end and back, out again and back, almost to the cemetery and almost to the Square.

"He wears a mustache," Elsie murmured. "Buster, I wonder if it's true, what they say?"

I knew what she meant; they said, "A kiss without a mustache is like an egg without salt." I exclaimed, "Elsie! You wouldn't!"

"Oh, I don't know!" she said airily. "People do."

"But then he wouldn't respect you."

"Well my goodness, how green do you think I am? It's all right when you're engaged."

"Well, but you aren't engaged."

"Oh, don't be such a boob!"

It was nerves. We were both quivering; we started and clutched each other every moment, fearful of every shadow, every little noise. Suppose someone recognized us? Suppose my mother learned that Mrs. Miller didn't know where we were? Suppose our fathers found out?

We paused by the dark bank. Lamps burned in Miller's store, in the drug-store and the barber shop and the hotel. Men stood in the shadows. We could hear their voices and see the red ends of cigars. Beyond the Square the starry sky came down to the long black depot and the railroad tracks. A switch light burned red and green.

I shivered. Elsie was risking everything for love, but what was I risking everything for? Still, I could not honorably desert Elsie now. Nor could I bear to lose this chance to watch Elsie, to see how she fascinated Mr. Andrews.

Number Five's whistle wailed beyond the cut. Elsie gripped my arm.

Everywhere the darkness stirred; all along the sidewalk men moved, sauntering through the patches of lamplight toward the depot. A burst of noisy voices came out of the barber shop. Men hurried from livery-stable and drug-store, and the hotel roustabout pushed the baggage cart down the middle of the street.

Trembling, Elsie and I watched this masculine life of the night. A few men passed us, not seeing us in the dark. Hearty and unconstrained, they were not like men seen in the daytime.

Nearer, louder, the wild train-whistle came rushing toward us. The railroad tracks hummed. A glare shone on the twin steel rails, and the train came roaring, its bell clanging. Lighted windows flashed, a long streak of light in the dark. A jolting crash of machinery deafened us, and Number Five was there.

Under a plume of smoke, the long powerful train stood motionless, puffing.

Black shapes of men crowded the depot platform. Above their heads we saw the passengers sitting in red velvet seats, in a brilliant light that gleamed on polished wood. They were aloof, indifferent to us.

We stared at them until the bell clanged again. Lanterns swung signals from engine to caboose. The engine's great wheels began to turn. More and more rapidly they spun, while jolt after jolt ran down the length of the train. Number Five roared away into the night, its whistle screaming.

Elsie and I fled. Safe at the end of the board walk, beyond the last house, we waited until no more homecoming men clicked gates shut behind them. The last window went dark. But the drug-store did not close till nine, and Elsie was almost sure that Mr. Andrews would go to the drug-store to buy cigars.

Stealthily we passed all the still houses. The only light on the Square was in the drug-store. We waited. Every shadow seemed to have eyes.

The drug-store's door opened ; a man came out, and Elsie nudged me. Bravely we advanced. I saw that the man was not very tall, that he wore a pale vest and a derby hat. Elsie's little shriek made me jump.

"My goodness !" she cried softly. "Why my goodness gracious me, it's Mr. *Andrews !* Why, where on earth did *you* come from ? This *is* an unexpected pleasure ! How *are* you ?" I had never heard her speak so elegantly.

"Well, well, well, well !" Mr. Andrews said. He

seemed pleased. He took the cigar from his mouth, lifted his hat with a flourish and set it on his head at a jaunty angle. "Well, well, and how's little bright-eyes?"

"Oh, fine!" she said. "Just fine! Fine and dandy!" She laughed her peal of laughter. It was more silvery than usual, and longer. She slapped at him playfully. "Don't you call me bright-eyes, you fresh thing, you!"

One of the lamps in the drug-store went out. I was paralyzed. Mr. Hutton was closing up; in a moment he would step into the street and see us, out at night, and with a traveling man. Our characters would be ruined.

Mr. Andrews chanted, chuckling, "Just because you made them goo-goo eyes!" Almost he chucked Elsie under the chin. She evaded his touch with dignity and formally said, "Mr. Andrews, meet my friend Miss Blake."

He lifted his hat again and said he was pleased to meet me. I said gruffly, "How do you do?" Our peril unnerved me; desperately I wanted to get away from that spot, but I didn't know how to do it. We all seemed immovable.

Not a word was said; silently Mr. Andrews took us each by an elbow and on either side of him we went walking away. Even in my infinite relief I knew I had learned nothing; I would be just as helpless, next time. Behind us the drug-store's door slammed, the key turned in the lock. But we were so far away that Mr. Hutton couldn't recognize us.

"Mind if I smoke," said Mr. Andrews.

"Oh no, no indeed, not at all!" Elsie replied vivaciously. "I just love the smell of tobacco, it's so manly. I like the smell of a good cigar, I really do, I'm different from most girls that way, but I always say, Don't mind me at all, just go right ahead and smoke as if I wasn't there, because I enjoy the smell of tobacco, I really honestly do. Most girls don't feel that way about it, but I—"

Mr. Andrews gave each of us a whole package of Sen-Sen.

The darkness of the trees was on the board walk. Only dim starlight dappled it. My feet had a solemn sound in my ears. Slowly we walked all the way to the end of the walk, and slowly back again. Elsie and Mr. Andrews were talking all the way. I tried to make sense of what they said, but I couldn't. "Oh, you kiddo!" Mr. Andrews often repeated, and often Elsie retorted airily, "Skidoo for you!" But she hung on his arm and laughed. "Oh, them goo-goo eyes!" Mr. Andrews said, as if greatly pleased with himself.

Nobody had ever held my arm before. I didn't know whether he was doing it quite properly. His hand closed warmly from time to time, as if the pressure meant something. But it couldn't mean anything, so I decided not to notice it.

Now and then he drew my arm snugly closer and looked at me. He had a round, jolly face; the glow from his cigar showed little wrinkles at the corners of his eyes. The mustache was a sandy color. Softly he said to me, "Hello."

It didn't make sense. I couldn't think what to reply. "Hello," I answered every time.

All at once I saw that he and Elsie were holding hands. I didn't know how it had begun. Her arm was in his, her hand lay on his extended palm, their fingers were interlaced. In fascinated embarrassment I pretended not to see those hands. So that was how Elsie did it! But precisely how had she done it? And how did she dare?

Mr. Andrews said good night debonairly. "Well, kiddos, the best of friends must part. I got to get some sleep, got a big day tomorrow."

Elsie was easily elegant. "Well, thank you for a very pleasant evening, Mr. Andrews, and good-by till we meet again." I couldn't say anything like that. I said, "Good night."

When we were alone Elsie squeezed my arm rapturously. "Oh Buster, isn't he wonderful!" she breathed.

"He's all right I guess," I said crossly. "How're we going to get in, and what'll we do if your mother catches us?"

Elsie didn't know. She was light-headed with happiness, and reckless because of so many dangers passed. But I was worried.

Like thieves we stole across the dewy grass, past the iron deer. The house was dark and still. It must have been ten o'clock, or even later. The front door was locked.

Elsie's aplomb did not desert her. Shamelessly, in

the open air, she stripped to her cambric underwear. Her corsets and her best dress wrapped in the silk petticoat she tossed onto the porch roof. More modestly I removed only my shoes; my mother still made me wear a Ferris waist and my dress was only gingham. We climbed the porch-post, crawled through Elsie's window, and listened.

There was a faint stir in the house. Steps came cautiously down the hall, a hand felt for the doorknob. We had barely an instant to leap into bed and draw the covers up to our chins. The door opened, and it seemed that anybody must hear my loud heart.

Elsie stirred and gasped. She whispered, "What's that? Buster! Buster, you awake?"

"Sh!" Mrs. Miller hissed. "What time did you get in?"

"My goodness, mama," Elsie complained. "Waking us up in the middle of the night, scaring us to death!"

"When," Mrs. Miller repeated with emphasis, "did you get in?"

"How do I know?" Elsie asked peevishly. "What would I look at the clock for, and you know you won't make papa let me have a watch. If I only had a watch, I—"

"Sh!" Mrs. Miller hissed more imperatively. "You'll wake your father up." She went out, closing the door stealthily.

Elsie began, "Well, I've certainly got him going, haven't I? He's just crazy about me, I guess you saw

that. My goodness, anybody could see that much!
You did see how crazy he is about me, didn't you,
Buster?"

"Yes," I said.

She settled down cosily. "And he's such a man of
the world, that's what I like about him. I always did
say I was going to marry a nobby dresser. Why, just
the way he wears his hat, you can see he's perfectly
at home in the best society. And Buster, you know
what I think? I think—"

Until sleep overpowered us I listened, while the
knowledge burned into me that I was nothing but
a dub. I could never be anything but a good, worthy
girl. Other girls would get all the men.

I made only one effort to imitate Elsie. That week
Charley Boggs saw me home from Christian Endeavor. Charley had red hair and freckles, and he
was only a country boy working his way through
school. I didn't really want him, but in my dis-
couragement I felt he was the best I could do.

On the way home he didn't say, "Oh, you kiddo!"
He didn't say "Them goo-goo eyes." He didn't say
anything much. I did my best. I said, "The stars are
lovely, aren't they?" I said, "Isn't it a lovely night?"
I said, "I don't think it's going to rain, do you?" Desperately I thrust my arm into his. My heart thumped,
the ground lurched under my feet, but I clutched his
hand.

He started. Both of us stared straight ahead; our
hands remained clasped as though paralyzed. Neither
of us said another word until at last, hurriedly, we

reached my gate. I cried out, "Good night!" Flee-
ing, he muttered, "Good night." He never asked to
see me home again.

My mother worried. "I declare," she said, "I've
half a mind to give you a good dosing of sulphur and
molasses, for all you've had one this spring."

"A good dose of housework's what she needs," my
father said.

"Don't nag at her, Joe," my mother murmured.

"You stop her gadding with that girl of Miller's,"
my father told her darkly. "Or you'll wish you had."

"She's a good girl," my mother replied, hoping to
prick my conscience with her praise. "I can trust
Ernestine never to do anything that'll make talk."

Guilt gnawed at me. A musing look on my
mother's face, an unexpected glance from my father,
alarmed me for hours. But I could not give up the
bitterness of watching Elsie's romance.

Again we escaped and met Mr. Andrews. This
time Elsie had my promise not to walk the whole way
with them. "He's polite to you," she said. "But I
guess you could see he'd like to talk to me by myself.
I guess you saw that, didn't you?"

Yes, I had seen that.

He met us even more jovially than before. I saw
again the round, jolly face, the laughing eyes, the
sandy mustaches stylishly trimmed and waxed. The
cigar clenched in his teeth was so masculine. His
derby was jaunty, the shoulders of his coat were perfectly padded, watch-charms hung from the chain
looped across his checked vest. His ox-blood shoes

had the very latest knobby toes.   He clasped my arm warmly.

But I had promised Elsie, and half-way out the board walk I stopped.   Mr. Andrews' clasp tightened. "What's the matter, kiddo?"

"I don't want to go any farther," I said.   "You and Elsie go on. I'll wait here."

"Well!" Elsie cried.   "Well, of all things!   Why, Buster Blake, I never!   Well, if that's the way you're acting, and after all I've done for you, well if you want to all I've got to say is, You just can!"

In a gentlemanly way Mr. Andrews said he hoped nothing had offended me.

"I just don't want to walk any farther," I said.

"Well, we'll just turn around and go back," he said. In the moonlight Elsie frowned at me ferociously.   I was bungling everything.

Desperately I blurted, "I've got something in my shoe."

There was an instant of embarrassment, but Mr. Andrews was truly a man of the world.   "Why, that's all right," he said gallantly.   "Don't worry about that. I'll turn my back and you go right ahead and take it out; I won't look."

Elsie was equal to the situation.   "Why, Mr. Andrews!" she gasped.   "Why, as if Buster could — Why, the very idea!   You come right away from here!"

I sat on the edge of the sidewalk while their loitering steps and Elsie's voice receded from me in the moonlit night.   Sitting there in my loneliness, I knew that, like Agnes in "David Copperfield," I must smile sadly, serenely, and let Elsie have him. I couldn't stop her. I had never known anyone like him; I knew that I loved him as I could never love again. I hated Elsie.

Nevertheless, I admired her with passionate intensity, and I would not let my mother separate us. If she did, I could never again meet Mr. Andrews. And day after day I knew more surely that I loved him, and that this was true love. Mrs. Browning said so.

> *Unless you can love as the angels may,*
> *With the breadth of Heaven betwixt you,*
> *Unless you can muse in a crowd all day,*
> *On the absent face that fix't you—*

I could do that. I did. And one morning before breakfast my mother filled a tablespoon with molasses, stirred into it a teaspoonful of sulphur and grimly said to me, "Open your mouth." Even this I bore with Agnes' pure, pale smile.

When Elsie asked my advice about a note to Mr. Andrews I gave it to her, sweetly and serenely. She didn't take it. She said that "My dear Mr. Andrews" was too intimate. "He isn't, well, not exactly — mine. Yet," she said. "Dear Mr. Andrews," was too bold. She decided to begin "Dear Friend," and to sign the note with the same restraint, "Your true friend, Miss Elsie Miller." She would not let me read the note, but after she had copied it on pink stationery we went together to mail it.

Next day she suddenly began to cry and would not tell me the reason until I had solemnly promised not to get mad. She had told Mr. Andrews to enclose his reply in an envelop addressed to me.

"Oh Buster, I just had to!" she sobbed. "You know papa'd never let me write to a traveling man. I was scared he'd find out from Postmaster Boles. Oh, papa'd be terrible! He'd just ruin my whole life! Buster, please, *please!* Nobody'll pay any attention to your letters, they know you wouldn't be getting letters from a man. And when I'm married you'll always be my best friend and I'll do anything for you. I'd give you my rhinestone combs now, only mama'd make such a fuss. Oh Buster, *please!*"

I made her promise to let me read his letter when it came.

Every day we confronted Mr. Boles at the post office, and I asked him, "Any mail for me?" One day he handed me a letter.

Elsie and I hurried away from the Square. "Oh Buster, feel how my heart's beating!" she said, pressing my hand against her corset. What I feared was that she'd hear my own heart.

An imposing picture of a hotel, surrounded by scrolls, was printed on the envelop. The penmanship was beautiful, so complex with fine flourishes and inky down-strokes that one could hardly decipher it. "Miss Ernestine B——" That was all I saw. Elsie snatched the letter.

I turned on her in fury. "Elsie Miller, you give me that!"

"I won't!"

"You will!"

"I won't do any such a thing!"

"You promised."

"I don't care! I guess I'm not going to let anybody read my very own love let—"

I slapped her. We parted vowing never to speak to each other again as long as we lived.

We met that evening at the Ladies' Aid ice-cream social. Sweetly Elsie slid her arm into mine and we strolled away from the crowd gathered around the long tables under the lantern-lighted trees.

"Oh Buster," Elsie murmured, "I could hardly wait to see you. Buster, I've made up my mind to something, and I wouldn't do it for everybody, but just for you because you're my very best friend and getting his letters for me and everything, and I know he likes you, too. So Buster—" She paused; a solemn instant. "I'm going to name my oldest girl after you."

"Are you going to let me read that letter?" I asked her.

"Why, Buster!" She gazed at me, softly pretty, her fair hair shining and her brown eyes limpid in the light of the Chinese lanterns. "Why, of course. Why, I said you could! My goodness, you didn't think I meant—" She laughed. "My goodness, Buster, what a big boob you are!" Her hand squeezed my arm fondly.

We walked up and down, on the trodden earth by the empty hitching-posts. In the center of the Square the churchladies, in second-best dresses and aprons, were spooning ice-cream from the dank freezers standing on the grass and carrying the heaped saucers and plates of layer cake to eaters sitting at the long tables, all in their Sunday clothes under the candles flickering in Chinese lanterns. The gay scene made our aloofness romantic. All the girls were envying me because Elsie and I had so much to confide to each other that we disdained even ice-cream, to walk together apart with arms interlaced and heads bent close. Now and then a boy sauntered near, pretending to be not much more aware of us than we were of him, but Elsie dismissed each one by turning away brusquely. "We don't want to be bothered with boys, do we, Buster?"

I answered somewhat weakly, "No."

If my mother had let me go home with Elsie to stay all night, I might have read Mr. Andrews' letter. But that evening my mother clamped down on me with tight-lipped determination. She would not let me go home with Elsie. She never let me stay all night with Elsie again.

I got perhaps half a dozen letters from the post office for Elsie, and gave them to her. But I never was able to read one of them. Elsie's archly smiling references to them were tantalizing. Her generous attempt to get another traveling man for me was hard to bear; Dora had never tried to get a lesser man for Agnes. Yet the effort's failure was a catastrophe.

It was not my fault that I could not meet Elsie that night, and Elsie forgave me for it so kindly that

I wanted to slap her again, but helplessly couldn't. "Though I must say I don't know how Mr. Andrews feels about it," she said. We had only a hurried moment together in Miller's store; my mother had sent me on an errand, warning me to be back in ten minutes, and I knew that her eye was on the clock at home. A letter had come from Mr. Andrews, the first since the dreadful night when I had not met Elsie, and Mr. Andrews and his unknown friend had no doubt waited for hours in vain. I had got the letter from the post office and Elsie had hidden it in the front of her shirtwaist.

"Well, you'll find out what he thinks when you read that letter," I told her. "And you've got to let me read it."

"Waiting there all that time," she went on. "My goodness I don't know what he thought! Men hate to be kept waiting and I don't want you to think I blame you one bit, Buster, I honestly don't, not one bit, because I don't want to hurt your feelings, or anybody's, and how can you help not being smart enough to get away somehow? Because I always say, nobody can help how God makes them and my goodness gracious I guess you would if you could. So I know it's not your fault but honestly Buster just for your own good you ought to try to be smarter. Men don't care what grades you make in school and things like that, they like a girl that's really smart, and you know in some ways you've got brains, you really have, because look what grades you make in school. So maybe if you'd try to be anyway a little bit smarter it wouldn't matter so much how you look, because I bet no matter how I looked, the boys would be just as crazy about me. Oh my goodness!" she exclaimed, touching the crackling piqué over the hidden letter. "My heart's beating so I can't hardly breathe! Oh Buster, if he's mad at me because you kept him waiting! I'll die! I'll just *die!*"

"Yes, but Elsie," I said hastily, "I'll get away to Christian Endeavor right after supper. You meet me on the church steps, and bring that letter."

There was still daylight in the sky when, panting, I reached the church. The door was open but only the town's handy man was there, lighting the lamps. His eye asked me what mischief was afoot now. "No, I ain't seen Elsie Miller nowheres, as I know of," he told me, and muttered, "Christian Endeavorers! Look at them hymn books! Young Christian Endevils is what you are!"

I met Elsie loitering past the drug-store with Blanche, and separated them brusquely. "What did he say?" I demanded of Elsie. "Where's that letter?"

"What letter?" she asked, and answered airily, "Oh, *that!* Why my goodness, Buster, I don't know where that old letter is, I guess it's lying around some place." She laughed merrily. "My goodness, Buster you're awf'ly silly! Why, I've just been fooling you the whole time. I don't care a bit for any old traveling man, and I never did."

"Why, Elsie—! Why, of all the— Why, you told me this very afternoon you'd die—"

"I never said any such a thing and anyway, if I

did, my goodness are you such a boob you believe everything you hear? As if I'd die for any old silly *man!*"

Something terrible had happened; I was sure of it. "Elsie, what was in that letter?"

She laughed again. "Oh, I don't know! I didn't pay much attention, my goodness gracious I get so many— No, wait, Buster." Her arm slid into mine. "Why, you can read that silly old mushy letter if you want to, I don't care, it's nothing in my sweet young life. But listen, Buster, the way I feel about it, I guess maybe I'm peculiar that way, but the truth is it just makes me kind of sick to read such mush. I don't think it's manly, I don't think any real man writes such awful mushy letters, and the way I feel about it, if anybody's as gone on me as all that, why he can just go 'way back and sit down! I guess you think that's awful funny, but that's the way I am, I guess maybe it's because I've been spoiled by so much attention, but honestly Buster if I can find that letter any place why then you can read it if you want to, I don't care any more about him than if he'd never been born. You know, Buster, I have awf'ly high ideals of what my Prince Charming will be like when he comes along, and—"

"You don't mean you're through with Mr. Andrews!" I couldn't believe it.

"Why, my goodness yes! My goodness gracious, I should say so!" she cried with evident sincerity. "Why, I wouldn't cross the street to wipe my feet on a dozen Mr. Andrews! The silly old, mushy thing!"

Her voice grew shrill. "Oh, he'll be trying to see me, all right! But skiddoo for him! I'm just absolutely through with him, there's no three ways about that."

There was no doubt that she meant it. She disdained even Mr. Andrews; she spurned him. In my complex emotions, I didn't know what I felt. This meant that I would never meet Mr. Andrews again, and I loved him, but I had never admired Elsie with such a fervor of envy and if Mr. Andrews had appeared before us then I would have been irresistibly impelled to spurn him, too. Nevertheless I suffered. We had almost reached the lamplit church when Elsie, glancing at me, stopped short and cried, "Buster, what's the matter? Are you sick?" I couldn't say that I was knowing I'd never meet Mr. Andrews again.

Yet I did meet him once more.

One November evening Elsie and I were strolling on the board walk. Imperceptibly our friendship was waning. I listened without hearing what she said, while we stepped carefully over the cracks between the wide boards. The shadows of the leafless branches were melting into twilight. Even the fact that my mother didn't know I was with Elsie had lost its savor.

We were far out on the lonely end of the walk, when we heard a man's steps behind us. We were terrified. Clutching each other, we looked over our shoulders, ready to run. The man was Mr. Andrews.

Elsie gasped. Then tearing her hand from my arm, she snatched up her skirts and without a word fled past him. She didn't stop running. Too amazed to follow her in flight, I stood and gazed at the receding flutter of petticoat ruffles. So did Mr. Andrews. Swiftly the thudding of her feet diminished. She was gone.

"Well, I'll be —!" said Mr. Andrews. He turned to me, and beaming satisfaction spread over his face. "Well, girlie! You're a smart kid!"

With horror I realized that I was alone with him. I couldn't imagine why Elsie had done such a thing as to desert me. I didn't know what to do. Not a word would take shape in my mind.

"I wouldn't 've believed it," Mr. Andrews said. "Well, girlie!" he repeated. "Well, kiddo! Here we are."

His arm was around me. His face came closer, grew larger in the dusk. It had a look of artless pleasure. "Hello, kiddo!" he said softly.

Even in that petrified moment, I tried to explain to myself why he said that. It still didn't make sense. "Hello," I heard myself replying feebly. My eyes fixed themselves for an instant upon the sandy mustache, impeccably clipped and waxed; then they shut. A light blow, with a prickling around it, suddenly struck my mouth. Briefly my lips encountered the hardness of my teeth. Swifter than thought, I knew I was being kissed. Kissed! without making the slightest objection!

The kiss had happened even more quickly than my

convulsive start. Mr. Andrews' arm still clasped my
shoulders and I was struggling. But I felt irretriev-
ably misunderstood; I was struggling, but too late to
prove that I would have struggled sooner, if only I'd
had time to.

"Don't!" I gasped. "You mustn't! I didn't
mean —"

Mr. Andrews' arm released me so suddenly that I
staggered. He whispered fiercely, "*Leave your hair
alone!*" I discovered that my hands had automati-
cally gone to my back hair. Then I perceived that
someone was rapidly coming up the board walk. Mr.
Andrews' hand clasped my elbow, my other hand
gathered up my skirts, and my trembling legs moved
weakly forward in step with his.

"Yes, Miss Blake," he said. "It is unusual weather
for the time of year. Here it is almost Thanksgiving,
and —"

I recognized my father, and my knees melted. My
father came striding terribly toward us. He thundered, "What does this mean?"

"Papa!" I gasped. Mr. Andrews began hurriedly,
"There's no —"

My father roared, "Shut up, you smart-aleck dude!
What do you mean, fooling around with my girl?"

Mr. Andrews said, "But there's no —"

"Shut up!" Mr. Andrews retreated before my
father's rage. "Shut up, or I'll jam your lying teeth
down your throat! I'll have you understand my
daughter's a lady. You let me catch you so much

as speaking to her again, and I'll wipe up the ground with you." His fingers sank into my arm. "Now, young lady, you march."

I stumbled blindly along beside him. My whole arm ached from his grip, but I didn't dare speak.

My mother was filling the water glasses for supper when he propelled me into the dining-room. She faced us, aghast.

"Let her gad the streets, will you?" my father roared.

"Joe! What's happened?"

"I told you what it'd come to! It's a traveling man, that's what. Sneaking off on the sly, making herself a sneer and a by-word! That's what's happened, and you might as well know it." His hands were shaking. He jerked a chair from the table and sat down heavily. "God, if she's got so much as a shred of reputation left —"

My mother tried to speak. She put a hand to her throat. Huskily she said, "Ernestine, is this true?"

"No," I faltered. "That is, yes, kind of. Only —" Her face stopped me. She, too, sat down.

"Only it wasn't like that, mama," I began again desperately. "Honest, mama, I didn't know — I didn't mean to. I was just walking. I just went for a little walk, and —"

"Don't add lies to the rest of it," said my father. He took a letter from his pocket. I saw, upside down, the picture of a hotel and the beautiful penmanship dwarfing the envelop with its fine flourishes and heavy down-strokes. "Postmaster Boles handed me this. Said he thought he ought to let me know what's been going on."

I thought wildly that Elsie must have lied to me; she must have written to Mr. Andrews, and this was his answer. I cried out, "No, no, no! Papa, no!"

He looked at me. Everything blurred; I crushed a fist against my mouth. The uproar, the scandal, the scorn that Elsie and I must bear was falling on me all at once.

My mother said sternly, "Ernestine, we've got to get to the bottom of this. Go on, Joe. Read it. Out loud."

My father cleared his throat. He read, "Dear friend Buster—"

"What?" I cried, strangling.

He repeated,

"Dear friend Buster, Well here I am in Evansville and no answer from you. I guess maybe you thought I was too fresh to write to you the way I did. Can only say I have always been a gentleman in every respect and would for no consideration hurt a sweet little girl's feelings. Can only say no disrespect was intended and I hope none taken. Well little girl I am still thinking of your big blue eyes and will try to make your town on the freight Friday. If so will stroll out the board walk about five o'clock hoping you will do the same and would kindly appreciate you bringing some other friend that will not talk too much ha ha. Well will say no more at this time, so no more till I see your big blue eyes from Yrs. Respectfully, A. B. Andrews (Andy)."

I was sobbing loudly and uncontrollably. My mother guided me to a chair. She said, "You leave this to me, Joe. I'm thankful it's no worse."

"Worse!" My father exploded. "How do we know how bad it is? For all we know, the whole town's talking. How long has this been going on? What does he mean 'some other friend that will not talk too much?' What's this, they want hushed up? Who's *been* talking?"

I began to laugh. I couldn't stop laughing, nor stop crying. My mother slapped me. "You leave this to me, Joe," she repeated imperatively, giving me a glass of water.

She put me to bed and sat on the edge of it while I told her everything. Everything except the kiss; I couldn't tell my mother that I had been kissed. Once she said grimly, "I feel it my duty to take this up with Mrs. Miller." But she seemed willing to do her duty.

When I had finished she was silent awhile, then she patted the quilt on my shoulder and stood up.

"You girls nowadays think you're altogether too smart," she said. "I must say I don't know what the world's coming to. Disobedience, disrespect, lying, sneaking, running the streets at all hours. You might know what it would end in. Meeting strange men! It's only the mercy of God it hasn't got out and ruined your character for good and all. If folks did find out, Ernestine, you know as well as I do, you'd never be able to hold up your head again." She paused. "But I see you know you've done wrong, and repent it.

Let it be a lesson to you." She blew out the lamp. "Now try to get some sleep, and you'll feel better in the morning."

I felt better already. I felt snug and cosy, thinking of Elsie, thinking of her reading that mushy letter. Mr. Andrews had written it to me, and now Elsie would know that I knew he had written it to me. Now I knew why that letter had made her so mad, why it had ended her love for Mr. Andrews. I wondered what he had written. But I didn't want ever to see Mr. Andrews again.

For a moment I made a feeble attempt to regret the kiss; no doubt I would someday be bitterly remorseful because I hadn't saved my first kiss for my future husband. Strangely enough I no longer felt the slightest fear that I would be an old maid. In the dark my eyes felt very big and blue, positively starry.

VII

COUNTRY JAKE

AB WHITTY must have come to town on Saturdays when the farmers came in to do their trading. He must have been one of the ragged, barefoot boys riding on wagons loaded with cooped hens and butter jars, apples and potatoes. On winter days he must have come trudging beside a load of wood; he may have knocked on our own side door. When my mother opened it he would have swiped a mittened hand under his nose, licked chapped lips and said,

"Want any wood today, ma'am? It's good seasoned oak, sawed stove-length and split, and I'll cord it up neat in your woodshed."

"How much?" my mother might ask.

"Well'm, it's big measure. I been figuring it oughta be worth fifty cents."

"No thanks." My mother would shut the door quickly and shivering back to the heater she'd exclaim, "Brrrr, but it's freezing! The very idea, fifty cents for a load of wood!"

We must have seen Ab Whitty in this way, now and then. He was born and brought up on a farm four miles from town. But of course we did not know country boys.

Country folks were respectable enough; they were not like people living south of the tracks, where men drank and wives took in washing. But country folks were gawky and poorly dressed, and there was a certain crude heartiness in their manners. They were not refined. It was not their fault that they had not had our advantages, but we did not associate with country folks. We went to Ladies Aid oyster-suppers in the Opera House and to decorous ice-cream socials in the Square. Country folks went to boisterous corn-huskings and to spelling-bees and box-suppers in their country schoolhouses.

Thirty years have affected memories strangely. Today everyone in our town remembers Ab Whitty from his infancy. Nearly everyone remembers saying at the time that that boy would make his mark in the world. Even Bob Mason fondly recalls going to school with him. I can't at all remember that unanimous admiration for Ab Whitty. Indeed I don't remember seeing him until he came to our school when he was seventeen years old.

It was the first day of school, as important as Easter Sunday. For weeks fathers had been besieged, mothers had been frantically sewing; social standing was at stake. On First Day of School only girls from south of the tracks had to wear made-over dresses and pretend they didn't care. Only the poorest boys wore last year's suits with trouser legs let down, and thrust their hands deep into pockets to hide their wrists.

The last bell had not rung yet, and in the Principal's room all the young ladies were clustered around Leila

Barbrook. Leila had lived in the city till she was eight years old; her father had been a city man and he had left Mrs. Barbrook well off. She owned her own home and had an income of thirty dollars a month. From the day she bought the large white residence by the schoolhouse, everyone had recognized Mrs. Barbrook's superiority. She was a severe, reserved woman who held herself straight as a ramrod, and always buttoned her gloves in privacy.

"Never let me see you buttoning your gloves on the front porch again," she once reproved Leila, while I listened in awe. "A lady never appears in public till she is fully dressed. That's one sure way to tell who's a lady."

When I repeated this to my mother, she flushed hotly. After that, no matter how my father tried to hurry her, he could never get her to step over our threshold until she had buttoned her gloves.

But no other lady could be quite as ladylike as Mrs. Barbrook, and no other girl could equal Leila. Her manners were perfect, her hair-ribbons were always pressed, her dresses always freshly ironed. We discovered that Mrs. Barbrook brushed Leila's hair a hundred strokes every night and bathed her in the washtub every single day.

"Acting like she's better than ordinary folks!" Mrs. Rogers sniffed. "Well, cleanliness is next to godliness, and if there's a godlier day than Sunday, I'd like to see her point out chapter and verse! I guess we'll go right on bathing Saturday nights and washing Mondays, for all of any stuck-up Mrs. Barbrook!"

"Well, anyway. One thing's sure," my mother said hurriedly. "She's ruining that child with her finicky ways. If she don't turn out a spoiled little minx, I miss my guess."

It was incredible that my mother could miss her guess, but she did. Leila was not spoiled. She was superior, of course, but she couldn't help that. Her charming manner begged everyone to overlook that and like her, anyway.

Her complexion seemed transparent; her golden hair was long and heavy; her darker lashes seemed sprinkled with golden dust, and when she lifted them you saw only her sweet look. No other mother could make clothes as stylish as Leila's, no other girl could keep her pompadour so high and smooth, her belt so snug, her placket so neat. Yet even Leila's most intimate friends said nothing about her behind her back that they couldn't have said to her face.

They were fluttering and preening around her on this first day of school, and she was the most ravishing of all, though she wore only a plain thirteen-gored skirt and a foulard waist. The boned lace collar fitted perfectly under her ear-lobes, and when she turned to glance out of the window I saw the incredible neatness of her back hair — a huge twisted doughnut of gold.

"Oh, girls!" she cried. "Look at the hayseed!" All young ladies could laugh musically, but Leila's soft laughter bubbled from her throat as if she didn't think about it.

Elsie Miller and I rushed to the other window. In

the yard the hayseed was getting off a raw-boned mule. He wore new overalls and a .new felt hat. The town boys stood looking at him while he tied the mule to a tree and lifted a sack from its shoulders. Elsie was excitedly telling us who he was; she knew, because her mother couldn't keep her out of Miller's store on Saturdays.

"It's that Whitty boy!" she cried. "From Poverty Flat. He's an orphan, his father'n mother's dead, and his grandfather's an old soldier. He lost a lower limb in the Civil War and they're poorer 'n Job's turkeys. He can't be coming to school here in town, why, he couldn't pay tuition, why they can't hardly rake and scrape the interest on the mortgage — Oo, look!"

The Whitty boy was taking schoolbooks out of the sack. At that, Bob Mason yelled, "Hi, country jake! Who're you?"

Ab Whitty turned around and looked at him. Bob's new shirt and stiff collar and the cap set straight on his combed hair gave him an unnatural look, as if he were innocently good and couldn't help it. But he was the banker's grandson, and no country jake looked at him like that.

"Hello, dude," Ab Whitty said deliberately. "Who're you?"

All the young ladies were exclaiming, "Oh, it's a fight! Oh, somebody stop them! Look, they're going to! Oh, why doesn't somebody stop it!" when the Principal disappointed them; he stopped it. The bell ran two minutes early; the Principal stepped out and clapped his hands. The boys had to form in line to march in, and there wasn't any fight. But Ab Whitty was elbowed back to the end of the line.

It was horribly funny to see him come marching in. He was lean and gangling, his face was bony and his sandy hair was parted with painful neatness. His eyes stared fiercely blue from a blush that darkened with every squeak of one shoe. Leila was the only girl who didn't giggle, and the effort made her pink.

We never quite stopped giggling at Ab Whitty; there was always something embarrassingly funny about him. As if he were not outlandish enough already, he studied straight through his second-hand schoolbooks and looked up every hard word. There was always a muffled outburst when he bent over the big dictionary, doubled up like a grasshopper and scowling earnestly. In class he asked questions until the Principal sternly told him to confine himself strictly to the lessons set him, and then he asked, staring, "Why, sir?"

"Because I say so, and I'm going to have discipline here, young man!" the Principal thundered. Ab Whitty looked funnier than ever, then.

Bob Mason ignored him, so all the other nice boys did, too. He didn't make friends with boys from south of the tracks. At recess he walked by himself, at noon he fed and watered the mule and ate his lunch alone. After school he clattered away on the mule; he had the farm work to do and it would be dark before he got home. On Saturdays he hauled wood to the schoolhouse; he was paying his tuition with wood.

No one guessed that Leila Barbrook had ever spoken to him. I hadn't dreamed that a proper appearance might conceal improprieties until the day our clock stopped. For seventeen years that clock had not missed a tick; my father had wound it regularly every night and regularly every month he had oiled it with the tip of a chicken-feather. No one could account for its stopping now. My father hurriedly ate his way through dinner, eager to get at the insides of that clock and see what ailed it. He was unhooking the pendulum when the school bell rang.

We thought it was the last bell. Frantic, I ran all the way to the schoolhouse at the end of the empty street. I was panting up the stairs before I felt the silent hollowness of the building, and in immeasurable relief I collapsed against the upstairs bannisters. After an instant a voice spoke eerily in the vacant school-room.

"What am I getting out of it? I know everything in the books by heart, what's the good of reciting it to that dub? I had a fool idea an education'd be — well, like reading Shakespere, only more so. But all I'm doing is wasting time."

There was a pause. It chilled me to think of Ab Whitty, lonely and discouraged, talking to himself. Then his voice again, quivering. "Leila! You mean — You don't really mean — ?"

I was electrified. Mrs. Barbrook chaperoned Leila so strictly that Bob Mason had to see them both home from church. I couldn't believe my ears. But my eyes, peeping around the door-post, confirmed them.

Leila was sitting on the bench by the heating stove, gazing down at an apple in her hand. Somehow I knew that Ab Whitty had given her that apple; I knew they had often talked together like this. How it had begun, how she contrived to get back to the schoolhouse at that hour, what she told her mother, I couldn't imagine. Ab Whitty was leaning toward her, waiting. There was a proper distance between them, but the look on his face petrified me.

Leila said softly, "Well, I think schooldays are awfully important, because they are the time in life to — to get educated, so I think we should always improve our opportunities and you will regret it in after years if you leave school —" Her lashes slowly lifted. I had not known that anyone could look as Leila Barbrook was looking at Ab Whitty. She said breathlessly, "Because mama's going to give me a party and I wish you'd come?"

The look out of her eyes was like the ray of light down which angels came scooting, in Bible pictures. Only it was Ab Whitty's face that was sliding down that look, nearer and nearer to Leila's. His big hand hesitated near the long collar-ribbon flung stylishly back across her shoulder.

She drew back with pretty dignity, his hand retreated, and at that instant she saw me. Her face became as red as the apple, but she didn't start or giggle.

"Hello, Ernestine," she said, and lifting the apple she bit it, then held it toward me invitingly. "Have a bite?"

Her self-possession staggered me. All at once I knew that she'd never ask me not to tell what I had seen. And because she wouldn't beg or try to bribe me, I couldn't tell. The tremendous advantage of being a lady had never struck me before. But what monstrous injustice gave her that advantage over me? I cast a wildly helpless glance at her and fled. Ab Whitty passed me, plunging downstairs. But I had not the courage to face Leila alone. Shaken, I waited in the hall until someone else came.

Fortunately I could talk about the party. Leila announced it at once, and for weeks the whole town was talking about it. It was to be a formal party and no one quite knew how people behaved at formal parties. I was not worried, being too young to be invited, but I did wish that I might be invisible and see that party. No one else knew how Leila had asked Ab Whitty to come to it.

A few of Leila's intimate friends helped her write the invitations, and they said that Leila said she thought she should invite Ab Whitty; it wouldn't be polite to ask everyone else in the class and leave him out. But Mrs. Barbrook said firmly that it would be a mistaken kindness to ask him. "He's nothing but a country boy," she said. "No doubt he is clean and honest and as good as anybody, but one must draw the line, Leila."

Nevertheless, the men in the post office saw Ab Whitty get the big white envelop. He tried to take it carelessly and he did not open it there, but he didn't deceive any of them. And that Saturday he traded

Jim Miller a calf as part-payment on a hand-me-down suit.

Then one afternoon I came home from school to find my mother all of a flutter. Mrs. Barbrook had called, and she was asking Elsie Miller and me to serve the refreshments. The party was to be so formal that Leila and her mother wouldn't hand around the plates.

On the fateful night Elsie came by for me. Bathed, and all dressed up, with clean handkerchiefs in our pockets and new ribbons on our braids, we scurried up the dusky street. The April day had been sweet with rain, the air smelled of spring and our overshoes splashed in puddles. Every house was alive with lamplight and shadows on bedroom window shades; mothers were emptying bath-water in back yards, while young ladies were curling their hair and young men were getting into Sunday suits.

Mrs. Barbrook's house was cleaned in every corner. In the kitchen Mrs. Barbrook was opening cans of cove oysters and brushing nervously at a few sluggish early flies. Elsie and I were awed by rows of little pie-crust cups, by three kinds of layer-cake, and by a crock full of chopped oranges, bananas, and cocoanut. Even Elsie Miller had never heard of ambrosia.

"It's what the Greek gods lived on," I told her. I didn't confess that I hadn't known it was made of oranges, bananas, and cocoanut. Then Leila came rustling in, so beautiful that I forgot everything else. She hugged me playfully, and rapt in her perfumed silkiness I felt a vibration like the telegraph wires

faintly humming on still, hot Sunday afternoons.
Suddenly I remembered that Ab Whitty was coming.
The gate clicked and lantern-light flickered. Leila
felt the back of her belt, Mrs. Barbrook whisked off
her apron, and both put on company manners. The
party had begun.

More and more guests crowded the porch, un-
buckling overshoes and blowing out lanterns. In the
bedroom the young ladies took off their coats and
fascinators and shook out their flounces, then vivaciously they went into the parlor, all in their best
winter dresses, with elastic gold bracelets on their
wrists and gold watches pinned to their bosoms. The
young men jostled around the hat-rack in the hall,
hating to go into the parlor, and they were suddenly
still when Leila said, "Oh, how do you do, Mr.
Whitty!"

She was lifting his hand in a stylish handshake. I
hardly recognized him. The padding of the new suit
made his shoulders appear enormous, a massive watch-
chain hung across his vest, a coral stick-pin was in
his tie. But above the painful collar was Ab Whitty's
country face and plastered sandy hair.

"Mama, you know Mr. Whitty," Leila said breathlessly. "Let me take your hat."

His hands clamped on its brim while he bowed
blindly toward tight-lipped Mrs. Barbrook. Leila
gently tugged at it. Then all at once the young men
surged into the parlor. When the confusion was
over, Ab Whitty had got a chair in the corner behind

the piano. His shoes were planted side by side and his hands looked dogged on his knees. But everyone was constrained, all the faces set in polite smiles.

It was an elegant scene. Pictures in heavy gilt frames almost covered the parlor's white-and-gold wall paper. Blue silk drapes were looped on big gilt rods above the lace curtains, and the lace curtains were looped back on either side of fringed, scalloped window-shades. There were hand-painted roses on the lamp shade and bigger red roses all over the pale Brussels carpet. Crowded on the sofa and demure in chairs set close together against the walls were the young ladies in brown and blue and wine-colored dresses, with satin yokes and collars, satin reveres covered with silk lace, velvet and satin ribbons, and gold chains, bracelets, rings, and the loveliest hair-ornaments. All the young ladies were looking their dressiest. But Leila was beautiful.

She was more than beautiful, that night. She was somehow translucent, softly glowing as if a light were shining through her lovely face. Nothing she said or did was unusual; she merely sat conversing politely with those beside her on the sofa. But all the eyes kept going back to her even while other young ladies, at Mrs. Barbrook's request, were playing the piano.

At last the party was almost over. Mrs. Barbrook went to the kitchen and stirred flour into milk for the oyster patties. The scent of coffee boiling in the borrowed Ladies Aid coffee-pot spread through the house, and everyone relaxed a little. When Leila suggested just one game of Spin the Platter, the eager voices were almost natural. I ran to get the platter.

Leila's lashes hid her eyes when she stopped over it, but her face was a sparkle of daring. Daintily she caught back her flounces, the tip of a shoe peeped out, she hung poised from the curve of her slender waist. Bob Mason was on the edge of his chair, ready to spring.

Leila blushed softly, her smile quivered. Thumb and finger set the platter spinning and she called, "Ab Whitty!"

Bob Mason was on his feet when the shock stopped him. All around the walls there was a gasp. Some quality of Leila's low call seemed to echo. The platter was spinning. Then with a mighty upheaval Ab Whitty came headlong. His big hand grabbed the platter, his coat slid toward his neck, and on his doubled rear crackled a sheet of sticky fly-paper.

He must have been sitting innocently on it, all that time.

Bob's yell started the uproar. Young men rocked and young ladies shrilled hysterically while Ab Whitty whirled about and the fly-paper flapped. He whirled again, ferociously; the young men fell against each other and tears ran down the young ladies' cheeks. Then he clapped a hand to his rear, and Elsie and I collapsed on the floor.

Leila was frantically saying something that couldn't be heard. Ab Whitty tore at the paper and bits stuck to his fingers. Bob Mason was yelling and pointing. We all saw Ab Whitty's watch-chain dangling, and the bent safety-pin on its end. The chain was a sham; he didn't have a watch.

The next instant Mrs. Barbrook stood terrible amid wild whoops and gasps. The front door slammed behind Ab Whitty while Leila ran toward it, crying, "No! No!"

"Leila," Mrs. Barbrook said. Her tone would have recalled anyone to his senses.

"Yes, mama." Leila was gasping, but her back stiffened and her mouth set in a smile. Bob Mason choked and young ladies were strangling behind their handkerchiefs. Leila looked down at the platter.

"I'll have to spin it again, won't I?" she said in a tinkling way, smiling. Suddenly she lifted clenched fists and shook them. "Oh!" she said deeply. "I hate you! You mean, mean, horrid — I hate you all!"

An earthquake would have been no greater shock.

"We will serve the refreshments now," Mrs. Barbrook said evenly. "If you will excuse Leila a moment to pour the coffee — ?"

Everyone was hushed as at a funeral. Elsie and I tiptoed about, giving each guest a fork and spoon and napkin. In the kitchen Leila and her mother didn't exchange a word. Mrs. Barbrook had a grim, "I could have told you so," air. Leila poured the coffee. Mrs. Barbrook swiftly put on each plate an oyster patty, a pickle, a dish of ambrosia and a slice of each kind of cake. Elsie and I carried the full plates and cups into the parlor, where Leila again sat conversing politely. Her face was like tallow.

Mrs. Barbrook had been superb; she had made it possible for everyone to pretend that nothing had happened. When refreshments were over, the guests put on their wraps and filed out past Leila and her mother, each young lady saying vivaciously, and each young man mumbling, "Thank you for a very pleasant evening."

"I'm glad you enjoyed it," Leila repeated, properly smiling. "I'm glad you enjoyed it, so glad you could come."

The town didn't begin to laugh until the livery-stable and barber shop opened next morning. The livery-stable roared when Ab Whitty passed it, and the whole street laughed when Jay Willard yelled, "Where's your hat, and what's your hurry?" Ab Whitty took his books from the schoolhouse that day, and Mrs. Barbrook mailed him his hat.

Only the men were heartless enough to laugh. The women said with pleasure what a pity it was, to think of Leila Barbrook, of all girls, making such an exhibition of herself. And Mrs. Barbrook such a finicky housekeeper, too; the last woman you'd think would forget and leave sticky fly-paper in a parlor chair when company was coming.

"Well, pride goes before a fall," Mrs. Rogers said complacently. "I know I have my faults, but I will say, I never was uppity."

Mrs. Barbrook and Leila held up their heads, however. Ab Whitty was gone, and after awhile there was no more to say about that party. In a few years it was almost forgotten.

Leila was eighteen years old ; then she was nineteen ; then she was twenty, and all her friends were married. It didn't seem possible that Leila Barbrook could be an old maid, but there it was. Mrs. Barbrook said everywhere that she'd always urged Leila to take her time. "Marry in haste, repent at leisure," she said firmly.

"I wouldn't worry if I was you, Mrs. Barbrook," Mrs. Rogers said right out before everybody at Ladies' Aid, "I guess there's no danger Leila'll marry in haste." Mrs. Barbrook couldn't say a word.

Everyone had expected Leila to get Bob Mason. He was still paying her attention, and Mrs. Barbrook chaperoned them less and less. Bob was a handsome, lounging fellow, and though it was whispered that he sometimes drank, he was the best catch in town. He was cashier in his grandfather's bank, getting forty dollars a month at a job he couldn't lose. Old man Mason was worth fifty thousand dollars if a cent, and there were only seven grandchildren, so Bob had good expectations. From the way he looked at Leila, you'd have thought she could land him. Still, she hadn't, and she was getting no younger.

It would have been slander to accuse Leila of flirting. But her manner with young men always reminded me of someone who, laughing a little, was fending off a thrown ball with the palm of her hand.

We had all forgotten Ab Whitty. No doubt he came to town on Saturdays, but the men brought home no news of him. Most of their talk was about hard times. Straight-front corsets had come in, and full blouses, and circular skirts that couldn't be pieced out of old gores and flounces, but every man in town had become tight-fisted.

"I knew this was coming," my father said darkly. "Years ago I told you the Trusts 'd ruin this country, if Bryan wasn't elected."

"Well, I won't have Ernestine's figure ruined," said my mother. "Maybe mine don't matter, but she's got to have a straight-front, if it does cost a dollar."

My usually indulgent father exploded. "Gol darn it! You women-folks talk as if dollars grew on blackberry bushes! Corsets!" he said bitterly. "You better be thankful you got a roof over your head. Be thankful we're not tramping the roads, like folks did in '93. Not yet we're not," he added darkly. His anger rose again. "You get it into your head once and for all, we're going to be dum lucky to get enough to eat. New-fangled fol-de-rols are for rich women — rich women and their poodle dogs! I tell you the Trusts've ruined this country with their devilish Gold Standard. The common man'll never see good times again."

I was a little frightened, but after he had gone my mother said his stomach must be upset. "Men will get into tantrums over their politics, but election's more than a year off. I'll steep him up some wormwood."

My father hadn't told us the news. When I went to get the mail that afternoon, I saw the loafers watching a young man in overalls on a ladder set against the front of the G.A.R. hall. He was whistling cheerfully and painting the weathered gray boards a dazzling white. I didn't recognize him; of course I passed swiftly without looking, holding my skirts with care to conceal my ankles. But when I saw Elsie in Miller's store I went in to find out what was happening.

Ab Whitty was moving to town. Old man Mason had foreclosed the mortgage, and the Whittys had less than $200 from selling tools and stock. Instead of putting his grandfather in an old Soldiers' Home and hunting a job, Ab Whitty was starting a Boston Racket Store in the vacant room under the G.A.R. hall. He was setting up in opposition to Miller's big store, where everybody had traded for years.

Jim Miller wasn't worried, and all the men laughed when Jay Willard said, "It won't be sticky fly-paper this time, it'll be a tin can."

By Friday afternoon, downtown hardly seemed the same place. The new store stuck out like a sore thumb. Against that violent whiteness, Ab Whitty had painted the window-frames dark blue and the sashes Turkey red. The panes glittered with cleanness. Behind them Ab Whitty set up the mail-order catalogue, open at its cheapest plow and propped against a plow priced fifty cents cheaper.

Out of the G.A.R. window he hung an enormous tomato plant. Its branches were spread out fanwise and their tips almost touched the sidewalk. Every man in town counted the little yellow tomatoes on it. There were almost three hundred; no two men could agree on the exact number.

On Saturday Ab Whitty handed out free sticks of fine-grained pine for whittling, and the store was crowded. He did some trade in jack-knives and groceries, but nobody bought the plow. All the talk was about hard times, and the town was laughing at what Ab Whitty said.

"Are these hard times?" he asked, surprised. "I don't notice any difference from what I'm used to."

"That explains why the poor dub don't know any better than to set up in business, these days," my father said. "What he was thinking of beat me."

That Sunday night Ab Whitty saw Leila Barbrook home from church. There hadn't been such a sensation since Jay Willard bet he could kiss Miss Sarah.

Ab Whitty still had his gawky country air. His peg-top trousers and knobby-toed yellow shoes were as up-to-date as Bob Mason's, but the padding bulged on his shoulders and his neck was rigid in a starched collar. He looked ready to fight anybody when he walked down the church steps with Leila's hand tucked into his arm and her silk muslin ruffles swishing at his ankles. Her cheeks were as pink as the roses on her hat. Mrs. Barbrook's black silk skirts hissed angrily.

No one but Mrs. Barbrook heard what Ab Whitty and Leila said to each other. It couldn't have been anything but polite conversation. But my mother and I hadn't got the washing out next morning when Mrs. Rogers, leaving her own tubs, ran in to tell us that there'd been a ruction between Leila and her mother. Mrs. Rogers had been borrowing a cupful of blueing from Mrs. Miniver, who lived next door to Mrs. Barbrook.

"Mrs. Miniver says of course she wouldn't listen — though I don't put it past her, a born gossip if ever there was one, and my land I don't know how she looks folks in the face, the things she says behind their back, but butter wouldn't melt in her mouth — and she told me not to tell, so don't tell I told you. But Mrs. Barbrook was laying down the law to Leila, and mad enough to bite nails. Mrs. Miniver couldn't make out just what she said, but she kept it up an hour or more, and Leila only spoke up once or twice. And more than that —"

Mrs. Rogers lowered her voice. "In the middle of the night, Leila was crying as if her heart would break. She'd crept out of the house and she was huddled up on the back steps, in her bare feet and only a shawl over her nightgown, crying low to herself. The most pitiful thing she ever heard in her life, Mrs. Miniver says, it was all she could do to listen to it. Now what do you make of that?"

"I never heard of such a thing," my mother said.

"If you ask me, Mrs. Barbrook's lost patience," said Mrs. Rogers. "I wouldn't wonder if she said 'old maid' right out to Leila."

"But my goodness, the poor thing's doing the best she can!"

"If Ab Whitty's the best she can do to get Bob to the point, she might as well give up," Mrs. Rogers replied. "It looks like she can't get anybody worth being jealous of. And what kind of an idea is that, to give a man?"

"That's true enough," my mother agreed.

I couldn't bear to pity Leila, who had been so lovely and so perfect. Indeed I didn't dare pity her, for if Leila Barbrook had come down to being pitied, what might I come to? It was embarrassing to encounter her on the sidewalk that evening. She was scurrying along in the dusk and didn't see me until we almost collided.

"Oh!" she gasped. "I'm — I was — I'm coming to your house, Ernestine. To return this." She held out a stiff paper roll, one of my Battenberg lace patterns.

"Well, I'm on my way home," I said.

She had passed our house, and Mrs. Rogers', and Mrs. Cleaver's. We stood there not knowing quite what to do. Her nun's-veiling dress was almost the color of the twilight; only her pale face and golden hair were clear under a little tilted hat. She seemed tired, worn, almost desperate.

"I have a headache," she said. "I thought a little walk in the fresh air —"

In my confusion I could only cling to politeness. It was polite to believe her, so I did. I said I hoped her headache was better now, and still we stood there.

"Ernestine," she pleaded. "Would you keep a secret for me? Even from your mother? I know it seems wrong, but I wouldn't ask you to do anything really wrong. You know that, don't you?"

"Yes," I said.

"Then please, please just go on home and don't tell anybody you've seen me. I'll be there right away — only five minutes —"

Her hand tightened on my arm. A man was coming down the walk. In the dusk I couldn't see who he was. Beyond the fence spread the livery stable's pasture; I smelled the clover, and the roses by the vacant house across the street. Then I saw that the man was Ab Whitty.

When Leila said, "Good evening," I remembered the evening she had spun the platter. Her voice had that same tone in it.

He glanced at me uncertainly and said, "Hello, Ernestine." I said, "Hello." The situation was beyond my social powers; I stayed where I was because I couldn't think of the proper etiquette for getting away. Probably he decided I was there for propriety's sake. He turned to Leila and said gently that he had got both her notes, and couldn't quite figure them out.

"I didn't mean the first one," she said, and then, quickly, while he seemed to leap at this, "That is, I didn't want to write it the way I did. I had to, mama made me. But it's true. I can't go buggy-riding with you. Or let you see me home from church again, or anything."

"You mean you can't?" he asked. "Or don't you want to?"

Leila hesitated. Than she said bravely, "I can't."

I was appalled. This was not only brazen; it was fatal. No man would want to go with a girl if he was sure she wanted to go with him; he couldn't respect her. "You do want to, then? You do!" Ab Whitty almost whooped. Somehow he was holding both her hands in his, he was gazing passionately down at the top of her hat. Leila slightly retreated, but her hands stayed willingly in his. Dazed, I stooped and picked up my Battenberg pattern.

"Oh, please—No, no, you mustn't think—" Leila was protesting. "That other note was only because I—I only wanted to see you just once, to explain, so you wouldn't try to see me home from church again. Where people are looking. Because I'd have to say no. I'd have to."

He was repeating, "Leila!" He said it two or three times, then he seemed to pull himself together. "What's the matter? Your mother?"

"I can't disobey her, Abner," she said. "As long as I'm living in her house and she's supporting me, I have to do what she says. It wouldn't be right not to."

"No," he said, letting go of her hands. "No. I know it wouldn't." The air seemed to grow heavy and still. I thought of just quietly going away, without saying anything. Then Leila moved a little closer to him and touched his sleeve.

"You won't be mad at me, will you?" she said. "Because I can't help it."

"Look, Leila!" he said strongly. "I'll work like the devil. It won't take me so long. Would a rented house do, just to start with?"

This couldn't, surely, be a proposal. But if it wasn't a proposal, what was it?

"I don't care what kind of a house," Leila murmured.

"Oh, darling!"

The bonds that held me suddenly broke. I uttered some strangled yip, and fled. The thuds of my shoes on the boards were loud in my ears till I trod on my petticoat and heard an ominous rip. Leila's smothered appeal followed me, "Ernestine! Wait!"

It was some little time before her light feet started toward me. In the darkness I pinned up the ripped gathers at my petticoat's waistband. My head was a whirl. When Leila reached me I asked her, quivering, "Leila, are you engaged?"

She answered as if she were singing with joy. "I couldn't be engaged without mama's consent."

I was unable to ask her any more. No nice girl should be kissed before she was engaged at least, yet in spite of my suspicion I felt that Leila was a nice girl. My faith in my mother's teachings was profoundly disturbed.

Perhaps this helped to make my own affairs engrossing that summer. If Leila and Ab Whitty met again, I didn't know it. They could hardly have exchanged notes; not a small boy in town could be trusted not to tell. In church I saw him gazing at her, and sometimes I was sure her lashes hid a glance at him. But Bob Mason saw her home, and bought her ice-cream at the Ladies Aid socials.

Ab Whitty was doing better than anyone had expected. He was getting Jim Miller's country trade. The traveling men called on him, and his empty shelves filled with goods. He opened a bank account. This did not increase his popularity. The little store was always full of old soldiers smoking their pipes, so he did not get the ladies' trade. Jim Miller was down on him, and Jay Willard called him a tightwad. He didn't spend a cent. He and his grandfather lived in the rooms behind the store and spaded up the back yard for a garden. When he wasn't behind the counter, or scrubbing floors and washing windows, he was hoeing.

Neither my mother nor I had been able to get new summer dresses, and I was still without a straightfront. One morning in a storm of tears I declared that I wouldn't wear that old wasp-waisted thing one more day, and my tight-lipped mother was mixing my father's favorite oatmeal pudding for dinner when he came home at ten o'clock.

She looked up at him, and I saw that instantly she had forgotten even my existence. "Joe!" she cried, and then, swiftly, "Whatever it is, it's not as bad as that. We're all right, Joe, we've got our health."

I couldn't speak. I stood looking at my father, and I was cold all over.

"Well," he said heavily, "it's all we've got."

There was no money in the bank. Our savings were gone. Everybody's savings were gone.

"Never mind," my mother said. "We've got the house, and the garden. We'll manage, somehow. The hens laid four eggs this morning, and I'm making you an oatmeal pudding for dinner."

My father raved. "I told you the Trusts 'd ruin us! They set out to do it in Cleveland's time, and now they've done it. Bryan would 've saved us if —"

"Oh, stop talking politics!" my mother cried. "A pest on politics! The question is, What're we going to do?"

"Do? There's nothing we can do. Morgan himself couldn't stop this. The Trusts 've got all the money, and they're got all the property in this country. The Trusts can't keep going, themselves. How can they sell anything, when they've got all the money to buy it? Any dum fool can see there's no way out now. It'll come to revolution, that's what it'll come to. What's to become of decent folks, between the Trusts and the Socialists?"

"Not — Socialists?" My mother went paler. Socialists would destroy the home, separate husbands from wives and take children from parents.

The first shock was followed by report after report from the depot, where the telegraph operator got news from the wires before the afternoon local brought yesterday's papers. Every day it grew more clear that my father's worst fears were justified. Not only our town, our county, our state, but America was collapsing. Nothing like this had ever occurred before.

Money had vanished. The banks were not closed, but they were helpless. Trade had stopped; wages couldn't be paid; farmers couldn't sell anything. Times had been hard in '93, but nothing like this; this was the end.

Respectable women were getting food on credit. My mother, who had never charged a cent in her life, laid in a supply of flour and sugar and did not pay for it. "Whatever money we've got, we'll hang onto," she said grimly; she had sixty-three cents in her purse. "But just the same, we're not going to starve. Anyway, not for awhile."

As in a tornado, hidden things were being revealed. Mrs. Barbrook's home was mortgaged to old man Mason; the interest fell due and she could not pay it. A diamond ring, collect on approval, was at the depot for Bob Mason; he couldn't get it out. Leila denied that she was engaged to him. In the excitement, we did not get all the details of a furious scene between Bob and Leila and her mother. My father came home one evening and told us that Ab Whitty was done for.

"Jim Miller can hold out awhile longer; the wholesalers 're letting him ride. He talks some of getting out scrip, other folks are doing it everywhere. But Ab Whitty's got to pay a four-hundred-dollar bill for goods, next Saturday, or they'll sell him out. He had the money saved and in the bank, but that's no good to him now."

"How can they sell him out, if nobody's got the money to buy?" my mother asked.

"Jim Miller's fixed it up. He'll take over Whitty's stock and stand good for it, and the bank's standing behind him. But Ab Whitty can't get any backing out of Bob Mason."

My wail startled him. "Oh, papa! Can't he get the money somehow?"

"Four hundred dollars? There's not that much money in the whole country."

That evening Ab Whitty walked up Mrs. Barbrook's steps and tried to see Leila. Mrs. Barbrook met him at the door and shut it in his face. Mrs. Miniver said he acted like a man distracted. He went back to his store, wrote and mailed a letter to Leila, and left town. He went in his overalls, riding the blind on Number Five.

"Bumming his way out of here to God knows where," my father said. "So that's the end of him. Too bad; he was an enterprising young fellow. But the time's past when a poor man could get somewhere in this country. Ab Whitty was licked before he started, if he'd only known it."

The Boston Racket Store's white front was like a tombstone. Inside, a few old soldiers sat with Ab Whitty's poor old peg-legged grandfather. What would become of him? What would become of us all?

The stores were open but nobody bought anything; the first flurry of buying on credit was over. There was no laughter even in the barber shop. The town was like a stopped clock. The freight went through without stopping; the afternoon passenger local carried only two coaches, empty except for a man or two traveling on passes, or on scrip.

Friday evening my father said the man had come, to sell Ab Whitty out. My mother said he'd been cowardly to run away; he should have stayed and faced the music. "What good would that 've done him?" my father replied.

My mother sighed, "His poor old grandfather — I wonder how he'll get along?"

"Oh, he'll be all right," said my father. "He's got his pension."

Saturday morning the farmers' wagons came in as usual. They still brought a little produce to trade at the stores, though they had to take most of it home again. Still they came to town on Saturdays because farmers had always done that.

About nine o'clock riders began to come in. We were not doing big Saturday bakings now, so I sat on the porch crocheting, and so many riders went by that I wondered how they would find room at the hitching posts. But I was not disturbed until my mother came out on the porch.

She said she wondered if the man ever lived who knew enough to come to his meals on time. "It's twelve o'clock now, and dinner's been ready to dish up for five — What's that?"

It sounded like some excitement uptown. We listened, and looked at each other, and listened again. The street sloped down to the plank bridge and then climbed past the pasture to the livery-stable and the blacksmith shop facing it on top of the hill. We could see the roof of the drug-store beyond the black-smith shop, but we couldn't see the business blocks or the Square.

The sound uptown grew more distinct — the sound of many men's voices, excited. My mother worried, "I wish he'd come home."

Screen doors slammed here and there. More and more women came out of their houses to listen at their gates. The peaceful day became ominous; even the sunshine seemed to grow pale.

"Ernestine, you go in the house and stay there," my mother said.

The kitchen was smoky from potatoes scorching on the stove. I snatched them off, and without pausing to set the pot in cold water I went out the back door. The sound was louder now, and yells rose above it, like the yells of boys at a dog-fight.

Some women were at Mrs. Rogers' gate. My mother was among them. Mrs. Ben Herrick, Minty-Bates-that-had-been, was there, and Mrs. Estes, and Mrs. Miniver. Bare-headed and in her mother hub-bard, Mrs. Miniver was waving a big sheet of paper.

I heard her say, "My country cousin —" and "— all along the roads —" My mother cried out a word that sounded like, "Derbies!" All their voices rose, but I had to turn back to get through our gate.

When I reached them, my mother was taking off her apron and rolling down her sleeves, saying with asperity, "My good land, I'd like to see some man, just once, that had some sense a woman didn't have to pound into his head! Derbies, indeed! and after all I've put up with! Joe's coming right straight home right now, I don't care what anybody says! Come along, Annie. Nobody'll bite you!"

The others watched her and Mrs. Rogers hurrying away. I snatched a glance at the big sheet of paper in passing. Its corners were torn, where it had been nailed to something. Enormous scarlet letters said:

GET YOUR DERBY!!

FREE!!! GRATIS!!!

PUT ON STYLE AND CUT A DASH!

Latest STYLE derbies
Only 62 cents
Every Tenth Derby

GIVEN AWAY!! FREE GRATIS!!

SATURDAY ONLY.

At the top of the hill my mother's courage had ebbed. She and Mrs. Rogers stood there, and she didn't say a word when I joined them.

In front of Ab Whitty's store a vast crowd of men surged and jostled, yelling and leaping with up-stretched hands at hats sailing over their heads. Above them we saw Ab Whitty's tousled hair and sweating face; his collarless shirt was open in front, his sleeves rolled up, and his arms moved almost too

fast to be seen. The crowd boiled around him, bills
fluttered up at him, and more and more derbies poured
up into his hands and through them while he yelled,
"Seven! Eight! Nine! and here's the tenth, boys,
grab it! One! Two! First come, first served!
Three! Four! Stand back, don't crowd! Six!
Seven! Not many left! Nine! Hurrah, boys!
Grab it!"

There was unutterable and helpless exasperation on
my mother's face. Now and then her mouth opened,
and closed without a word. Mrs. Rogers stared, gasping exclamations. My own eyes felt stretched in my
head when I saw my respected father staggering out
of that crowd as if he were drunk, two new derbies
on his head and three in his arms. A certain helpless-
ness came over him, too, when he saw my mother.
He came up to us with hesitant boldness.

"Well!" he said. "Uh —"

Frightened by what might happen to us all in that
encounter, I looked at my enraged mother. Her eyes
smiled at him and she said with immense gentleness,
"It's dinner time, Joe."

Mrs. Rogers and I followed them, listening with
all our ears. Most of the way home my father was
jubilating over his bargains, but he did mention that
Ab Whitty had come back from St. Louis on the
midnight Cannonball. He must have made special
arrangements to get it to stop. Between midnight and
morning he'd covered the county with handbills, and
a carload of derbies had come on the morning freight.

Women were still fluttering at their gates; a dozen dinners must have been cooling or scorching. Behind us the clamor did not diminish. My father declared, "I always said he was an enterprising young fellow!" Yet there was an unwonted meekness in him. He ate the scorched potatoes without comment, and when, over the pie, my mother asked if he could let her have some change, sheepishly he gave her twelve dollars.

"I might as well pay up that grocery bill," she remarked. "And Ernestine needs a few things."

The excitement uptown continued. All up and down the street women were listening and talking. Loaded with derbies, men came straggling home. The afternoon wore away, and farmers streamed past, every one wearing a new derby. My father reported at supper that Ab Whitty had sold more than eight hundred derbies at sixty-two cents.

"It'll be a long, cold day before they lick that young fellow!"

"Where did he get the money from, to buy them?" my mother wanted to know. My father couldn't tell her.

While I was washing the supper dishes it occurred to me that Leila Barbrook might explain the mystery. We had never learned what Ab Whitty had written her in that letter; I had taken for granted that it was a heartbroken farewell. But it couldn't have been. Setting the scorched potato kettle aside to soak, I threw out the dishwater, hung up the dishpan and tidied my hair. I remarked to my mother that I thought I'd just run up the street to see Leila a minute.

The whole feeling of the town had changed. Even the moonlight seemed cheerful. Rockers rocked briskly, voices were animated, and children were running and yelling in the street. But I found Mrs. Barbrook and Leila sitting silent on their porch.

There was only a chance of getting a word with Leila. I borrowed a crochet pattern, talked politely for a few minutes, then said good-night. Leaving, I added, "Come walk a piece with me, Leila? Please. Can't she, Mrs. Barbrook?"

Mrs. Barbrook hesitated. "Well, don't go far, Leila."

"No, mama," Leila said. Outside the gate she drew a long breath.

Arm in arm, holding our skirts in our free hands, we walked slowly and talked about Ab Whitty. She did know how he had got the carload of derbies. He knew every old soldier in the county, and they had all lent him their pension certificates.

A pension certificate was exactly the same as gold, because on the certificate the government promised to pay it in gold. Though there was no money in the banks, Ab Whitty knew that if he took those certificates to the government office in St. Louis he would get the gold; whatever else failed, The United States Government kept its word.

"Why, of course," I said.

"Yes. But wasn't he smart to think of the pension

certificates, when no one else did?" said Leila. "He wrote me not to be worried, he wasn't licked yet, and he had almost two hundred dollars in pension certificates. Well, of course the government gave him the gold, and of course in times like this he'd get goods cheap in St. Louis, for cash. Don't you think he's wonderful?" she asked me wistfully.

Even in the moonlight I could see her blush when I asked if she was going to marry him. She said it wasn't quite proper to think about that, yet. "But perhaps, sometime, when he can provide for me, and if we care for each other enough, and if mama —"

The livery buggy was passing us before we noticed it. Livery buggies didn't usually set out at that hour. The horses trotted by, and Leila gasped. Ab Whitty was in the buggy. It turned in a swirl of dust and pulled up beside us. Ab Whitty started to wind the reins around the whip, but the horses plunged; he pulled them up again, cramping the wheels.

"I'll have to hold 'em, Leila," he said. "Come on, hop in!"

"Why, what — wh-where?" Leila asked, trembling. Her face was white.

"Hartville!" Ab Whitty sang out. "We'll be there by morning!"

Hartville was the county seat, twenty miles away. Eloping couples went there to be married. Leila felt her back hair and said weakly, "But I'm bareheaded."

Ab Whitty never touched a drop, but he seemed drunk then. "I don't owe a penny!" he almost shouted. "And there's money in the bank! You

bet we'll get it out! Everything's going to be all
right. Come on, Leila! We'll grow up with the
country! Sweet are the uses of adversity and we'll
have plenty of it. There is a tide in the affairs of men
that, taken at the flood — Sweetheart, darling, you little
goose, come on!"

Leila Barbrook gathered up her skirts in both hands
and jumped the weedy ditch. She put a toe on the
buggy step, Ab Whitty caught her hand, and the
swirl of blue muslin was between the buggy wheels
when the horses reared and plunged.

I clapped a hand over my scream. But her golden
hair shone safely beside Ab Whitty's derby. With
both hands he was controlling the horses. Their
hoofs thundered across the bridge and dust ran swiftly
after the wheels, up the hill and over it.

My knees weakened when I realized that before
morning I'd have to face Mrs. Barbrook.

VIII

THANKLESS CHILD

No ONE in our town had ever known such a wholly
devoted mother as Mrs. Estes was.

"Maybe it's natural," Mrs. Rogers said uneasily.
"When you think she's buried five. But my land,
she don't have a thought in her head but Lois. She
just lives and breathes in that child."

My mother didn't glance at me, but her reply did.
"Well, and no wonder — such a good, sweet, obedient
little thing. Anybody'd be thankful to have a little
girl like Lois you didn't have to keep nagging at the
livelong time to make 'em half-way behave."

Mrs. Rogers agreed. "Yes, if ever there was a little
angel on earth —   And those curls, just like sunshine."

The worst of it was that we could not take it out
on Lois. She was a constant good example, but somehow we could not wholeheartedly detest her. Her
goodness did not seem to be entirely her fault. She
was good as if she couldn't help it. "Mama says I
mustn't," she'd almost whimper.

"All right for you, fraidy-cat!" we'd answer, leaving her. It must be said for Lois that she was no
tattle-tale. Of course she was never questioned; no
one could ever have suspected that she even knew

about our naughtiness. Quite often she didn't. She was a rather lonely little girl.

Mrs. Estes lived in a tiny, unpainted house on the back street, behind the Gifford's barn. Of course Mr. Estes lived there, too, but he was a little man with walrus mustaches, always answering advertisements which promised a live hustler an opportunity to make as much as $10.86 a week. We connected him vaguely with books, perfumes, complexion soaps — things no sensible woman would spend good money for. Once he frightened us with the notion of burning gasoline; it was a mercy that outlandish lamp didn't explode and burn everybody out of house and home. Then he tried to sell mats of a new thing called asbestos. He said fire wouldn't burn it.

"Mercy on us, what next?" my mother said. "How poor Mrs. Estes ever puts up with it all — and she trying to hold up her head with the best, the way she does."

"Those dum mats won't burn, for a fact," said my father. "Most the men in the barber shop bet money on it. Jay Willard planked down a round silver dollar. So we all went across to the blacksmith shop and got Murfee to blow up his fire full blast, but to save our lives we couldn't make the dang thing —"

"Joseph Blake!" my mother interrupted. "You mean to tell me you bet good mon —"

"I am not telling you any such a thing!" my father almost shouted. "Do you want to know what goes on up town, or don't you?"

"Go on," she said coldly.

"That's all," said my father.

We ate in silence, till at last she said, "So it wouldn't burn."

"You said yourself it would," he accused her.

"And it did turn brown and start smoking. We — that is, Jay let out a yell you could've heard from here to breakfast and begun joshing Estes, when dummed if the dang thing didn't turn white again."

"You might just as well swear outright as use such language," said my mother.

He ignored this. "Estes was all set up, pleased as Punch and grinning like a Chessy cat. Said he finally got hold of the right thing, this time. He sold Jim Miller a couple mats right there, ten cents apiece is all they are, and you can boil a kettle of potatoes plumb dry on one of 'em, Estes guarantees they won't so much as scorch."

"Let me catch you squandering ten cents for one," my mother said ominously. "When did I ever burn potatoes, I'd like to know? If that Estes comes around insinuating I let my cooking burn he'll get short shrift, I promise him! Even if it would keep anything from burning, which I doubt; a trick of some kind's what it is. And ten cents don't grow on bushes. Not for me they don't," she added, rubbing that bet in on my father.

I don't remember what Mr. Estes died of, nor exactly when. His death was as vague as his life. Mrs. Estes did not put Lois in black; she herself had never got out of mourning for her children in Heaven, and she could not afford widow's weeds. We had always thought of the house as her house.

How she made both ends meet, no one quite knew. Women who came down to taking in washing must have earned more money than she earned by dress-making. But Mrs. Estes was determined to keep a social position for Lois.

It was true that she lived only for Lois. As Mrs. Miniver said, that woman did not seem to have a selfish bone in her body. My mother suspected that she scrimped herself even on food, to keep that child looking like a little doll.

"We might as well admit it, our lives are as good as over with," she said once to my mother, who accepted the fact as if it didn't taste good. "I never had anything I wanted, and now I never will. But Lois is going to. She's not going to do without, like I have. Not if I work my fingers to the bone."

She was a gaunt woman with a sallow complexion and mud-colored eyes set deep against a big nose. Even as a girl she couldn't have been pretty; likely Mr. Estes was the best she could do. They had been country folks and at least he had ambition enough to move to town, though in the upshot she hadn't bettered herself much. It must have been a consolation to her to have the prettiest little girl in town.

It is hard to say why I felt that Mrs. Estes was like a hungry tiger. She was always a lady; I never saw her make a brusque gesture or heard her voice raised. She slept in her corsets to keep her straight, inflexible figure, and at dawn she encased herself in starched calico with a tall collar. Her back hair was always neat. Nothing less tigerish can be imagined than Mrs. Estes, swiftly making buttonholes or whaleboning a bodice, her full skirts concealing feet planted on the thin, clean rag-carpet of her front room and her mouth shut neatly.

Lois and I would glance at each other with diffidence. Mrs. Estes was an even tighter constraint than one's own mother.

"Well, I'm going now," I'd blurt. "I only came to bring the pickle receipt, mama made me."

Mrs. Estes' look at Lois disturbed me. It was a pouring-out look, as if all of Mrs. Estes came out of her eyes and ate up the delicate little face, the golden curls topped by a blue bow, the big brown eyes and fringing lashes, even the pretty dress, the unwrinkled stockings and the shoes with not a button missing.

"Say good-by to Ernestine, nicely, now." Her voice was like a mother-cat's loud purr, licking her kitten. And that look would follow Lois. None of us had such perfect manners. A crinkle went over me. Somehow it was as if Lois really were a doll — one of those figures held on a ventriloquist's knee and speaking unnaturally with the voices he put into them. They seemed all wrong inside, too, so that I didn't like to hear them and was uncomfortable without knowing why. Lois would murmur, "Good-by, Ernestine. I am glad you came. Come again."

I would be glad to get away. And for no reason, while I wandered homeward, rattling a stick along the

Gifford's picket fence and dragging one foot after the other, I'd chant, "I don't care, I do as I please, I do as I please, I do as I —"

My mother's voice would end that. "Ernestine! You stop that caterwauling this minute, you hear me? Shame on you! Shame! And how many times have I got to tell you to stop scuffing out your shoes as if we're made of money? My goodness! I don't know what gets into you."

Days were limitless then; summer was summer forever, and each year's end was too far away to be seen from that year's beginning. When did we leave childhood's eternity, when did space begin to close upon us and time begin to hurry us toward the end too clearly known?

There was no moment when we might have felt a pang of hesitation. Yet it seems to me now that quite suddenly we were young ladies. Our battle was for recognition. "My goodness, mama, I'm not a child! I'm going on sixteen, and I can't wear skirts way above my ankles! Please let me have long skirts, mama, please. Please, mama!"

Elsie Miller not only wore long skirts; she put up her hair with rhinestone combs and barette. The rest of us had to fold our braids on the neck, under a black ribbon bow. But out of sight of our mothers, with surreptitious hairpins we pinned those braids up on our heads. Only Lois still wore dangling curls, a rich mass now almost reaching her waist. Every morning Mrs. Estes brushed each of those curls around her finger till it was a shining, perfect tube. We thought they were babyish. But we did not ask Lois why she didn't make her mother let her stop wearing them.

It was not that we ignored her, as we ignored poor girls from south of the tracks. She was with us in school and in Sunday school; she was always invited to parties, and came, beautifully dressed and with beautiful manners. At Easter she was chosen for the tableau, Rock of Ages. Clinging to a gilded cross, her golden curls spread down a long white robe, her gaze fixed faithfully on Heaven above the rainspot on the church ceiling, and green cheesecloth waves agitated beneath her while Mr. Gifford, choking, held the hot shovel from which tableau powder fumed a blue light, she was so beautiful that tears filled my mother's eyes.

We did not dislike Lois. We didn't like her, either. You could not say she wasn't there, when she was, yet in some indefinable way she really wasn't. Elsie said, "Oh, she's just namby-pamby." But I felt that there was a real Lois, far down inside her somewhere, and I was sorry for her. She was always so good, so proper and ladylike, and if you suddenly asked her whether she wanted this or that, an odd confusion came into her eyes. She didn't know what she wanted; she had to have a rule to go by, and she'd say, "Well, I don't know what mama would —"

"Oh, shoot your mama!" Elsie shocked us all. "I guess I'd have a mind of my own, mama or no mama!"

"That is not a nice way to speak, Elsie," said Lois, perfectly reproducing her mother's dignity. Even

Elsie was squelched. Lois was right, of course; it was not a nice way to speak.

We were fifteen then. All of us were beginning to have beaux, except Lois. She said, "Mama says I'm too young," and did not seem to mind. In spite of her beauty and her clothes, no boy paid any attention to her until the night Dan Murfee taught her to skate.

She was out-dressing us all that winter. It was the winter that Mrs. Gifford died; not that we marked time from that event. The Gifford's square white house was only a little way from ours, across the street, but I had seen Mrs. Gifford only when she was polishing windows or hanging out clothes. She slaved her whole life away taking perfect care of that big house that no one ever set foot into; not even Mr. Gifford, for in order to save the house they lived in the kitchen and its lean-to bedroom. A bedraggled wisp of a woman, she was so timid that if you knocked at the door she wouldn't come to it, fearing tramps. So no one missed her except Mr. Gifford. But her going had been, you might say, a blessing for Mrs. Estes. Mr. Gifford was the station agent; he made good wages and had no time to cook. Mrs. Estes sold him bread and baked beans, pies and cakes, and spent the money on Lois.

"The way to a man's heart is through his stomach," Mrs. Rogers said, but my mother pooh-poohed her.

"Mrs. Estes 'd never set her cap for any man and his wife not cold in her grave. No, all she's thinking about is more fol-de-rols for Lois."

I wasn't interested. The mill pond had frozen,

and for a little while a madness came upon us; we forgot we were young ladies now. Our mothers shook their heads dubiously, but on those starlit evenings sparkling with frost they couldn't keep us indoors. A bonfire crackled and blazed by the pond; the keen air bit our cheeks and blew in steam from our mouths, and all the good ladies were faintly scandalized by the noise we made.

Elsie and I were tightening our skates in the firelight when Dan Murfee came swooping toward us, and my heart thumped at my ribs. Dan was black Irish, like his father the blacksmith, and he set any girl's heart thumping. It was impossible to say why. Mothers didn't approve of him. In that instant while he was flying toward us on one skate, I remembered how wild he was, he'd fight anybody at the drop of a hat, he played cards and was suspected of smoking, he loafed around the livery stable and the barber shop and spent money as fast as he got it and would never amount to anything, but my heart was pounding with a hope that he'd skate with me instead of with Elsie.

He wasn't even good looking. His nose had been broken in a fight and one of his flashing white teeth was crooked. He was wearing ragged overalls and an old jacket and he had lost his cap somewhere. His black hair was intensely alive; a lock was always tumbling across his forehead, and when, with a quick jerk of his head, he tossed it back, my very bones seemed to melt. Dan Murfee could have gone with any girl in town, no matter what her mother did. But no girl had ever got him.

His eyes narrowed when he smiled, and the dancing twinkles in them would dance out of reach if you tried to catch them.

"Hello, girls!" he said, and without a pause, "Come on, Lois."

Elsie and I were too staggered to answer him. We had forgotten Lois. She was there only because my mother wouldn't let me come alone, so I'd brought her. Elsie had lent her an old pair of skates and she'd buckled them on, but didn't dare try to step.

"Oh — th-thank you — I ca-an't," she said, teetering. Dan Murfee didn't say anything. He gripped her mittened hands firmly, drew her arm across his, and the next instant they were gone. She couldn't fall; he was too strong, and he was the best skater on the pond.

He did not leave her, and every time I passed them I was more astonished. Lois wasn't like herself. I saw her, breathlessly laughing, tear off her coat and fling it on the snow. Most of us had taken off our heavy coats, but not with such abandon. Her pale blue, beaded fascinator kept slipping over her eyes till she flung it away, too. The tossing curls grew more and more tangled and she laughed as I'd never heard her laugh. So did Dan. Everyone was noticing their behavior, and Lois didn't care. That was the incredible thing — that Lois didn't care. Her laughter made me feel queer.

I was sober, feeling responsible because I had brought Lois. Indeed, we all grew quieter than usual, except Dan Murfee and Lois. Long before ten o'clock I took off my skates and said to Elsie, "I've got to take Lois home."

"You've got to, all right," said Elsie. "But will she go?"

"Lois?" I said. "Why, of course she'll —"

Those two came swinging down the middle of the pond, so swiftly careless that others got out of their way. They were swaying as if they were one person and with each flying stroke they yelled a wild crescendo whoop. Lois, her hair uncurling, her mouth open, yelling, and her shape showing under the blown cashmere dress, flashed by so quickly that I almost succeeded in not believing what I saw. Before I could catch my breath, I lost it again in fright. Headlong, Lois and Dan were going straight into the heaped snow at the end of the pond. At the last half-instant, Dan swerved. I saw Lois spinning around him at arms' length. Still on one skate, her petticoat ruffles plainly to be seen, twice she circled around him, then they crashed together in what might as well be called, outright, a hug.

Lois was merrily laughing and Dan yelled, "Oooo-peeeeeee!"

"Well, if that don't cap the climax —!" said Elsie.

I walked straight up to them and said, "Lois, we're going home."

"It can't be ten o'clock," she said, and suddenly I felt that she wasn't Lois. Her voice wasn't the same, nor her eyes. Even her rosy face seemed less soft, as if her whole body, like her voice and her eyes, were rounded out, full of a girl I didn't know. I was not sure that I could cope with her.

Dan said Number Five hadn't gone through yet. "If you've got to go, run along," he said. "I'm taking Lois home."

She laughed at him, "Are you?" I knew he hadn't asked her. "Oh, don't go yet, Ernestine," she said carelessly. "I want to skate some more."

From another girl the words would have meant nothing. But to hear Lois say them, in that sure voice, almost unnerved me.

"I am going," I said firmly. "And what will your mother say?" I knew well enough that no mother would allow a girl to behave as Lois was behaving that night, especially with Dan Murfee, and I'd brought her, I could be blamed. Mrs. Estes always aroused my sense of self-preservation.

The color went out of her cheeks and I knew she'd come with me. There was never any resistance in Lois. After all, she had been brought up to do as she was told. Hesitant again, she looked at Dan to tell him goodnight. He spoke first.

"Rats!" he said, swinging her into skating position. "I'll get you home by ten o'clock." They were so far away that I did not hear her reply.

I could do no more. Besides, Lois was no longer making an exhibition of herself. She and Dan were skating decorously, swinging along together and talking, when my beau took me home. He stayed some

time at the gate and it was precisely two minutes to
ten by the dining-room clock when, all but frozen,
I went in. My mother had been sitting up for me;
she put away the sock she was knitting.

"Did you and Lois have a good time?" she inquired
kindly, and I replied, "Yes, mama."

It was no conspiracy which kept Mrs. Estes from
knowing what was going on. With parents it was
always prudent, as well as respectful, to be silent until
spoken to. And there was nothing definite to tell.
We simply knew that Dan Murfee was gone on Lois
and that she was not discouraging him. Their eyes
said that. In one way and another they saw a great
deal of each other, not secretly, yet not quite openly.
She didn't, for instance, let him see her home from
church; all that next summer they did not go buggy-
riding, and when he asked to buy her ice-cream at
the Ladies Aid socials she said, thank you, she didn't
care for any.

I think they quarreled about it. One autumn
evening I passed them at the corner of Mr. Gifford's
yard, where the side road went to Mrs. Estes' house.
They were standing there, talking. Chrysanthemums,
I remember, were ghostly along the fence and there
was a scent of burning leaves. Dan was speaking
vehemently.

"But why can't I? What are you afraid of?
What can she do?" he demanded. Lois must have
made some warning gesture; they were both silent
while I went by. But walking soundlessly across the

street's velvety dust I heard his voice again, low but vibrant. "We'll have to tell her sometime, won't we? Lois? Won't we?"

When I told Elsie, we were thrilled. We were sure that Lois was secretly engaged. This was the single romance known to us which was one bit like the romances in books. For a time we cultivated our friendship with Lois as we had never done before, partly from curiosity and partly from a mystic feeling that some magic might be communicated to us. I wondered endlessly how she had got him to pop the question.

She was changed, and not only because at last her mother had put up her hair. Mrs. Estes arranged it beautifully in a huge pompadour and piled coils. Beneath that marvelous golden weight, her face was like the flower-faces in children's picture books. But if she had been vague before, now she was quivering. The slightest incident, even a word, might throw her into excited laughter, or tears. "Oh, I don't know!" she'd answer, sobbing. "It isn't anything. It's my hair, it makes my head ache." We could understand that. But once she said appealingly, "Oh Ernestine, don't you wish we didn't have to grow up?"

I hadn't thought about it. "Well, we don't have to *do* anything," I said. "We just do grow up."

It must have been a May evening when my mother and I noticed the light in an upstairs window of the Gifford house. We were sitting on our front porch. I remember the slender moon and a feeling of spring-time, and the maple leaves were young. "What can

be going on in that bedroom?" my mother wondered.
"He can't be dressing up, it isn't prayer meeting
night."

Our side gate clicked and Mrs. Rogers came around
the house, holding her skirts above the dewy grass.
"You suppose he's moving in, up there? Poor soul,
she must be turning in her grave."

"Take the other rocker," my mother said. "Well,
it's no disrespect now if he does get some good out
of that big house. Let's see, was it a year in January?
I remember the ground was frozen."

"February third," said Mrs. Rogers. "And you
can't tell me he didn't begin taking notice again, way
last winter. All that traipsing back and forth; it
wasn't just pies and cakes he was after."

We could make nothing of the shadows on the
window shade. The lamp went downstairs; light
glimmered briefly through the colored glass in the
front door. Then the house was dark, until a lantern
came from behind it. Pepper-and-salt trousers legs
moved scissors-like in the moving light.

"His Sunday clothes!" Mrs. Rogers exclaimed.
The lantern went twinkling down the side street
beyond the pickets. My mother settled back then,
and Mrs. Rogers exclaimed, "There! What did I
tell you!"

"And a good thing for both of them," said my
mother.

"Yes, she won't refuse him, a good man and a good
home and all. I wonder how Lois'll like a step-
father?"

"Lois'll have nothing to say about it," my mother replied. "If you ask me, it's high time her mother's mind was on something else for a change. You mark my words, if Mrs. Estes don't let up on that girl, Lois'll break out somewhere in a way you'd least expect."

Next day, like a bomb, the news burst upon us that Lois and Mr. Gifford were engaged.

I couldn't repress a gasp, but my mother remained properly composed. Sitting in our parlor, her hands folded in her lap, she smiled and said, "Well, I'm sure I wish you every happiness, Lois."

"Thank you, Mrs. Blake," Lois murmured. The thick lashes hid her downcast eyes and she had never had much color. The air seemed heavy, yet dangerously unstable. I didn't dare speak.

"Mr. Gifford is a good man," my mother said carefully.

"Yes, a most suitable match in every way," said Mrs. Estes. Her sallow skin glowed, and so did the small eyes set against her big nose. She was a lady from the hem of black skirts to the velvet-and-jet toque she'd made from scraps of Mrs. Miller's dresses, but I thought of tigers, of a tiger's purring triumph. She purred satisfied love and pride. "He's all I ever dreamed of for her."

She had saved the announcement until the end of their call. Now she rose, and so did Lois. I had to say something. "Oh Lois, I hope you'll be awfully happy!"

Her eyelids quivered upward. She seemed even

more confused than I was. My mother was supposing they hadn't yet set the date. Mrs. Estes almost caroled, "June. I always said Lois' must be a June bride." Then we all began saying, "Good afternoon, good afternoon, I'm glad you called, you must call on us, yes, call again, good-by, good-by."

My mother and I watched till they entered Mrs. Rogers' gate. Then weakly my mother sat down. "My goodness gracious me, never in my born days — All this time she's been maneuvering it! For Lois. We might 've known it. But — but my goodness — Keep watching, Ernestine, and tell me when they leave."

Before sunset the town was a stirred beehive. Mrs. Rogers declared it was a sin and a shame, marrying that poor girl off to a widower old enough to be her father. Mrs. Miniver said the sooner a girl was settled the better, nowadays; what with all the wild goings-on, there was never any telling. My father came home early, only to be disappointed when my mother told him the news before he could tell her. She said that, after all, mothers had only a girl's happiness at heart, and knew what was best. But I knew that she was saying something quite different to Mrs. Rogers, after she'd left me alone in the house to do the supper dishes.

I was meditatively stirring the cooling dishwater round and round in the pan while through some vaguely blissful dream I watched voluptuously the patterns formed by the congealing grease, when thunder and whirlwind came upon me. Uproar focused in Dan Murfee's wild face. I had to help them, he shouted; the door banging behind him, pans leaping on the walls. "You're her best friend, you've got to! Don't stand there like a fool! I tell you I won't stand it! You've got to!" He propelled me out of the kitchen, his grip hurting my arm while I tried to dry my hands and take off my apron, making incoherent protest and inquiry.

"You can get in," he told me. "You're going in there and get her." He swore at Mrs. Estes with a fury that intoxicated me. I had never heard such language. There had been a violent scene of some kind. "She can't throw me out, she can't get away with it," was his description. Trotting beside him and pushing loose hairpins into my hair, I prayed that my mother wouldn't see me from Mrs. Rogers' porch. We hastened through a faint haze lighted by the unseen moon. Mr. Gifford's house looked flat as pasteboard and trees loomed gigantic.

"But I don't know — what can I say? How —" I hesitated at Mrs. Estes' gate. The house was dark, the shades down; only a thread of light showed under the warped door.

"What do I care? Get her out here," Dan ordered.

In the center of drama, I didn't feel as adequate as I had always thought I would be. Something told me that it would be wiser to postpone action. I tried to convey this wisdom to Dan. "But," I began again. "If you really love her, don't —"

"If I — you don't know what you're talking about!" he exploded.

"Sh-sh," I breathed. "But after all, maybe—"

"Yes, she does," he said harshly. "I tell you I know she does, and she knows it, if only she had the nerve to. She knows it, only she's so—God damn it, will you stop asking questions and get her out here!"

Desperately trying to contrive a plausible lie, I stole up the walk. In Mrs. Estes' front room there was the faint recurrent swish of skirts in a rocking chair. I knocked.

What I'd interrupted was clear from the little sounds I heard before the opened door let a shaft of yellow light pierce the misty vagueness. Past Mrs. Estes' silhouette in the doorway, I saw the small, closed, lamplit room where she had been holding Lois in her arms. The chair still swayed. Lois stood near it, her lips slightly parted, her eyes wide.

"Good evening, Mrs. Estes," I began, breathless. "I thought I'd run in just a minute to—Oh hello, Lois. I—"

Mrs. Estes blocked the doorway, immovable. "I am surprised at you, Ernestine," she said in that cold tone which indicates no surprise whatever, indeed the grimmest expectation realized. "Your mother will not approve when she knows this, I am sure."

"But— Why, Mrs. Estes! I don't know wh-what—"

"You can tell that young man that Lois wants nothing whatever to do with him," said Mrs. Estes, and Dan Murfee was there in one bound.

He was terrific and pitiable. After crying out, "Oh no, Dan, no!" Lois wept. Mrs. Estes remained impregnable. Her manner said that Dan's actions and words were in the worst possible taste. As always, she was right; they were.

Again and again he refused to leave until she let Lois talk to him, though she told him that Lois didn't want to. At last she turned to Lois, huddled sobbing in the rocking chair. "Lois, have you anything to say to this — young man?"

For a long moment there wasn't a sound. Then Lois sobbed again.

A roar came from Dan. He swore, he raved; wildly accusing Mrs. Estes, calling her mean, cruel, abominable, he begged Lois to be brave and to do something, it wasn't clear what. She couldn't marry him, of course; he hadn't a penny.

"You are making an uproar to start the whole town talking and ruin her character," Mrs. Estes told him. That was true. "She wants you to leave her alone. Don't you, Lois?" Sharply she repeated, "Lois!"

"You devil!" Dan shouted. "Lois, don't let her! Darling, sweetheart, tell her to go to hell! For God's sake, Lois. Darling. Stand up just this once and —"

"Will — you — go, and leave my poor girl in peace?" Mrs. Estes said.

"Tell me it's a lie!" Dan raved. "You won't marry him, will you, Lois, you won't let her, speak to me, Lois for God's sake — Lois, you can't let her —"

"Lois, you must put a stop to —" her mother was saying, when Lois screamed, a thin, high, piercing screech. Her face came up from her arms, blind, convulsed, screaming. "Go away, go away, go away and leave me alone! Leave me alone!"

Mrs. Estes softly shut the door behind us. My legs were shaking, I stumbled in the ruts of the side street. With a shock, I perceived that Dan was sobbing — walking along with his fists in his pockets and shoulders hunched, and sobs tearing his chest. I did not speak.

At last we came past Mr. Gifford's picket fence to the sidewalk. Two rockers creaked on Mrs. Rogers' porch, I could hear my mother's voice faintly, and I thought I'd better get home through the alley and our back yard. I yearned to tell Dan how sorry I was, and timidly I touched his sleeve. "Dan —"

"Oh, go to hell!" he growled, striking my hand away.

That was the thanks I got. I was not surprised next day when my father told us that Dan Murfee had got rip-roaring drunk and fought the night-watchman. "Took three men and his father to handle him," my father said, not without admiration. "That young fellow can lick his weight in wildcats when he gets started."

Of course that ended my knowing Dan Murfee. Even had I not given the solemn pledge that lips that touched liquor should never touch mine, no nice girl could know a man who drank. Reason told me that Mrs. Estes had acted for the best.

By a good fortune only too rare, I had reached our kitchen unseen and unsuspected. I longed to tell

what I knew, but I couldn't think how to explain
my own part in that scene; the first sight of my un-
suspicious mother told me that silence was safety, and
I was thankful that Mrs. Estes did not call to speak
to my mother privately. I knew very well that I
could not trust Elsie. I could speak only to Lois,
and she retreated into herself as swiftly as a snail.

"But Lois, do you love him or don't you?" I per-
sisted hardily.

She ventured out a little way, timidly. "How can
you— Do you know how to—to tell, for sure? Do
you, Ernestine?"

"You just *know*," I replied with assurance. "You
just don't have any doubts about it—not if it's Real
Love." We always spoke those two words with awe.

She murmured, twisting her handkerchief with
quivering fingers, "It's so important—so awfully important. All your life long— And if you make a
mistake—" She shivered. "Mama says nice girls
can't ever know. Not till they're married. Real
Love comes after you're married. If you marry a
good man you respect." She burst into tears.

Her weeping was so terrible that it frightened me.
I did all I could to soothe her, and I did not speak
to her again about Dan Murfee. She couldn't, of
course, respect him. He was becoming the town
scandal, with his wildness and his drinking. The
worst fate that could befall a woman was to be a
drunkard's wife.

We were all fluttering around Lois in envious excitement. She was the first of us to be a bride. And

she was making a match which we could hardly hope to equal. Her mother was sewing night and day, making her clothes. She had a diamond engagement ring. She would step right into that big house, with all its furniture good as new, its wall papers as fresh as the day they were put on. She was going to the St. Louis World's Fair on her honeymoon, and when she came back she'd be Mrs. Gifford. Not even Mrs. Miller could look down on Mrs. Gifford.

I had never really seen Mr. Gifford before; he had always been simply Mr. Gifford. Now I looked at him and could find nothing to dislike. His heavy gold watch-chain curved across a front more portly than most, but he was not unpleasantly fat. He had a gravely serious manner, suited to his position; he was a pillar of the church and superintendent of the Sunday school. He was really a good man, too; strictly business-like but not merciless to the farmers whose mortgages he held. His large face was serious and rather heavy, with thick-lidded eyes of no particular expression, and all the lower part of it was brown whiskers, cut short and square. They were always neatly trimmed and combed. His clothes were of good substantial material and his clean hands, with blunt fingers and uncalloused palms, showed that he was able to hire work done for him. Nobody could object to anything about Mr. Gifford. He had proved that he was a steady, reliable husband and a good provider.

I did not quite know why I felt a faint chill at the thought of being married to him.

Lois would not tell us how he had popped the question. Under Elsie's prodding, she admitted that she hadn't expected it.

"Did you think all the time he was making up to your mother?" Elsie asked her.

Lois was startled. "Why— Why, of course not! Whatever gives you such a—"

"Oh, I don't know! Nothing," Elsie said airily. "Only he's more her age, and all. I bet he's her ideal. Lois, I think you're just simply awfully mean not to tell us everything, but anyway tell me just this much: Is it just perfectly wonderful when he kisses you, or do his whiskers tickle?"

"Elsie Miller!" I exclaimed. Lois was red as a beet.

Elsie answered me brazenly. "Well, I don't care! I think Lois is just simply mean not to tell us, because you know they say a kiss without a mustache is like an egg without salt, and he's got mustaches and whiskers both."

"It isn't proper to be kissed till you're married," Lois said.

"Why, Lois Estes, it is too! It's perfectly all right to be kissed just the very minute you're engaged, and do you mean to say you've never even once let him—"

"Oh, leave me alone, please!" Lois cried, and I said severely, "You ought to be ashamed of yourself, Elsie Miller. The way you talk isn't one bit nice, and you just leave Lois right alone!"

It was a church wedding. The day was June's perfection, and everyone said to everyone else, "Happy is the bride the sun shines on." There was not a vacant place in the church. The flowery silks and lawns and the sprays and wreaths of flowers on new spring hats made the crowd look, my mother said, just like a garden. Though we had never seen a garden with anything in it but vegetables. Elsie Miller sang, "O promise me," and Mrs. young-Doctor Wright played on the organ, "Here comes the bride."

Lois carried white roses. Their fragrance went up the aisle with the shimmering pure lengths of China silk and the misty veil, and its passing by seemed the passing of all lovely things — the passing of simple faith and unconscious hope, of dawns and noons and evenings twinkling with fireflies, of sun and wind and stars and of all small homely matters, of life itself. So that our awareness of that moment even then, in our first perception of it, eluding us and lost forever, was too poignant to be borne without tears.

"Beats me why women have to cry at weddings," my father muttered huskily, and turned his face away from my mother's wet glance. When the bride's trembling voice repeated the irrevocable oath, "to love, honor, and obey . . . till death do us part," sobs could not be choked.

Mrs. Estes had worked her fingers to the bone to make it a perfect wedding, and it was. Everything went off without a hitch. Lois, pale and remote in a bridal daze, was more beautiful than words can say. Her wide eyes saw nothing, and she quivered at a touch. Mr. Gifford was solidly substantial in a new

pepper-and-salt suit. He plainly had a realizing sense
of his responsibility and was able and willing to shoulder it. Mrs. Estes got Lois into traveling clothes in
time for the train to St. Louis.

Climbing into the coach, she stepped blindly into
her skirts and stumbled; Mr. Gifford seized her arm.
Handsful of rice were pattering, every train-window
was full of heads, we were all laughing and cheering.
Lois glanced back at us across Mr. Gifford's grip and
my heart contracted; her eyes were silent screams of
terror. Trapped, I thought; no escape now, never
any escape, all her life long. Mr. Gifford's ponderous
back came between us, and the grinning black por-
ter mounted the steps.

It was over. The steel rails hummed behind the
diminishing train. There was no Lois any more; she
was Mrs. Gifford. In her fawn-colored suit with
bands and reveres of brown velvet, with the little
toque of massed violets on her golden hair and a tiny
dotted veil to the tip of her small nose, she must begin
now to love Mr. Gifford.

Tears dripped down Mrs. Estes' sallow cheeks. But
they were tears of joy, dried more by triumph than
by her damp handkerchief. "I haven't lost a daughter," she said. "I have gained a son." Nobody, she
repeated, could be more generous than Mr. Gifford,
more kind and thoughtful; a Christian and a gentleman in every way; she couldn't ask for a better man
for Lois. "I could die content, now," she said. "I've
got nothing more to wish for."

"Well, it's all been her doing," my mother said,

while we walked sedately homeward to take off our best clothes. "And anybody can see she's full satisfied. I'm sure I hope it all turns out for the best."

From delicacy, we crossed the street to avoid passing the blacksmith shop. Mr. Murfee's hammer was striking showers of sparks from iron on the clanging anvil; he would be ashamed to speak to us, for Dan, drunk and disorderly, had been arrested. Dan was even then in the calaboose, serving a two-day sentence.

"Well, that's so, you never can tell," Mrs. Rogers sighed. "But Lois might have gone farther and fared worse." The words were as final as an epitaph. In those days all stories ended with the wedding.

Indeed, when Mr. and Mrs. Gifford came home, she had settled down. She was quieter and if possible even more proper. We called, dressed for the occasion and carrying our cardcases, and sitting in the parlor with its rich carpet, lace curtains and heavy furniture of real mahogany, she showed us pictures of the World's Fair. We turned the album's pages delicately with gloved fingers and murmured what a privilege it must have been to see such buildings and such gardens, and lighting by electricity.

"Yes," Lois said.

"Look at this one!" Mrs. Estes was uplifted by pleasure. "They walked right along here — here, in front of that fountain. Just like being in Paradise. Wasn't it, Lois?"

"Mr. Gifford and I enjoyed it very much," Lois said.

Mrs. Estes had rented her little house. Mr. Gifford was glad to have her live with them, and she did all the housework. Lois did not know very much about housekeeping because her mother had never let her spoil her hands.

This exasperated Mrs. Miniver. "A married woman that don't do a hand's turn from morning to night! It's a wonder she don't get too lazy to breathe! Just downright selfishness is all it is, and the more you do for such folks, the more you can do. There's her poor mother just given her whole life up to that girl and what thanks does she get for it I'd like to know!"

At first we girls ran in less formally to see Lois and her house. We admired the large square rooms and the good furniture so well taken care of by Mrs. Estes. The lean-to bedroom was not used any more. Mrs. Estes had the bedroom over the kitchen, nicely arranged with her own things. Mr. Gifford and Lois slept in the large front bedroom, with its massive walnut bedstead and matching bureau and wash-stand. Lois had not changed this room at all, and left nothing of hers lying about in it; everything was precisely as the first Mrs. Gifford had kept it. The room was so neat that it seemed chilly.

"Yes, it's a nice room," Lois agreed. She agreed to everything we said about her house.

When Elsie asked her outright how she liked being married, she replied in the same colorless way that Mr. Gifford was a good man and she tried to be worthy of him.

She had not asked us to sit down; we stood in the

square room, looking at its pale green papered walls, the tobacco-colored carpet with large red roses on it, the pink washbowl and pitcher and soap-dish on the washstand. The slopjar was pink, too, and so was the chamber-pot set under the edge of the bed; even the crocheted silencer drawn over its lid was made of pink yarn. A golden light came through the translucent shades that covered the windows. Only the bed glared white in spotless counterpane and pillow-shams.

Elsie and I both knew that in this room, in that bed, Lois must submit to some dark and secret degradation. Submitting to that, whatever it was, was a married woman's duty. Lois knew what it was, now.

She had showed us that place, and now she expected us to go on to look at other rooms. I moved blindly toward the door. But Elsie didn't.

"Oh, don't be a boob, Lois!" She tried to say it airily. "Now you're married and everything and we're not going to let you off like that." She was choking. "You've just got to tell us—tell us what it's—" A desperate Elsie whose existence I had never suspected gasped, pleading. "Please, Lois. Because, someday, we've got to—and is it—is it always so awful?"

In the dark middle of the night, in bed, while we were spending the night together, after all lights had been out for hours and our throats were tired from whispering and our minds vague with sleeplessness, sometimes Elsie and I had ventured to wonder, to speculate about what being married was like. And

Elsie had said it couldn't always be so awful, because then why did bad girls have babies? They weren't married; they didn't have to. Of course it must be terrible at first, you'd just almost die of shame, but maybe, after awhile, you wouldn't mind it so much. Not if you really loved your husband. Because you could stand anything, for Love.

My whole face was burning painfully and I could not look at Elsie. I was ashamed to look at Lois, but I couldn't help it. Astonished, I saw not the faintest flush on her cheeks. She was pale and infinitely remote. I had the old feeling that she was not there.

Mechanically she spoke the only proper words that could come through the impenetrable barrier separating married women from good girls. "There are some things, Elsie, that it isn't nice to think about. You will understand such things when you are married." She added, "Would you like to see the spare room?"

Two or three times I was in the house when Mr. Gifford came home. He was dignified and bland. Lois met him at the door as a wife should, took the meat he had brought for supper and hung his hat on the hall rack for him. Young married women were beginning, among friends, to address their husbands informally by their first names, but Lois always said, in the old-fashioned way, "Mr. Gifford."

"Blind Booth is coming next week. Would you care to go, Lois?" he'd ask, and she would reply, "Just as you like, Mr. Gifford."

They would go sedately, accompanied by Mrs.

Estes, and sit side by side in the Opera House above the drug-store, hearing the blind negro play the piano. Then they would walk home again. She and her mother always accompanied him to church, and at his request she took a class in Sunday school. She was definitely a married woman. Our mothers still masked anxiety, but Mrs. Estes was complacent.

Lois would undoubtedly live all her life as she lived the first two years of her marriage. The stork had not yet visited her, and women ceased to speculate about it, agreeing that likely, now, it never would. Though she was so much younger than Mr. Gifford, there was no reason she should dread widowhood; her husband's health was as substantial as everything else about him. His father had lived to ninety-six, his mother to eighty-seven. He often referred to their long lives, and said that he didn't feel a day older than thirty.

My mother could hardly believe her ears when Mrs. Rogers ran in to say that Mr. Gifford was down with typhoid fever. "Not Mr. Gifford!" she exclaimed.

It was the beginning of a nightmare summer. Within a month, typhoid was in almost every home; whole families were down. Both doctors were working day and night; women abandoned housework, eating where they could and snatching a few hours' sleep whenever they could be spared from sickrooms. Disheveled and sandy-eyed from night-long vigils, we exchanged scraps of news in passing. More help was needed south of the tracks; Mr. Murfee had passed away; Gerty Bates was very low; both Mrs.

Miniver's boys were down now; old Mr. Whitty had barely lasted through the night. The church bell tolled. We counted the doleful clangs, one for each year of a life ended, and the summer weather seemed to have a chill in it, the sunshine to be a false aspect of darkness.

Mrs. Estes was wonderful. Nothing could induce her to rest. Lois of course helped all she could, but Mrs. Estes had never allowed her to do much. Now she took the whole care of Mr. Gifford upon herself. With passionate intensity she promised, "If constant prayer and human effort can do it, Lois, I'll save him for you."

Her whole self poured almost visibly into that effort. Her eyes burned deeper in her face, the sallow skin stretched taut. "My land, she looks like a skull!" Mrs. Rogers said. "But you can't do a thing with her. She's bound and determined."

Mr. Gifford's flesh had fallen off him. He was a foul and raving thing of bones and lax skin, on the walnut bed in the stifling room. Mrs. Estes bathed him hourly, day and night. She held him when he fought in delirium, she kept the covers over him when he struggled to throw them off. She would let no one else give him medicine, dole out his spoonfuls of water and broth. She was magnificent and terrible.

The doctor himself gave her no hope. For sixteen days the fever burned unbroken, steadily mounting higher. "Flesh and blood can't stand it," young Dr. Wright said. "He's literally burning up. If we can't break that fever today, Uncle Dave—" The old doctor nodded, agreeing. "We've got to break it," he said grimly.

That afternoon Mrs. Estes stepped into the hall with the dirty sheets, and Mrs. Rogers followed, urging her to lie down and rest for only a few minutes. Mrs. Estes had not slept for days and nights, nor rested properly for more than two weeks. She turned on Mrs. Rogers like a tiger.

"Get out of my way!" she said so fiercely that Mrs. Rogers turned pale. "My girl's not going to be left a widow! Not while there's breath in my body."

They could not break the fever. It burned even higher next day, higher still the next day. Old Dr. Wright told Mrs. Estes there was no hope whatever. There could be only one end.

Early next morning Mrs. Rogers came across the street to summon my mother. "We'll have him to lay out today," she said. Even Mrs. Estes admitted that he was sinking into the last sleep; Lois had been at the bedside all night. "Poor soul, I wonder how she's taking it?" Mrs. Rogers murmured. I did not know whether she meant Mrs. Estes or Lois.

It seemed strange that anyone could die on such a morning. Beneficence poured from the sky, hens cackled in barnyards, and a freight's whistle cheerily echoed from the cut. I swept the porch slowly, in a drowsy awareness of time's passing over the earth with the sunshine; summer was going, soon winter would come, then summer again, and at last the seasons passing over the earth would know nothing of me, nor I of them. But I did not believe it.

Young Dr. Wright had gone into the Gifford house and, shocked, I caught myself thinking how pretty Lois would be in a widow's weeds. Thoughts must be controlled; such thoughts as that must be destroyed in the mind. Triumphantly virtuous, I did not think of Dan Murfee. Nothing, I was saying to myself, was farther from my thoughts than any slightest connection between Mrs. Gifford and Dan Murfee. And a terrible shriek ran up my spine and crinkled under my back hair.

I stared at the Gifford house. The shriek broke into wild, uncontrollable sobbing. In a flash, while I ran, I saw that scene of tragic widowhood and wondered whether, with all that money, Lois would marry a mere blacksmith. The front door stood open to the unkempt hall and, astonished, I saw Mrs. Rogers coming hurriedly down the stairs. She urged me back to the porch.

"Sh, we must keep him quiet," she murmured.

"Him?" I gaped at her. "Who?"

"Mr. Gifford's better, the doctor just said he'll likely get well if —" Mrs. Cleaver reached us, and two or three others were coming. The sobbing upstairs was almost suppressed now; my mother's firm tones could be heard.

"But — that's Lois? crying? like that?" someone said.

"Yes. It's — shock," replied Mrs Rogers. "I guess." The pause quivered with words that might be said, but were not. "Anyway, that's what the doctor said :

shock. Of course we all expected — He was getting cold at four o'clock this morning."

Mrs. Cleaver gasped, "Well, of all —" and made it hurriedly, "Well, no wonder. Poor soul." All the others said hurriedly, yes, yes of course. Of course it was the shock, poor thing; such sudden good news and she so high-strung, so worn-out after all those weeks of anxiety.

Mr. Gifford's recovery was miraculous. Mrs. Estes said solemnly that she would always believe it was a direct answer to prayer. After that morning when even the doctor's thermometer confirmed Mrs. Rogers' statement that he was growing cold as death, Mr. Gifford had only a trace of fever. He lay weak and thin but himself again. Day after day his strength increased; it was certain that he would get well. It was only a matter of time and of liquid diet.

"Wait till you're up and around again, good as ever," old Dr. Wright told him jovially. "Then you can eat steak and fried potatoes, all you want." The patient's outburst of bad temper was nothing to worry about, Dr. Wright said; it was another good symptom.

The epidemic dwindled away. It was over, and a blessed calm fell upon us. Wherever women met they said they thanked God it had been no worse. Cheerfully we attacked our delayed housecleanings and gossiped again across side fences. There was plenty of neighborly help in taking care of Mr. Gifford. He was mending slowly; daily his temper

grew worse and he demanded food so constantly and
so violently that even Mrs. Estes lost patience and
my mother told him tartly, "You get what the doctor orders and not one sip more. We don't want
to bury you."

Lois was angelic to him. His worst fit of temper
did not disturb her quietness. She was thinner;
shadows made her eyes appear enormous in the small
pale face and the mass of fair hair was too heavy for
her head, but she was still beautiful. Mr. Gifford's
eyes followed her while she went quietly about, carrying out basins and bringing towels, setting chairs in
place. "Come here," he'd say, and she came.

"Sit down a minute, can't you!" She did not
mind his crossness; she sat down. He'd ask her,
"Glad I'm getting well?" and she'd say, "Yes, of
course." She would sit for hours by the bed, doing
nothing, looking at the idle hands in her lap. The
thick gold wedding ring was loose on her finger.
When he spoke she said, "Yes, Mr. Gifford," and
fixed his pillows or brought him a drink of water.

I had seen this so often that I knew what to expect
when one afternoon I went into the still house.
Everything was clean and in order; doors and windows were open to the balmy autumn day; nothing
stirred but a fluttering curtain. The hush made me
tiptoe even before I realized that Mrs. Estes must be
asleep. Carrying my bowl of steaming broth, I went
noiselessly upstairs. The bedroom door stood open
and for an instant, on the threshold, my mind rejected
what it saw.

Mr. Gifford sat propped against pillows, and Lois was bending over him. Every curve of her expressed angelic tenderness and the sweetest of smiles beamed from her face. I know I was not mistaken; it was a scene of pure and selfless love. Her voice was full of the joy of giving. She said, "Don't you want another, Mr. Gifford?"

Her two hands held a platter heaped with steaming ears of corn. Mr. Gifford laid down a gnawed cob and grasped a plump ear. "Butter," he said.

"Lois!" I screeched.

She started and turned a clear gaze on me. The smile lingered in her eyes. "Mercy, you scared me!" she exclaimed. "What? What is it, Ernestine?"

"Don't!" I cried. "You mustn't!" The broth was slopping on my hands and I couldn't find a place to set down the bowl. Mr. Gifford gnawed wolfishly. "You know better!" I told her. "Stop him!"

"Stop him what?" she asked, bewildered. The sense that Mr. Gifford was a sick man weakened my attack. He left a partly denuded cob in my hand and seized another ear. "What on earth are you trying to do?" Lois asked me in shocked disapproval.

I said it would kill him. She murmured dreamily, "Oh, no." Mr. Gifford, munching, growled something about fool notions, starving a man. I noticed splashes of melted butter on his nightshirt.

"The doctor told you!" I said furiously.

"Did he? I don't remember anything like that," she replied vaguely. Suddenly a terrific power rose in her; in a voice I'd never heard, deep, resonant, vibrating with emotion, she said, "The doctor never said anything of the kind! Nourishing food will do him good."

All this had occurred with utmost rapidity. I couldn't have been half a minute in that room. I burst into Mrs. Estes' bedroom, shouting. I sped across the street to my mother and on her orders ran for old Dr. Wright. He was out on a country call. In a nightmare effort to hurry, I reached the other end of town. Young Dr. Wright was out, too.

I forced quivering legs to bear this news to Mr. Gifford's bedroom. It was crowded. He looked quite well. There was some color in his sunken cheeks; the barber had shaved them that morning, and trimmed his beard. He said doctors didn't know anything; he said he felt well enough to get up, right now. But he was watching the door.

Lois sat beside the bed, shrinking from all the eyes. "Well, I didn't know," she breathed, trembling. "I honestly didn't. I don't remember the doctor's saying —" While her worn-out mother slept, Lois had gathered that corn from the garden, stripped the ears and boiled them, and carried them upstairs to Mr. Gifford. He had eaten eight. "He told me to get him something to eat. He told me to," she pleaded. "He was so hungry, and he wanted sweet corn. I only did what he told me to." She twisted her handkerchief.

Old Dr. Wright came at dusk. Mrs. Estes lighted a lamp. Still dusty from the country trip, he listened while we told him what had happened; he took Mr. Gifford's temperature and pulse. Lois watched him with terrible intensity. The click of his watch-case, snapped shut, made us all start. Looking down at Mr. Gifford, he said cheerfully, "Well, well, so you been cutting up didoes, uh? Feeling pretty good now? That's fine. Take it easy, now, and don't worry. Couple these good ladies'll stay with you tonight, and I'll be around again in the morning."

We made way for Mrs. Estes and Lois to go with him into the hall. He beckoned my mother and Mrs. Rogers with a glance, and shut the door behind all of them.

Mrs. Miniver said immediately that she must get home to see about supper; so did Mrs. Miller, and I thought defensively about my father's supper, too. Mrs. Miniver opened the door. But the hall was empty.

Downstairs the parlor door was shut. We hesitated on the porch, murmuring that we didn't like to go without knowing — The parlor windows were open, and the lamp lighted. Beside the center table Lois stood trembling and crying; the others stood looking at her.

"But I didn't mean — I didn't remember you said not to," she told the doctor. "I don't remember now. I don't remember, I can't —" Her voice rose.

"There, there, of course you don't," the doctor said. "Of course not, Mrs. Gifford; we all know that." There was a queer look on his face. Watching her under his bushy eyebrows, he shook some tablets from a bottle into a twist of paper and gave it to Mrs. Estes. "Get her to bed right away. Two of these in water, and two more in an hour if she isn't asleep. Come, come now, Mrs. Gifford; you mustn't give way. Sorrow comes to us all."

"Come, Lois," Mrs. Estes said, but as if she didn't want to. She moved to put an arm around Lois, and quick as a cat Lois turned on her.

"Leave me alone! Don't touch me!" Her face was hideous. "I can't stand it! I can't stand it! Don't touch me! Leave me alone! I hate you, hate you!" Piercingly she screamed out the word that no one had said. "Murder! Murder! You did it, you made me! Don't touch me! Take her away! Don't let her!"

The old doctor picked her up, kicked open the parlor door and carried her, screaming and struggling, upstairs. Mrs. Rogers scurried after them, my mother ran to the kitchen. The hall was a babble. "Lord save us, she's gone stark raving —" "She don't mean it, Mrs. Estes. They always turn on them they —" "You don't mean she —" "What did she say? I didn't —" My mother appeared with a steaming tea-kettle. "Go home, Ernestine; you hear me?" she said from the stairs. I obeyed.

Mr. Gifford lingered two days in agony. The doctor gave him morphine. He died about four o'clock on the third morning.

The funeral was perhaps the largest ever held in our town. We had to wait half an hour at the raw, open grave before the last buggies began to arrive.

Mrs. Estes had aged terribly. Mrs. Miller and Mrs. Boles-that-was-Dorothy Hutton supported Lois, drooping in rich black crepe; the veil hid her face. Horses shook jingles from their bridles, stamped, and whinnied. The sky was deeply blue and great shining clouds floated in it. Looking upward, one felt that Heaven was a happy place to go to. We knew that Mr. Gifford, equipped with large white wings, was on his way there, or perhaps had already arrived and was even then playing a harp in the celestial choir.

The men with shovels settled to their work while the first mourners drove away. My father went to get our buggy from the grove where the horses were tied, and Mrs. Rogers said, "They'll have to patch it up somehow. Mrs. Estes hasn't got a thing in the world but Lois, and Lois can't turn on her; her own mother."

"And just given up her whole life to that girl," said Mrs. Miniver. We walked slowly down the grassy slope between the old headstones; the iris blades were turning brown at the tips. "I must say, I feel to sympathize with Mrs. Estes. I never in my life saw anything so horrible as the way Lois turned on her. So much as intimating it was Mrs. Estes' fault that Mr. Gifford passed away; I guess we all know who was responsible for that! I wouldn't put anything past Lois. You mark my words, poor Mrs. Estes is just beginning to find out how sharper than a serpent's tooth it is to have a thankless child."

My mother said, "Well. Mrs. Estes is a good woman, and a smart woman, and a lady if there ever was one, and she's acted only for Lois' good. But you can push a body just so far."

The moment had for me a pleasant melancholy; I was thinking that never again would I see the sunlight slanting on those graves and the iris tips turning brown. I was going away; for months the day had been set. In only a little while now I would be gone forever from this unsatisfying peacefulness, and for an instant the grass, the yellow gravestones, the long shadows of the pines, the buggy-wheels turning in the dusty road and the shining flanks of the horses had for me the unforgettable vividness of those things we know we shall forget.

The fateful day came. My father took my trunk in his dray, my mother and I walked together to the depot. The Gifford house was blank behind drawn blinds; no one knew what had happened between Lois and her mother. Dan Murfee was shoeing a horse when we passed the blacksmith shop. He clapped the iron on the upraised hoof and with rhythmic, sure strokes drove the nails in. In spite of his grime, there was something splendid about him.

My mother wrote me that Lois had sold the Gifford house. She and her mother had quarreled about that, but Lois would do it. Lois was boarding with Mrs. Cleaver; Mrs. Estes lived alone in her little house, taking in sewing again. "Mrs. Miniver says —" I skipped. "Dan Murfee has taken the pledge and keeps himself more spruced up nowadays. He comes to church regular and the new minister is well worth —" The town already seemed far away and dull.

Twenty-five years passed before I returned to the place where it had been. I recognized some old trees in the Square, and the Miller mansion was still standing. But I did not know the smiling woman who stopped her car beside mine at the gas pumps and cried, "Don't you remember me? We used to go to school together."

"Of course!" I cried, as one does. A stranger looked at me with affection through brown eyes sparkling with life. The silvery pale hair was cleverly cut and waved, the hat smartly defied gravity.

"You don't at all!" she laughed. "Lois Murfee. I used to be Lois Estes."

She was contented, merry, and full of pep. I rejoiced to think I looked as young as she, and the gaze of her two tall sons and a daughter made me feel older than Methuselah. "You must come to our basket-ball games," she said. "Ted's captain this year. Can you believe my youngest's a senior? and I'm almost a grandmother?" She nodded at the young man who came briskly from the garage. "There's Junior, now."

It was then that I saw the sign in Neon script above the plateglass windows proudly displaying the long, low sleekness of the latest models in cars. The sign said: "Murfee and Murfee."

I like Mrs. Dan Murfee. We have good times together. Her house is like her life, open to all weathers, overflowing with energy and fun. There is no pretense in her; she is sincerity itself.

Only last week we chanced to meet at the grocer's. The vegetable truck from the city was at the curb and its driver unloaded a case of southern sweet corn. Long ago I ceased to control my thoughts, and though I am fond of Lois Murfee I saw no reason to resist a curiosity invaluable to a writer. I picked up an ear of corn and parted the husk to the milky kernels. "This looks good," I said.

"Doesn't it?" she agreed. "But none of us care for sweet corn, for some reason. Dear me, I wish it wasn't so hard to get boys to eat vegetables!" Her eyes met mine. I had known that she didn't know why she gave Mr. Gifford that sweet corn. Now I know that she has forgotten she did it.

IX

NICE OLD LADY

Mrs. Sherwood was the nicest old lady in town. She was not a grandmother, she had no children, but she received with grandmotherly dignity the respect to which gray hair entitled her. When I first knew her well, she was more than forty years old.

"I declare it's an inspiration," my mother said. "To see her so well preserved and active and all, and not a missing tooth in her head."

"Yes, that's what I dread most, too, is losing my teeth." Mrs. Rogers sighed. "Well, the Lord giveth and the Lord taketh away, and it don't do any good to rebel, we'll all have to come to scraping apples. But seems to me somehow there's something about Mrs. Sherwood—" Her voice became stealthy. "You don't suppose she'd wear a — switch?"

"My goodness no," my mother answered calmly. "An honester woman never breathed and why would she want to? Married twenty years and more, and Mr. Sherwood perfectly steady. No, it's all her own hair, it just naturally don't match in back."

Of course we were always respectful to our elders. You must never interrupt them; you must never, never contradict anything they said; at table you waited while they took wishbone and drumsticks, leaving perhaps the neck for you. You must be polite when they looked at you and talked about you; politely, when asked, you must tell your name, your age, and say, Yes ma'am, you liked school, and Yes ma'am, you obeyed your kind teachers. Then if they began to say anything interesting your mother told you to go out and play, and you went out. When their talk was so boring that you ached all over, you sat being seen and not heard. Sometimes you were handed a picture book and then you must pretend to look at it.

To really old people, with gray hair, even your elders showed deference. Everyone stood up when old people came into the room. The most comfortable chair was moved a few inches and moved back again, for them. Something was done to doors and windows. A footstool was placed under the old feet. And when everyone was settled again, all the grownups turned toward this old person, their heads slightly bowed and tilted, and smiles of a special false brightness on all the faces. There was a special voice for old people, a voice cheerful and clearly distinct and gentle. But quite firm. If that voice said, "I'm afraid you're sitting in a draft," it made no difference what an old person said about liking fresh air, the window was shut. "There! Now that's better, isn't it!" that special voice would say with special cheeriness. Old people must be respected and taken care of. Like women.

Though I escaped when I could, when cornered I

was respectful to the aged. I ran to fetch shawls, I hunted for glasses and retrieved balls of yarn, I yelled into ear-trumpets and sustained by virtue's rewarding glow I listened attentively to reminiscences without hearing them. When I became a young lady, my kindness to old people greatly pleased both my mother and me. What the old people thought of it I don't know; I never really saw them. I saw Mrs. Sherwood, but that was because of her books.

Not every parlor center-table had a book on it. It was old-fashioned to keep the family Bible there; sometimes the Bible lay on the table's low shelf, sometimes it was not in sight at all. Some center-tables displayed the family photograph album, richly bound in plush and mother-of-pearl. But many women felt that nothing else gave a parlor quite the same air that a book did. Our own center-table held an imposing volume with its title in golden scrolls: Mother, Home, and Heaven. And on one of the little shelves jutting from our organ's mirrored top stood three more books: Tennyson's Poems, Scott's Poems, and Gates Ajar. This was fiction, and daring fiction. It was entirely dialogue with a mysteriously dying woman who, unrepentant to the last, believed that Heaven was not only pearly gates and golden pavements, but also meadows and brooks and even birds and dogs, if they had been good dogs.

But Mrs. Sherwood had bookcases, two tall bookcases full of books. And among all the old people I was kind to, indefatigably I was kindest to Mrs. Sherwood.

She lived in a comfortable house across the street from the Miller's turreted residence. Even from the outside her house looked comfortable; it seemed to rest more snugly on the ground than other houses did. It was painted snowy white, and so were the fence pickets. All along the fence was a bed of blue flags, and moss-roses grew by the serrated bricks that edged the path to the porch. Circles of bricks in the grass held, to the right a bed of cannas, and to the left a prickly low mound of cactus. In the summertime crowds of hollyhocks lifted their climbing blossoms at both ends of the house and the front porch was a mass of house-plants. Mrs. Sherwood's hens fluttered in dust baths under the maple tree, where no grass would grow. Mrs. Sherwood had set out that maple tree. She had lived more than twenty years in that house.

I had been increasingly kind to her for a long time before, having taken her a bunch of roses one June afternoon, I ventured to ask if I might borrow a book. Complacently I said, "I am very fond of reading."

Mrs. Sherwood, in her neat gray print and white apron, had come back from the kitchen with the roses in a vase. Setting them on the shelf by the dining-room clock, she said, "Are you? What have you read?"

I was staggered. It didn't matter what one read; merely to like to read was the distinction. Girls confided to young men taking them home from church for the first time, "You know, it's funny about me, I'm so different from most girls. Now there's nothing in the whole world I enjoy more than just to be all by myself with a book." Nobody ever asked them, "What book?"

In my confusion I could remember only books my mother must not suspect I'd read, or even knew about. *Capitola the Madcap*, or, *The Hidden Hand*; *The Damnation of Theron Ware*; *Maid, Wife or Widow*; and that baffling mystery, *The Woman Who Did*. Mrs. Sherwood's old maid sister sat sewing in the bay window and while I tried to think of a religious story she bit off the thread with decision and said, "Novels, I'll be bound!"

"My mother allows me to read novels, Miss Alice," I said with respect but firmly. "She says nowadays young folks do things that would make her mother turn in her grave, but she'd rather I was open and aboveboard than to sneak and read on the sly. And she says a good, moral novel now and then doesn't do any real harm." The name came to me. "She says 'In His Steps' is a very improving book. She approved my reading it."

"Stuff and fiddlesticks!" said Miss Alice, crossing her ankles the other way on the hassock. "The Bible's all anybody needs. I don't say but there's lofty thoughts in Longfellow and Tennyson, but no good ever came of novel reading or ever will. Wastes your time, wears out your eyes for nothing, and fills young minds with all kinds of trashy, harmful notions. It's an entering wedge. You mark my words, Jenny," she added with meaning.

I pinned my hope on Miss Alice's being the younger,

and only an old maid. She was old-fashioned, too. Old ladies hadn't worn caps for a long time, but when Miss Alice was forty she had put the little pancake of lace on the parting of her brown hair. "I'm an old lady now and I'll make no bones about it," she'd said to Mrs. Rogers. She had a vague quaintness, in her full-gathered skirts and cap, with the scent about her of the dried rose-petals scattered in her bureau drawers. But Mrs. Sherwood was up-to-date. Her hair was combed up to the big, darker coil on top of her head and a barette clamped the stray locks in back. Of course she hadn't adopted the pompadour when it came in, but on the other hand she didn't wear an old-fashioned lace cap.

"I feel I should speak to your mother, Ernestine," she said. "But you may look at the books now, if you like."

She took a key from her workbasket and going into the parlor she unlocked the bookcases' glass doors. I was overwhelmed. It seemed to me that the whole wide world that I didn't know anything about, was there. For two years I was to share with Mrs. Sherwood an intense, hidden life of exploration beyond the limits of anything we had ourselves experienced. But what we said when I looked at those books for the first time, I have forgotten. I remember that I took home a book which she was sure could do me no harm. It was the first volume of Gibbons' Decline and Fall of the Roman Empire.

I remember, too, how I first became aware of Mrs. Sherwood as a real person. About two months had

passed; it was a Saturday afternoon in August. A
thunderstorm hung in the sultry air. Not a leaf was
moving, and in their dust baths the motionless hens
panted with open beaks. I had bathed early that
Saturday, in preparation for the call on Mrs. Sherwood, and I felt pleasantly fresh and crisp in starchy
petticoats and sprigged lawn. I wore a white hat with
a transparent brim and my white parasol made a tent
of pearly light. The moss-roses were brilliant on
the ground along the graveled walk.

Mrs. Sherwood was sitting behind her house-plants.
She was not even rocking, just sitting there, and when
I came up the steps she looked at me oddly. Her
dark eyes were usually vividly sparkling, but today
they were dull and somehow hungry. Looking at
me, she seemed to see something she wanted and
couldn't have.

For some reason that look made me feel extraor-
dinarily vigorous, and most kindly cherishing toward
Mrs. Sherwood. We spoke of the heat, of the
need for rain, of our belief that this sultriness was
a weather-breeder. I unfurled my fan, and prettily
offered it to her. She said no, thank you. "Wouldn't
you like me to get your own fan for you, Mrs. Sherwood?" I asked. "Or a glass of water? A nice
fresh glass of cold water from the well? I'd be glad
to get it for you, Mrs. Sherwood." She thanked me
and said, no.

A moment later I urged her not to let me keep
her up if she'd like to lie down. I knew she didn't
take afternoon naps, but many old ladies did, and her

languor distressed me. "Mama says there's nothing like a little afternoon nap to keep up a body's strength, Mrs. Sherwood, and this heat is so hard on elderly people. Maybe if you'd —"

Suddenly she said, "Do you know what I mind most about it all?"

The last three words confounded me. I hadn't known she minded anything. Those three words, like a lightning flash, revealed a vast panorama of grievances, obliterated before I could see what they were.

"I'll tell you!" she said. "It's the bath-water."

"Bath —" I couldn't believe I'd heard it.

"I'll be married twenty-five years next Thanksgiving," Mrs. Sherwood said. "And every single Saturday for twenty-four years and eight months and three weeks I've dipped water out of the rain-water barrel, and strained it, and lugged the washtub into the kitchen to set on the supper fire to heat for Mr. Sherwood's bath. And put out the washrag and towel and soap for him, and laid out his clean underwear and his socks. And seems to me sometimes I'll scream. Seems to me I can't do it one single Saturday more. I been sitting here thinking and I ought to go do it and seems to me I just can't. Nobody'd want a better husband or a kinder. But if only once he'd get his own bath-water ready. Or not take a bath. Even not take a bath. Just anything different. I'm an old woman now and no use looking forward to anything any more but seems to me I could stand it all if only it wasn't for Saturdays and the bath-water."

She leaned forward and said with terrific energy, "Whatever you do, Ernestine, don't you get married! Don't do it!"

It was as if that energy shattered me to bits. Terror skittered among them. Before I could collect myself, she was merely Mrs. Sherwood again, placidly rocking.

"There," she said. "That's nonsense of course, I don't mean it, Ernestine; don't pay any attention to it. You noticed how my pink geranium's blooming? It's done real well this year. Remind me to give you that slip off it I promised your mother."

Everything was the same as it had always been, yet nothing quite fitted into the same pattern. I looked at Mrs. Sherwood with a different attention. Even her comfortable, well-cared-for house seemed to have another meaning when I thought that every day, since before I was born, she had done the same things in it at the same recurrent hours. And I saw Mr. Sherwood as I had never seen him before.

He was a good-natured, dryly joking man, thin and slightly stooped and growing bald. The hair around the bald spot had been fair and, faded now, it hardly showed the gray. He wore bushy but neat mustaches, stained on one side by his cigars. Any afternoon you could see him sitting behind the words painted on his dusty office window: Jos. M. Sherwood, Real Estate, Farm Loans and Mortgages, Universal Harvesters, Insurance, Notary Public. His feet were usually on his desk, his vest hung open, and with a thumb hooked in suspenders he talked with a man or two lounging in chairs tipped back against the wall. Two deep grooves curving from his nostrils disappeared beneath his mustaches; as a child I had fancied that those flexible wrinkles had something to do with his not being prominent in the church, though he was a member in good standing. Everyone thought well of him. He had a good business head, too; the Sherwoods would never want for anything.

He didn't touch liquor and he was a light eater, being subject to slight attacks of heartburn. All he asked was beefsteak every day for dinner. Other women said in exasperation that they envied Mrs. Sherwood; she needn't rack her brains to think what to get. "Yes," she said. "At our house it's always beefsteak." His punctuality was a model, too; the neighbors could set their clocks by him. Every morning at the stroke of eight he left the house, and he returned promptly at twelve and again at six. Mrs. Sherwood was never annoyed by his being late for meals. He didn't go down town after supper except on Saturday nights, when he went to the barber shop for his shave. And every Sunday morning, without trying to make any excuses, he put on his Sunday clothes and walked to church with Mrs. Sherwood and Miss Alice. He made no objection at all to giving Miss Alice a good home as long as she lived.

And now when I looked at him, I wondered what he had been like when he was young. It seemed impossible that he had been young; surely not young, like the boys I knew. But he must have been. And Mrs. Sherwood had been a girl. When I was old, would I be like her?

I asked her once, "Mrs. Sherwood, when you were young did you want— What did you want to be?"

"Oh, it's hard to say," she replied. We were in her dining-room; outdoors was a winter's day bright in the cold light of snow, but the heating stove surrounded us with drowsy warmth. I sat by the table, eating an apple. Miss Alice, in her cap and little crocheted sacque, was tatting, and Mrs. Sherwood was knitting Roman-striped blocks for an afghan. "Girls have all kinds of notions," she said.

"Tell the truth and shame the devil, Jenny," said Miss Alice. "You know you were always bound and set to travel."

Mrs. Sherwood flushed. "Well," she said a little tartly, "I never did and I never will, so there's no use bringing it up now, Alice."

I bit deeper into the winesap's juiciness, and giving the core my beau's name, silently I counted the slippery plump seeds. "One I love, Two I love, Three I love I say, Four I love with all my heart, Five I cast away—" It wasn't polite to be silent so long.

"Didn't you ever go anywhere at all, Mrs. Sherwood?" I asked.

"No," she said, "I never did. We planned to go to Niagara Falls on our honeymoon, but Mr. Sherwood thought best to buy this house and couldn't afford the trip at the time. And what with one thing and another, it kept getting put off from year to year till I saw I might as well stop fretting and make up my mind to it; we'd never go."

She spoke mildly, and Miss Alice's flurried manner surprised me. "Now, Jenny, there's many a woman would be glad and thankful to be in your shoes."

"Yes," Mrs. Sherwood said. "Yes, Mr. Sherwood's a real home-body." Her voice changed involuntarily. "He got all the travel out of his system when he was young."

Everything jolted and stopped, horridly changed. I knew I shouldn't have heard that; I wasn't wanted there now, and I didn't want to be there. The warm room, the bay window full of house-plants, the table covered with its between-meals red-checked cloth and the bowl of apples on it, and the good oak chairs ranged against brown-striped wall paper, the rocking chairs with nice crocheted tidies, the worn but still serviceable ingrain carpet and the black what-not with gilt wearing off its spindles; all these seemed a prison.

"Let me out, quick!" I screamed. What I actually uttered, of course, was some murmur about mama's expecting me, and thank you so much for the Les Miserables; yes, it did seem to be getting colder out, and yes, I'd be careful not to slip on the ice, and goodby, Mrs. Sherwood, goodby, Miss Alice.

With Quo Vadis and The Conquest of Peru gripped under an elbow, my hands clasped in my muff and my footing precarious on the icy path between ridges of snow, I struggled homeward. My heart was cold with fright. I knew now what all those books meant to Mrs. Sherwood, reading about strange places and foreign people. She could not hope to see them. She never could see them, married, trapped when she was a girl, and now too old.

But I? Though I was only a girl, at least I wasn't old. If I had the stupendous courage to do it, I could get away. Perhaps. Did I dare? Could I?

My mother didn't know what had got into me; she said to save her life she didn't know what I wanted, and indeed I didn't know. I was almost sure what I did not want, but I could not say that to my mother. Like every girl, I had always said I wouldn't get married, for fear I might not be asked. We were involved in a prolonged struggle, a war fought with arguments, pleading, furious outbursts and hours of sulking on my part, and tears on both sides. The one encounter with my father was terrible. We were poor, but not so poor that my parents could not maintain a decent pride; they needn't take charity, go into debt, nor let a daughter earn her own living. "But Ernestine, you don't have to!" my mother said a thousand times. She offered me a piano.

"Your father and I have talked it over, and if it will content you, he'll manage it somehow. Piano playing's a nice accomplishment for a girl, men admire it. And Ernestine, if only you'll wait just a little while longer— Girls marry later now than they used to, and you won't be eighteen till spring."

Trembling, she said, "Ernestine, we can't let you go out alone among strangers, with nobody to take care of you. You—you don't know the awful dangers — You don't know what happens to girls in cities."

The vagueness was more terrifying than if I had known. I was too deeply frightened to be at all sure that I didn't want to be taken care of. But grimly I stuck to it that some girls did take care of themselves, nowadays. It was true that we didn't know one, but we read about them. They were called Bachelor Girls. Charles Dana Gibson had drawn a picture of one, and what could be more respectable, more fashionable, than a Gibson Girl? You could tell by looking at his Bachelor Girl that she was perfectly nice, and not afraid of anything.

"You simply can not go to the city alone." My mother brought up the heavy artillery. She was pale. "What would people say? Your character would be ruined. Ruined."

We stared at each other bleakly; the instant became an eternity in which I knew that if courage failed now I was beaten, and with a supreme effort I shouted, "I don't care what people say!"

It was not true, I knew it was not true, but I had said it. And dizzy with that liberating lie, intoxicated by freedom, I heard defiance ring out again. "I don't *care!*"

My mother's drawn face crumpled, she sobbed into her lifted apron and I sank into a chair and wept. But I knew I had won. Nothing could stop me now. I was going to business college. The truth is that I was terrified, but I was going.

All that Mrs. Rogers could say, to us, was, "I don't know what the world is coming to."

"Well, I must say I'm thankful my girl's got gumption," my gallant mother replied, lightly stressing the possessive pronoun. "I made up my mind to it, she wasn't going to marry some boy here and stick in this little town all her days." She gave me a fondly proud smile. "Ernestine's a good girl, and she's a smart girl; she don't have to take the first thing in pants comes along. When she marries, she'll surprise folks!"

"Yes, it will surprise us," Mrs. Rogers innocently agreed. "But my land, you never can tell, and what I say is, Ernestine, don't give up hope."

Through a soft May afternoon I walked to the post office to mail the fateful letter to the business college, inquiring about terms. My mother had also written to the minister of her church in the city, offering the best references as to my character and anxiously trusting that he would find room and board for me in the home of some Christian woman who would take a motherly interest in my welfare.

With these two letters in my gloved hand and every nerve quivering, I walked decorously under the maples' translucent young leaves. The yards were golden with dandelions, and apple trees were in bloom. From the blacksmith shop the clanging of hammer on iron rang like band-music.

In the post office Mr. Sherwood was at the registry window and Postmaster Boles was weighing a

heavy envelop. They were talking about Tommy
Webb, who had run away from home. Mrs. Webb
was frantic and the whole town aroused until a loafer
at the depot said he'd seen Tommy leaving on the
brake-rods. Now everyone was saying that Mr.
Webb should have whaled the stuffings out of that
young scalawag years ago.

I bowed circumspectly and Mr. Sherwood palmed
his cigar and raised his hat. They went on talking
while I stood before the letter slot. I couldn't make
myself mail those letters.

"It won't hurt the youngster a damned bit —" Mr.
Sherwood had forgotten me, hidden by the lock-
boxes. "I was the same kind of young hellion, myself.
Run away with a circus when — but guess I've told
you. Well, those were great days. Damn fine days."

I didn't stir. This is the way men talk, I said to
myself in deep excitement. "Yes siree, sir, I bet
there's not a water-tank from here to Arizona they
didn't throw me off at. Never got to the Pacific,
though ; wish I had. But let me tell you I covered
some territory ! Denver, Chicago, Cleveland, Buffalo — Now there's a fine town, Buffalo. I spent
three solid days just standing and looking at Niagara
Falls. Man ! You ever see Niagara Falls ?"

"Tell me it's something to see," said Mr. Boles.

"Say ! it is. It is for a fact. It sure is. Niagara
Falls. Well — And Florida. I've picked oranges
right off the trees. Seen pineapples growing. And
there's turtles down there so big you couldn't believe it if I told you. Spanish moss, kind of a long

gray moss looks like hair, hangs off the trees. And palms. Big tall palms growing all over the place, you get no idea of 'em from these little things in pots the women-folks raise around here. There's snakes down there as big around as your arm. And alligators — say, I've seen alligators in Louisiana forty feet long. Seen 'em dozens at a time. You'll read in books they look like logs; let me tell you, you know damn well they ain't logs. They got long flat jaws like — well, you don't take 'em for any logs, let me tell you. And vicious mean little eyes. And hides you can't shoot through with a high-power rifle; that's a fact sure as I'm standing here. Nobody'd believe the things I've seen. Seen 'em with my own eyes."

"Guess you've seen a plenty, for a fact," said Mr. Boles' voice.

"Mm. You're damn tootin'. Right today, I wouldn't take a million dollars — If I hadn't been a darn fool kid with an itching foot, I'd 've made a million, at that. The chances I let slide. Yes sir, I could 've been a millionaire today."

"Oh well, that's the way it goes," said Mr. Boles. "You got no complaint coming, Joe, at that."

"Oh no. No, I can't complain. Got a good little business in a fine, neighborly little town, good home, something put by for a rainy day. A man's pretty lucky." But this recital of blessings sounded hollow. "Damn lucky," the voice insisted. Then it filled again. "But I say a young fellow, Tommy f'instance, he ought to break loose. Get out and see the world,

raise a little hell!   Won't do him any harm.   What's
the sense of being a stick in the mud all your life?
Damn it, we'll be a long time dead.   A man's entitled
to something."

I was furious.   A man's entitled to something, indeed!   And what about poor Mrs. Sherwood?   He
hadn't let her have even a wedding trip to Niagara
Falls.   Had he talked to her like this, before they
were married?   And then he'd never taken her anywhere at all.   I thought of the atlases and guidebooks
in her bookcase; the album of World's Fair pictures.
Everybody wanted to go to that Fair in St. Louis,
and the Sherwoods could have afforded to go, easily.
"We did speak some of it," Mrs. Sherwood answered
when asked.   "But Mr. Sherwood feels he can't get
away just now."   I hated him.   A savage and pro-
found hatred welled up in me, and blindly I must have
thrust those letters into the slot.   They were gone.   I
had missed whatever Mr. Boles said.

"Oh, sure.   But he'll settle down, he'll run across
some good-looking girl and marry her and settle down
with his nose to the grindstone," Mr. Sherwood's
voice replied.   "Oh sure, you're right about that; a
rolling stone gathers no moss.   That's what I tell Mrs.
Sherwood.   And say, know what she said, quick as
a flash?   Right away she says, 'That's the truth,' she
says, "and who want to be a moss back?"   Quick as
that!   Pretty good, uh?"

They laughed.   They dared to laugh!   "Yes, she's
smart as a whip.   Mrs. Sherwood is," Mr. Boles agreed.
"Well, that'll be twenty-seven cents, Joe, first class

registered. It's pretty steep, but you got a lot of weight there." Coins clinked, then Mr. Boles' fist thumped the stamps. "Guess you got all the travel out of your system, uh?"

"Oh sure. Yeh. When I was a young fellow." The brute! The mean, selfish brute! "Sure, this town suits me right down to the ground. Don't care if I never —"

Blazing, I swished haughtily past him. It was a slight relief to see his consternation. At least I'd let him know how his vile profanity had affronted feminine ears.

I had intended to call on Mrs. Sherwood, but I didn't want to see her now. I went straight by Miller's windows full of spring dress-goods, stonily passed the barber shop and the livery-stable, sped down the slope and slammed our gate, slammed my room door.

If I had glanced back, I would have seen the excitement uptown. If I had gone to Mrs. Sherwood's I would have been in the thick of it. But we knew nothing until Mrs. Rogers rushed in for my mother. Even then I was left at home to get supper.

Mr. Sherwood was dead. He had stepped from the postoffice corner without noticing where he was going, and Jay Willard's buggy was coming down the street at a fast clip. The horses were almost on Mr. Sherwood before he saw them; he stepped back, staggered, and fell. Old Dr. Wright had seen this happen, and he was among the first to reach him. Squatting down there, the old doctor said a strange thing. "Well, Joe," he said. "At last you're going to get a good, long rest."

"But Doc!" Jim Miller couldn't believe it. "A little fall like that, he can't be —"

"Heart," the old doctor said. He opened his medicine case and did what he could, but while he was doing it he sent for my mother and Mrs. Rogers. The old doctor himself went ahead of the others to break the news to Mrs. Sherwood.

"Poor thing, she's like a lost soul," Mrs. Rogers said when she and my mother came home. I had been sitting up on our porch, and went through the moonlight to meet them. Mrs. Sherwood was bearing up bravely but Miss Alice cried like a child. Mr. Sherwood was laid out in the expensive coffin that had so long been a white elephant in the furniture emporium.

"Well, they don't have to worry about means," Mrs. Rogers said. "He must have left a big insurance, being in the business and getting his commissions off."

Next day, of course, everyone went to Mrs. Sherwood's. The flag's crisp blossoms and the unfurling leaves of cannas seemed heartless, so near the sad house with the big bunch of crepe on the door. Tiptoe in the hushed parlor we bent over Mr. Sherwood's waxen face. The eyelids faintly showed the imprint where coins had been laid and his cheeks were hollow against the white band. Those deep grooves from the nostrils looked patient now, and tired. He was not in a shroud. Mrs. Sherwood had always kept his wedding suit, and seeing it aired one day in housecleaning time, he'd said he would like to be buried in it. Getting it out of moth-balls was the last thing she could do for him.

She and Miss Alice sat swathed in crepe. Miss Alice softly sobbed and blew her nose behind her veil, but Mrs. Sherwood's hands clasped a folded handkerchief as if she had forgotten it. When it came my turn to bend over her, she clung to me a moment and then still gripping my arms she leaned back and looked up at me. I could feel her intense looking through the veil that hid her face. "Ernestine, he was always good to me," she said. "I never was sorry I married him, never for one minute in all the — years we —"

She couldn't go on, and tears poured down my face while I thought she'd never again have to get his bathwater ready and I tried to say what I felt, feeling her piteous and soft and hot under the mass of crepe with its smothery odor and longing to comfort her and desperately trying not to want to get away. I never could really enjoy another's sorrows as everyone else did.

Already we knew there was no insurance. The whisper was in the kitchen where women rummaged, noticing how Mrs. Sherwood kept cupboards and hidden corners, and warming a little food to keep up her strength. It was on the crowded porch and among groups meeting in the sunshine on the graveled walk. "He didn't leave any insurance." "What! You don't mean—" Then silence, a grim nod, and glances chill with surmise. For everyone's husband was making payments on insurance that Mr. Sherwood had sold. My mother's lips set and she said, "I'll never in this world believe that Mr. Sherwood wasn't honest as the day is long."

The funeral was over, the last calls made; all the food that neighbors had brought was gone, and Mrs. Sherwood and Miss Alice began living alone in the house that felt empty even to me, though I had rarely seen Mr. Sherwood there. He had left Mrs. Sherwood very well provided for, but he had not bought a cent of insurance. Then one evening in Miller's store old Dr. Wright blew up.

"Not one of you'll ever be knee-high to Joe Sherwood!" he told the men talking there. "I've kept my mouth shut for twenty-five years because he wanted me to, and anyway a doctor can't talk. But now by gravy! I'm going to talk!" And he did. "So let that hold your horses," he said, and not a man spoke. "Furthermore, while I'm mad enough to, I'm going to Mrs. Sherwood and tell her." He stamped out of the store and went to Mrs. Sherwood's.

The truth was that Mr. Sherwood had no intention of settling down when he married. He had in mind to travel with his wife around the country, selling insurance. And wanting to provide well for her, he made out in her favor the biggest insurance policy he could afford. Man-life, he put off closing it up from day to day until just before the wedding. Then he dropped into Dr. Wright's office for the medical examination.

He was feeling fine. "Twenty-six years old, doc, and never been sick a day since I was a boy!" he said. "Guaranteed sound in wind and limb, not a blemish on me, and I'll go like the wind in single or double harness!"

The doctor joshed him back, at first, then he stopped and said, "Ever have scarlet fever?" Joe Sherwood said he sure had, he well remembered his mother's sending him to sleep with a neighbor's boy who had it. He had had a good mother who never spared herself trouble in taking care of him; she'd seen to it that he caught everything — both kinds of measles, chicken-pox, whooping-cough, scarlet fever, mumps, all the regular children's diseases that it was best to get through with while you were young. That was why he was so healthy.

Then the doctor had to tell him that he couldn't pass him for insurance. His heart was no good. Any little shock, surprise, sudden excitement, and he'd go, like that! It might happen any day. Any minute.

Joe Sherwood couldn't take it in at first. Then it slowly dawned on him, and not saying much but, "Well, thanks, Doc," he got up and left. This was on Monday. He was to be married Thursday.

In a couple of hours he came back and insisted that there must be some mistake. The doctor let him listen to his heart himself, and he read what the doctor showed him in the books. He left again without saying much. On Thursday morning, early, he came in and asked the doctor to keep the facts under his hat.

The doctor asked him if he'd told the girl, and he said he hadn't exactly told her, but he had talked to her and he knew she'd stick to him if she did know.

The way they both felt about each other, he said, they'd stick through hell and high water. He said it was open-and-shut; marry her or jilt her, and he hoped he was a decent enough man not to jilt a girl even if he wanted to. He tried to carry it off with a joke, saying, "What they don't know don't hurt 'em, Doc."

Dr. Wright said it might be some comfort to him to have a wife who knew what he was up against, but Joe Sherwood said he didn't look at it that way. He figured it was up to a man to take care of his wife, not the other way around.

He never left town after that. He did not want to leave her and he could not take her anywhere with him, knowing he might die any minute and leave her alone and unprotected among strangers. For twenty-five years he had gone on living carefully, kidding people along in his quiet way, putting by as much money as he could and never telling anyone what was in his thoughts.

"To think of all those years—" my mother said. "Lonesome all the time. Because he didn't want to worry her."

"And I don't suppose we'll ever know how she took it when the doctor told her," said Mrs. Rogers. "Well, the poor man's gone to his reward now. One thing, it won't be so much of a shock to her as to most of us when we meet our husbands on Judgment Day and the secrets of all hearts are revealed."

I hardly saw Mrs. Sherwood that summer; it was the summer of the typhoid epidemic and we met only in houses of sickness and mourning. But the time came when I must face alone the hazards of an all-day journey on the train, to the city, where the minister had arranged that a good lady and her husband were to meet me in the depot; the lady and I were to wear identical bits of blue ribbon, to guard against my making a dangerous mistake. The day before I left, I called on Mrs. Sherwood to say good-by.

Yellow leaves were drifting from the maples and along the weedy ditches the goldenrod was turning gray. In the shade of the blacksmith shop men were pitching horseshoes. A few dogs lay in the dusty street, lazily snapping at flies; two or three horses dozed at the hitching posts, and in a chair tilted against the front of Miller's store Mr. Sims was asleep. And all these familiar scenes, which I was so eager to leave, hurt me because I was going away and might never see them again.

There were the flags' narrow blades drooping brown-tipped along the picket fence, and the cannas' last wilting bloom, the moss-roses' brilliance along the graveled walk. Again seed-pods hung on the hollyhock's stalks and only a few topmost blossoms flaunted silky petals. The house-plants gave the porch a scent of moist earth and of rose-geranium, and Mrs. Sherwood came to meet me, taking both my hands in hers. "Well, my dear! So you came to tell an old lady good-by!"

She seemed resigned in her widow's weeds. But eagerly she urged me to tell my plans and hopes, and she wavered between the encouragement she wanted

to give me and the advice she should give. Like my
mother, she warned me never to reply if a stranger,
even a woman, spoke to me. "You must pray to be
preserved from the city's dangers," she said. She
spoke wistfully of the privilege of attending services
in a big city church. "And if you are ever invited to
eat in a public restaurant, Ernestine, do it! That is,
of course, properly escorted and chaperoned." Wistfully she said, "You'll see an automobile. I don't suppose one will ever come to this town, there's nothing
to bring rich people here. And they tell me our roads
are too rough for an automobile, anyway. So nobody here could ever have any use for one."

I couldn't bear it. I made some wild suggestion that
she and Miss Alice visit me in the city, after I was
established there. They were pleased, but the idea
was of course a fantasy. Two old ladies would
hardly travel so far alone, and there was no near relative to accompany them. My daring was part of
youth and the changing times, but they were no longer
young, and Mrs. Sherwood shook her head regretfully, smiling.

When I was taking my leave she asked me to wait
a moment, and going into her bedroom she brought
me a flat gold breast-pin as large as my finger, lightly
engraved in scrolls. She had worn it, she said, as
a girl. "I want you to have it, my dear, for a keep-
sake."

I tried to thank her properly, but couldn't, and
she put her arms around me and kissed me. "God
bless and keep you, Ernestine. Wherever you go,

if you're ever in temptation, remember I'm praying for you. And my dear, I want you to know I couldn't ask God to give you a happier married life than I had, or a better husband."

At intervals, for years, I could feel her tragically softer cheek against my firm one, and the pathos of her heavy widow's veil. Memories were all she had left, and it was intolerably cruel that they were not the memories she had wanted.

Letters grew rarer and at last were not written at all, but I knew how she was growing older in that aging house with Miss Alice. Every spring they would have the heaters taken down and set the house-plants on the porch; every autumn they'd have the heaters set up again, and range the plants in the bay-window. Summer afternoons they would spend slowly rocking on the porch and through the winter days they would keep themselves busy with little tasks in the warm house. They would go to church twice every Sunday, and weekly to prayermeeting, monthly to Ladies' Aid. Old neighbors would call and they would return the calls; old friends would die and they would go to the funerals. Nothing would ever change and everything would slowly grow older. Year after year it would seem less worth while to cook, when all they wanted was a cup of tea. At Mrs. Sherwood's age, it would be frivolous to go into half-mourning. She would not seem lacking in respect for the departed; until she died she would wear good black and the flat bonnet with the long crepe veil.

And all this while, gloriously we Bachelor Girls

would be living our own lives. We had escaped, we were free, and battling for woman's freedom. When I was twenty I knew exactly what my life was going to be; I controlled it. I had no intention whatever of meekly accepting and making the best of anything. Intoxicated by the discovery of my own intelligence, I planned my future and knew how to make it the best.

At that time I did not plan ever to leave my own country. I had never heard of Albania, and certainly had no desire to visit the Balkans. Sixteen years later I was driving down a familiar road from Tirana to the sea.

The day was such a day as comes only between a rainy season and a dry. It was a shock of beauty. Impossible to believe that clouds so ineffable were drifting in the incredible blue. From every hillside one could hear the shepherds' pipes and the faintly tinkling bells of flocks grazing on their way to the mountains. The shifting lights on that mountain wall shutting off the eastern half of the sky made breath catch in the throat.

Small below Dajti's gigantic mass, Tirana was a green grove pierced by seven white minarets, and on the mountain's shoulder ivory-colored Kruja with its mile of red roofs was a little jewel.

After the road crosses the plains and winds over the Kazani hills, it comes down to a long, straight causeway across sea-marshes, and ends in white-walled, red-roofed Durazzo, once a pleasure-resort so gay that Cicero, ruffling it there with other young scamps, squandered his last coin and had to write to friends in Rome for money enough to get home. The same brick walls he saw while he strolled about the harbor waiting for the rescuing Roman post are still supporting balconied houses high above the water.

From the causeway I observed some excitement in the bazaar, and while we approached the huddled small shops that line the way outside the old city gates, I mentioned it to my kavass. Albanians think that women must be taken care of, and in deference to public opinion I never left the shelter of walled court-yards and gardens without an armed kavass. The next moment I slammed on the brakes; the cobbled narrow street was a boiling mass of men, donkeys, gendarmes and water-buffaloes attached to tall wicker carts.

Across turbans and fezzes and between the rifles then carried on every Albanian's shoulder, I saw two gendarmes struggling to put a woman onto a dreary horse. Aloft in a side-saddle, another woman sat watching. Her hat, her gray hair, the back of her coat were unknown to me. Tourists were then un-usual in the Balkans, and in any case the street was blocked; I sat still, wondering if these travelers were Americans. Two women unaccompanied were in-evitably English or American, and if not English, I would speak to them.

With a shout of "Ya Al-lah!" the woman was pro-pelled upward; she wobbled, clutched desperately, and with a mighty flounder landed in the saddle. Several voices fervently exclaimed, "Per Zoti! Mashallah! The praise be to God!" She gasped, "My land, I —"

"If you can't ride a horse, Alice, what will you do on a camel?" her companion said, with finality. I did not recognize her, but these were unmistakably voices from home. Alertly the kavass opened the car door, cleared my way through the crowd, and amid water-buffaloes, Scanderbeg jackets, turbaned heads and bristling rifles I met Mrs. Sherwood again. The shock was terrific.

We went to that tiny café looking south across the harbor. Only two tables are set in the open air there, but the coffee-maker has not let Europe corrupt his art. When you clap your hands the green beans go into the roaster and the copper coffee-mill is heated. The coffee comes foaming and aromatic in the tiny handleless cups set in silver filigree; the perfect coffee, "Sweet as love, black as sin, hot as hell." I did not quote this descriptive progression to Mrs. Sherwood.

"I must say it doesn't taste like coffee, but I like it," she said.

She was not greatly changed, nor was Miss Alice. Her hair was still coiled, under a sensible hat, and Miss Alice's braids were still wound into a knot in back. They wore good dark tweeds, dark silk blouses and oxfords. I noticed that their ankles were trim in silk, and they didn't wear gloves; they carried them. They were old women, candidly wrinkled, and looking at their eyes I knew that my own were not as young.

Something, I felt, had gone wrong with Time. I was not forty yet, and these old ladies and I were the same age. I did not know why I was so profoundly disturbed; arithmetic told me that they were barely in their sixties, and they were not the first elderly women I'd met traveling in Europe. There was no reason why they shouldn't be here, no reason why their being here should dislocate my universe.

"How did we get here?" Miss Alice repeated my question. They had come from Rome; Paris before that, and before Paris, Stockholm. "It does seem queer," she agreed, though I had not said so. She digressed, "You know we bought an automobile."

I hadn't known. "Yes," Mrs. Sherwood said. "Dan Murfee's selling them; he said it would be a pleasure to us. After the highway was graveled he used to take us riding, evenings. And he got such a nice young man to drive us to California."

"California!" I cried, and the kavass instantly leaped to my side. I lifted my chin, and he returned to sitting on his heels against the white-washed wall. Behind every latticed window overlooking that spot, dozens of feminine eyes were undoubtedly fixed upon us; we sat unveiled at a public café, drinking coffee like men. Yet the guardian kavass implied our respectability.

"Everybody goes to California now," Mrs. Sherwood said. "It's quite the usual thing to do. Mr. and Mrs. Miller went with us in their car as far as Colorado Springs. We had a real pleasant trip. We stayed four days at the Grand Canyon, and we saw the cactus on the desert."

"And the Painted Desert, and the Indians," said Miss Alice.

"Yes, and we went out on the Pacific Ocean in a glass bottomed boat. In California we picked oranges right off the trees. Some very hospitable people live in California, they showed us everything. Los Angeles is a beautiful city and it is growing rapidly, but I said no, I'll leave my money right where it is. No good comes of speculating. And I don't know's I'd care to live in California, but it's a beautiful place to visit."

I learned that Mrs. Sherwood had become prominent in church work. Women were more prominent in it now than they used to be, she remarked. She had been elected delegate to an international conference in Stockholm, and could it be possible that I saw a cat-containing-the-canary look pass briefly across her face? Miss Alice, of course, had gone with her. At the conference they met some very nice people who were going on to Paris, so they went to Paris. They had seen Paris thoroughly, with guidebooks.

"I doubt if Paris is wickeder than any city," said Miss Alice. "We did not see any special wickedness there. The French seem to be a very nice, thrifty people and fond of their families." They were now on their way to Egypt. Mrs. Sherwood had always wanted to see the Pyramids and ride on a camel.

"I see no reason why we shouldn't make a good job of this trip while we're about it," said she. "We aren't getting any younger, and the time to travel so far from home's while we're still blest with good health."

I did not yet know why they had come to Albania. They said they had been surprised to find it so near Italy. The fare across the Adriatic was only four dollars.

"They told us Albanians are bandits," Miss Alice said. "But Jenny said fiddlesticks. Your mother told us you'd been here, and you liked them, and you wouldn't like bandits."

"I must say they've been very pleasant to us so far," Mrs. Sherwood remarked.

"And there's been no holding Jenny since we got to Italy," said Miss Alice. Wickedly she told me, "We wouldn't have gone there, only she drank champagne."

"Mrs. Sherwood!"

"I'm sure I had no idea it was intoxicating liquor," Mrs. Sherwood protested, and unexpectedly added, "Not that I repent it, Alice! I've been a respectable woman all my days, and at my time of life one little champagne cocktail won't do me any harm."

I didn't even quiver. She explained that they had been sitting one evening in the garden of the hotel at Monte Carlo. They had come down that day from the fields of flowers at Grasse. Seeing a young couple enjoying these drinks, and thinking they were some kind of foreign lemonade, she had ordered and drunk one. She felt no ill effects.

Ah, that tropical garden between the mountains and the sea, that enchanted moonlight, those champagne cocktails, those heartbreaking, silly violins playing Un Peu d'Amour! And Mrs. Sherwood had been there.

That evening they decided to go to Italy. "The champagne cocktail had nothing to do with it, Alice! I simply made up my mind I was going to see Italy."

"Look," I said. There before us was the boundless water, the immense sky, and to the left a fingernail paring of creamy-pink land edging the bay. The Adriatic has its own blue. The Pacific is tumultuous with color, the Mediterranean is a sky-reflecting black, the Ægean glows wine-dark off the shores of Greece and the Caspian runs to sapphire and emerald on its salt-encrusted shores, but the calm Adriatic is blue. It is the soul of blueness, pure, intense and vibrant, not comparable to anything. One sees that blue sometimes in the skies of Kansas; nowhere else. At this moment sky and sea alike were that one blue. Sight was amazed and lost in its infinite purity. And high above the sliver of flesh-colored land a celestial vision was appearing. Palpitating form created itself from the blue, from instant to instant becoming visible, white flushing to pink, pink deepening to rose, quivering to ivory. Almost it reached solidity. Then it was gone.

Tears stood in Mrs. Sherwood's eyes. She looked at me mutely.

"Tomari," I answered. "A mountain in the south. Sixty miles away. Snow-capped."

"It shows the glory of God," she said huskily, and after a moment, "Seems like I can't get used to how beautiful the world is. Sometimes I just don't know how we're going to bear Heaven."

I wish I might have shown her Albania, and gone down with her to the sunset-purple land, the lateen sails and the deserts of Egypt. But an independent woman's time is not her own; I had to sail that evening. I offered her my kavass and the borrowed car. There were at that time only three automobiles in Albania and the roads were still those made by pack-trains, buffalo carts and private carriages; it was a primitive country. I explained to Mrs. Sherwood that women should not travel alone there; it would make talk. The kavass would take care of them.

Miraculously, as kavasses do meet every wish or whim, he produced envelopes and paper, and I was writing hasty notes when Miss Alice started convulsively and grasped my arm. Behind her two cones of black stuffs were moving across the cobblestones with an almost inaudible sibilance. My ear detected the click of a French heel and a slipper's rasp. Two heads turned toward us, presenting that shocking effect of facelessness given by veiled women. "Gracious!" Miss Alice gasped. "What's that?"

"A lady," I said, "and her servant."

"How can you tell?" she inquired, but Mrs. Sherwood was exclaiming, "Of all the outlandish—!" Her eyes sparkled with joyous excitement. "Veiled

women! Veiled heathen Moslem women, Alice!"
She was actually seeing them.

"I'll take you to call in a harem," I said. They
were all agoggle. After some thought I selected a
harem not too much like the parlors of my youth.

But there was a nice old lady there, and in that
harem I clearly saw what had happened. Mrs. Sherwood had not changed; she was still what Mrs. Rogers
would have called the salt of the earth, and she was
nice. She was a wholesome, sensible, conventional,
and to me charming elderly woman. But she was not
a nice old lady. At home, I saw, there were no nice
old ladies any more.

Some hours later we walked to the end of the long
pier where small boats were waiting to take passengers
to the steamer lying off shore. Mrs. Sherwood said
they were going straight home from Egypt. "Mrs.
Boles promised faithfully to water the plants, and
Elsie Miller-that-was is taking care of the hens. It
was real neighborly of them to offer, and I know
they're doing their best, but nobody takes care of
your things like you do yourself." She asked me
when I was coming home. Almost her farewell
words were, "All the home folks will be glad to see
you when you come."

In the boat moving liquidly over sunset-colored
water I was sadly amused because I felt so forlorn. I
had never wanted to go back to the little town, but
without thinking about it I had always felt that it was
there, that imprisoning security to which one might

go back. Now I knew that it was gone. I was rather tired, and not so sure that feminine freedom was what we Bachelor Girls had believed it would be.

At least, I thought, Mrs. Sherwood has what she wanted.